THE
Desperate Trials of
PHINEAS MANN

Praise for
THE DESPERATE TRIALS OF PHINEAS MANN

"Think 'medical thriller' and Robin Cook usually comes to mind. This should be replaced by Mark Anthony Powers, because the arrival of another addition to the Phineas Mann thriller series lends added value to the genre. In *The Desperate Trials of Phineas Mann*, these involve not just diagnostic medicine, but the accompanying human fallacies that introduce bias into medical and problem-solving situations. The fictional cases come across as especially realistic because of Mark Anthony Powers' real-world job as a medical consultant in pulmonary medicine.

As in the other Phineas stories, Powers creates satisfyingly rich details about accompanying issues and just the right mix of tension to intrigue readers. The result holds surprises for Phineas, delights for readers, and reviews of medical, social, and political conundrums which consider bias in all forms. Readers seeking a vividly realistic medical thriller will find this especially thought-provoking."

— Diane Donovan, *Midwest Book Review*

"*The Desperate Trials of Phineas Mann* grabs the reader from the first chapter, and we are immersed into the challenges and joys of life with Dr. Phineas Mann. The author uses his characters and story line to highlight the continued importance of high-quality clinical medicine which cannot be substituted by computer-generated algorithms. I strongly connected with Phineas as he strives to remain relevant to his colleagues, patients in need, and most urgently, his wife, Iris. A stirring capstone to a thoroughly enjoyable four-part series that I encourage all to read."

— Carol Hamilton, M.D., author of *Hitchhiking to Madness: A Memoir*

"A masterful reminder of the danger of bias and predisposition in the workplace and in life. Throughout his book, Mark Anthony Powers weaves his professional experience of circumstances surrounding illness and how it affects the whole family, ending in an unexpected catharsis."

— Ruben D. Gonzales, author of the *Black Mountain Mystery* series

"Nobody writes medical mystery like Mark Anthony Powers. This fourth installment of the Phineas Mann series continues a flawless medical thriller storyline. *The Desperate Trials of Phineas Mann* combines a desperate race to solve a life-threatening diagnostic dilemma while Phineas confronts his own mortality. Powers' latest is a compelling page turner that is genuinely surprising, scientifically accurate, and full of heart and humanity. A brilliant modern day medical mystery!"

— Christopher Ethan Cox, M.D., Professor of Medicine,
director of Duke University's Medical Intensive Care Unit
and board-certified palliative medicine specialist

"Mark Anthony Powers' latest novel is an insider's look at physician Phineas Mann's struggles with becoming invisible in his field as he and his wife age and face inevitable illnesses. In a thoughtful tour de force that takes us behind the scenes in hospital rooms and clinics, Powers explores the power of family, the bonds created in a long-term marriage, the ways pets communicate with their owners, and the resilience of the human mind, as he draws on Dr. Mann's bravery when facing a drama that can determine his life, death, and magnificent career. Like a Southern version of Abraham Verghese's medical novels, *The Desperate Trials of Phineas Mann* teaches, inspires, and pulls on the heartstrings."

— Dawn Elaine Von Wald, author of *Analyzing the Prescotts: A Novel* and President, Rewired Creatives, Inc.

"Another great book from Mark Anthony Powers. It's nice to join Phineas and Iris once again in this brand new adventure, even if the circumstances they face are frightening. This book is an absolute delight to read!"

— Eleonora Piazza, Editor-in-Chief, *Not for Vanity*

"Mark Anthony Powers gives us an authoritative glimpse of the human travail that accompanies the evolution of medicine, while encouraging readers to grapple with diagnoses, the shortcomings of doctors and medical institutions, and the value of persistence and broad vision to the world of medicine. An instructive and enjoyable read!"

— Francis Neelon, M.D., Associate Professor Emeritus of Medicine, Duke University

THE
Desperate Trials of
PHINEAS
MANN

MARK ANTHONY POWERS

The Desperate Trials of Phineas Mann is a work of fiction. Other than any actual historical events, people, and places referred to, all names, characters, and incidents are from the author's imagination. Any resemblances to persons, living or dead, are coincidental, and no reference to any real person is intended.

HAWKSBILL PRESS

https://hawksbillpress.com

Edited by Dawn Reno Langley, President of Rewired Creatives, Inc.
Book design by Christy Day, Constellation Book Services
Cover image by istock.com
Author photo by Amy Stern Photography, www.amystern.com

ISBN (paperback): 978-1-7370329-8-4
ISBN (ebook): 978-1-7370329-7-7

Printed in the United States of America

For my third grandson, whom I haven't yet met

Foreword

An author's universal goal is to tell an engaging story. I wrote *The Desperate Trials of Phineas Mann* for two additional reasons. The first is to showcase the potential complexities of diagnostic medicine. The second is to expose the poison and perils of bias.

While artificial intelligence and computer algorithms can aid busy clinicians, rare diseases and common disorders presenting in unusual ways can slip through the programmed reasoning of machines. Finding uncommon answers requires clinicians to study the full spectrum of diseases during training activities throughout our careers. And we are required to keep our minds open and to really *see and hear* our patients.

A diagnosis will only be made if a clinician thinks of it.

To perform at our best, we must resist the temptations of bias. Bias limits our ability to fully think through complex problems. And bias mistreats its victims.

Many clinicians won't have the opportunity to diagnose the diseases explored in *The Desperate Trials of Phineas Mann*. These fictional cases are presented like the real cases that I had the opportunity to see during my practice of consultative pulmonary medicine.

The art and science of medicine have become increasingly complex since my training began in 1974. I salute those practitioners who labor to keep up.

Mark Anthony Powers, MD

CHAPTER 1
June 30

The branches of Phineas' backyard fruit trees nearly touched each other except in one spot.

The first tree he planted so many years ago, an apple variety, at first produced to his high expectations but eventually, despite its teasing him each spring with an abundance of flowers, offered a steadily shrinking harvest. Even after he installed beehives close by, the tree's fruit set became sparser, and fewer fully ripened. Then the devil squirrels took whatever fruit was left before he could get it. They knew the instant its apples should be harvested—always hours before Phineas. In the late summer, it was not uncommon to spot one of the furry-tailed rodents sitting on the porch railing with a fresh picked apple between its paws and gnawing its way around the equator, mocking Phineas like some insolent cartoon character.

By the time Phineas followed a zealous arborist's suggestion to cut the aged tree down, it had begun encroaching on the younger and more productive fruit trees surrounding it. Sapsuckers then drilled precise circumferential holes in rings up and down its trunk, one more insult that kept it unproductive. Yet the holes gave it an elegance that Phineas admired, like henna tattoos on a bride.

The first years after he sawed the apple tree down, the others around it flowered more exuberantly then went on to produce less and smaller fruit. Had the old tree somehow benefited the orchard's ecosystem in ways that didn't weigh down its own branches with food? Phineas told himself that the remaining trees were simply putting more of their energy into expanding their root systems and branches into the newly abandoned space, but he couldn't help thinking the entire orchard was mourning their senior member's execution. Whenever he looked at the spot where the tree's stubby trunk had finally rotted away, he felt a twinge of melancholy.

Had he ever, as a young man, unconsciously favored winnowing out someone older and less overtly productive to make room for youth in their more vigorous growth phases? He knew in his soul, as one of those swept aside and tucked away, that the elders in a community can add in profound ways often unappreciated by all but the most insightful.

Now, when the university's younger medical faculty need an obscure bit of clinical knowledge, they turn to internet search engines and artificial intelligence during the shrinking patient time slots allotted them by distant bean counters. If those harried doctors don't readily find an answer in digital bytes, they conclude one simply doesn't exist. Yet, more than once, Phineas had later heard the unanswered question they'd asked, and more than once—to their astonishment—neuronal bytes in his brain's seventy-five-year-old hard drive bequeathed the critical piece of missing information. He had become their last resort for hopeless mysteries—but only if a baffled physician happened to remember that Dr. Phineas Mann still existed.

The first thing Phineas did each day was to press his shaking fingers onto the pulse in his wrist. When his heart functioned in a regular rhythm, his touch felt a glorious crispness with every beat, but if he awakened weakened by a bout of the dreaded and chaotic atrial fibrillation, that touch felt like his hands rested on the handlebars of a bicycle bumping over coarse gravel.

Three months ago, his doctor, an efficient young woman, advised him to embark on a trial of wearing a continuous positive airway pressure (CPAP) mask for sleep. She'd speculated that elusive obstructing apneas from his Parkinson's disease might be triggering his heart's episodic and troublesome nocturnal rhythm disturbances. He'd dutifully followed her advice and, so far, that efficient young woman's suggestion was coming up brilliant. He hadn't had any episodes negotiating those rugged, unpaved roads since.

Phineas gave silent thanks each morning when he found his pulse bounding in a steady cadence. No need on those days for him to swallow a rate-slowing beta blocker and a rapid-onset blood thinner to prevent the disastrous added burden of a stroke to his neurologic miseries. His clumsiness made him a "major fall risk," so when he was on those medications and lacking effective clotting factors, even the slimmest chance of a blow to his fragile noggin terrified all concerned.

But the CPAP added another measure of complication to his life. When he had to get up to pee in the middle of the night, removing that infernal contraption's head harness with his tremoring hands ended in frustrating tangles on numerous occasions and wetting the bed on a few. Phineas' attempts to use a urine bottle in bed were soon aborted. His shaking hands, like those of a priest blessing the congregation with holy water, had sprinkled *his* water all over the sheets. The indignity of a condom attached to a catheter solved the conundrum. Pragmatism trumped humiliation but, in addition to his CPAP air source, had raised his bodily tube count to two. An old intensive care unit adage taught that when patients have six tubes attached to them, survival is unlikely. Four more to go, and he wasn't even out of his own bedroom.

Through a gap between the drapes, the morning sun shot a crisp sliver of light onto Phineas' beloved wife, Iris. She lay facing him, her eyes closed, her breathing gloriously steady and relaxed. Her long silver braid disappeared under the sheets that caressed her curves the way he longed to once again with steady, capable hands. She'd kept those near waist length tresses because of him. More than once, she'd threatened to cut them short, but his sorrowful expression stopped her. At his age and in his condition, she must have understood that these could be the last times he delighted in their elegance.

Was that a sheen of perspiration on her brow? It wasn't *that* warm inside, and she went off female hormones many years ago. Maybe too many covers on a summer night? She must have kicked them to the foot of the bed, since only a thin sheet covered her now. He'd mention the unexpected perspiration if he saw it again.

And the angle at her hips. Had that become more prominent recently? If she's lost weight, she'd say it was because he wasn't cooking anymore, that she'd preferred it when he'd cooked, both the food's tastes and him taking a foodie's pleasure in what she viewed as a tedious chore. Lately though, he'd watched her push away half-eaten plates of even the tastiest takeout offerings. Worry about this recent change in her appetite gnawed at him. *Might a husband get in trouble if he asked his wife about her weight?*

When was she last examined and pronounced healthy by the internist they shared? Had she skipped that checkup? Been too busy? Her pitiful husband filled her days and nights with needs more constant than any spouse deserved. If he mentioned his concerns, would she say he was just a hypervigilant worrywart, that he now fretted over her alone, since he no longer had patients on a medical service to worry about? Was he concerned about her because he so depended on her for his personal care and tenuous emotional stability? If the latter unraveled, they'd be in an even worse mess. Was him fretting over her coming from concealed selfishness for his own needs?

He reached for the magnetic right-sided attachment on his CPAP harness. Before he could grasp and release the clasp, the ever-present tremor made the task like piloting a single-engine plane trying for an emergency landing in turbulent winds. *There. Done.* Now for the left one and guiding the hand with the worse affliction. This time his thumb and index finger only poked him in the ear and cheek before they located and clamped on their target. Weeks ago, he'd learned the hard, painful way that he should keep his left eye tightly closed. Triumphant, he snatched the straps from his scalp and lifted the form-fitting mask off his nose and mouth. The CPAP machine, relieved of his respiratory resistance, gasped and shot a final volume of warm, moist air through the mask. The screen lit up with two approving smiley faces but reported a disappointing six hours and twenty-five minutes of mask wearing sleep. His nightly goal was seven hours, but worry about the ambitious day facing him had kept his mind from settling down enough to drift easily into sleep.

Would this phase of his life be easier if dementia softened the realization that his physical abilities had entered free fall? If there was anything positive with his condition, it was that the prison of his rigid body now forced him to focus through its iron bars on everything around him. Subtle details in his surroundings, that his constant activities might have made him miss in earlier years, now came to his attention—details that able-bodied medical observers often failed to notice—and on occasion those unappreciated details turned out to be pivotal.

For instance, he didn't miss Iris now studying him, her glacial blue eyes peeking out under half closed lids. "Are you still going in today?" she asked. If he was, she would have to rally herself to help him get ready before she drove him to the hospital.

Phineas dreaded hearing his voice the first time each day. Tremor had also invaded his vocal cords and made him sound like he was speaking from a vibrating chair in need of repair. "It's...it's the new...new fellows... first chest...conference." His meek voice was barely audible. Unless he made an extra effort to project his words, listeners predictably responded with "What?" or "Pardon?" Sometimes even the demand, "Speak up." If only he could.

The blast of air from the CPAP device had already alerted his service dog, Ernest, that his master was now awake. Ernest spent his nights on a four-foot pillow that was close enough to monitor his master, but far enough from the bed to not block traffic. When he heard Phineas' distinctive voice, the black, block-headed, barrel-chested Labrador rested his muzzle on the bed's comforter and made eager eye contact. A soft whine escaped. Most mornings, the command "let's go" would signal Ernest to first notify Iris, then to pull the covers back on Phineas' side. Today, Phineas commanded only "move" then "sit." With this morning's planned teaching excursion and need for efficiency, Iris would have to handle the whole process. Ernest obeyed but fixed his pleading gaze on his master. Service was his business, his raison d'etre.

The last weekday of June was the day when brand new pulmonary fellows initially viewed the division's faculty members assembled, and each fresh trainee was sure to do a double take when they spotted the shaky old man hunched over and shuffling behind a rolling walker. They'd first wonder if a confused geriatric patient had strayed into the middle of their hallowed meeting. Then they'd see the University of North Carolina Hospital ID badge clipped to his shirt pocket. There'd be skeptical head shakes, sideways glances, and eyebrows lifted toward the other new arrivals. They'd undoubtably be thinking, "Is this pitiful old man supposed to teach us something?"

Would this be the final time he sized up a fresh annual crop of pulmonary and critical care fellows? His neurologic condition's trajectory screamed an answer in the affirmative. Was there still time for some radical and novel treatment to provide a miracle and preserve what life he had left? Could anything on the year 2028's horizon have a prayer at allowing him to function *even better*? Most days, with Siri's necessary help for all things computer related, he combed the literature. Eight miles down Tobacco Road at the Duke University Medical Center, a research group studied an intriguing intervention. Their project made the most sense to him but carried the greatest risks. Without informing Iris, he'd reached out to them with Siri's help.

Iris rolled into a sitting position on the side of the bed and stretched her arms over her head. "Let me get your urine bag before you sit up." She came around the foot of the bed and peeled the sheet back exposing his futile wobbly attempts to grasp and remove the condom attached to its catheter. She placed one of her hands over his and used the other to loosen the Velcro cinch and slip the apparatus off without spilling a drop. She disappeared into the bathroom with the collection bag that contained his night's production, while he maneuvered his legs over the edge of the bed and leaned onto his walker.

Ernest's eyes remained locked on Phineas' every movement. For the first years of his master's impairment, the dog had been a reliable mobility assistant, strong shoulders for Phineas to occasionally lean or recover his balance on. But Phineas' unsteadiness progressed to the point the metal walker became a safety necessity. A subtle quiver in the dogs muscular shoulders indicated his daily disappointment in his reduced role and his dislike of the metal barrier the walker imposed between him and his master.

Iris returned in time to monitor her husband's progress into the kitchen with a vigilance that suggested she was ready to pounce at his first misstep. She'd donned her robe and cinched the belt tight. *Is her waist even slimmer than before?* He made a mental note to address his observations and concerns with her today as soon as he returned from the teaching conference.

Phineas plopped into his usual chair arranged sideways to the table next to his favorite window, a window that faced due east and welcomed each new day. He then pivoted chair and legs in short, choppy installments until they were underneath this preferred meal and work station. The window stretched from knee high almost to the ceiling and gave Ernest and him full view of the front yard and surrounding woods. A birdfeeder and suet holder attracted showy cardinals, bluebirds, and woodpeckers—as well as those thieving squirrels.

Phineas' everyday realm had shrunken from his actively engaging in an outdoors world he'd once relished to an indoor perch from which he could only watch it. The Parkinson's disease had stolen his capacity to tolerate heat, and the outside world continued to get hotter. July days were predictably brutal.

At least his imagination and ability to relive his favorite past scenes hadn't also been stolen from him. His quiet times often slipped into the most vivid recollections of not only pleasing images, but sounds, smells, and tactile sensations from the past. Even memories of prior culinary treats sometimes resurfaced and triggered pointless flows of his saliva.

His capable wife now turned her attention to Ernest. "Time to get busy, Ernest." The command for a dog to head outside and relieve himself. Ernest trailed her out of the kitchen, his tail wagging as steadily as a metronome.

With dog freed and husband secured, Iris appeared more at ease while she retrieved two Carolina Blue mugs. "You want coffee, right?" She laid his morning maintenance carbidopa-levodopa dose next to a half-filled tumbler of water. The pale-yellow tablet was his only current medication for the Parkinson's disease, and he had to take it four times a day and then wait for it to kick in and offer a modest transient (and shrinking) improvement in his impairments. He'd suffered through futile trials of the other drugs and even been subjected to a pioneering ultrasound generated heat ablation procedure that penetrated deep into his brain, into the site identified as his globus pallidus. Each new therapeutic intervention had promised hope, but none had delivered benefit, only intolerable side effects or nothing.

"Just…Just a…short cup," he answered. She knew he didn't want to have to use the restroom at the hospital. He'd have more coffee when he made it back home later. Dehydration served him when he was in a public place. He detested wetting the disposable incontinence product, an adult diaper, that now replaced underwear for his forays outside their home.

Phineas enjoyed watching Ernest's systematic patrol of the perimeter of the yard, pausing to lift his leg at predictable intervals. The dog's luxurious coat shone under the morning sun as if he'd emerged fresh from a pond swim. When Ernest reached the most distant point of the property, he emptied his bowels and kicked his legs backward as if to spread his scent and declare the yard secure. While a disciplined, highly trained, and intelligent service animal, he was still a dog with a dog's primal instincts.

Iris held the pill in one hand and the glass of water in the other. "Time for your medicine." Phineas opened his mouth for her to deposit the pill like a baby robin anticipating its mother's earthworm offering. This time he handled swallowing without coughing.

She smiled her approval. "Will Marie meet us, or do I need to park and come with you to the conference room?"

"Marie...confirmed...she'd be there." Having their daughter-in-law working at the hospital was one of the main reasons he could still venture there for conferences and when he, on occasion, was called on to consult on a perplexing case that had baffled the younger faculty. Marie would make sure her Wednesday morning allowed her to at least meet Iris' car and then to deliver him back to it an hour and a half later. Some weeks, she even found the time in her busy schedule as co-director of the University of North Carolina Hospital Medicine Service to stay with him for the entire pulmonary fellows' conference. She'd recently remarked that she now often guessed the correct diagnosis and was becoming a decent wannabee pulmonologist.

Today, one of the senior fellows would show two cases with diagnoses so obscure, that it was unlikely that any of the new fellows had ever seen or heard of those rare lung conditions. This annual introductory lesson in humility would inspire them to read the literature avidly to avoid the embarrassment of drawing another blank at a future public forum. It would also give them a taste of the varied and fascinating world of pulmonary medicine.

Though he was no longer supervising any clinical services, Phineas had seen about everything in his fifty years studying respiratory diseases and physiology. He knew those disease patterns from symptoms to physical examination findings to laboratory and radiologic studies like a seasoned forest ranger identifying local flora and fauna.

Iris set a bagel spread with peanut butter in front of him. She'd assembled it and sliced it in half, so he could grasp one end of the semicircular tube and guide the other to his mouth. He'd given up on breakfast yogurt after it repeatedly dribbled from his flailing spoon and necessitated a thorough cleaning of his beard. Utensils were challenges to be avoided whenever possible, and he'd rediscovered his childhood love of peanut butter.

He could still chew and swallow bites of a bagel if he concentrated and tucked his chin. His speech therapy consultants hadn't yet declared him a swallowing risk for aspirating food and his own saliva. They hadn't yet demanded he endure a thickened liquid diet, one without the succulent solids he savored. After *that* miserable liquid stage, a feeding tube stabbed through his abdominal skin and into his stomach could be tube number three; but he wasn't going to allow it. That command was in black and white in his final instructions. With the assistance of palliative caregivers, he'd spare his Iris the steepest portion of his decline.

He did sometimes chuckle when he brushed his teeth, having once pointed out that his electric toothbrush was no longer needed, its rhythmic scrubbing motions replaced by his tremor. That was his only amusement during morning ablutions. His reflection in the mirror startled him daily. *Who is that white-bearded old man in a stone mask?* Where is the Phineas Mann he wished to see looking back at him? The one he wished would lie each night next to his beautiful Iris.

Last night, Iris had shaved his neck and washed him on his shower stool in preparation for today's outing. She'd even trimmed his protruding nose hairs and unruly, corkscrew ear hairs, those impudent rogues that had secretly arrived at night several years ago. When they first appeared, he was inspired to submit a poem to the Alpha Omega Alpha medical honor society's journal, *The Pharos*. It was titled *getting old* and went:

hairy ears
eerie hairs

His poem was rejected, without comment. Must have reached an older male editor with the same issues and no sense of humor—or a younger editor who denied his own certain future.

Iris relieved him of his toothbrush and held up a cup, ready for him to rinse. "Want to use the toilet before you dress?"

"Number one...this time. Number two...later, after...I return." He didn't need to tell her, but always did. Number twos were *always* reserved for later at home. The tremor that brushed his teeth made cleaning his bum too great a challenge. His TUSHY Ace bidet, with heated seat and warm air dryer, turned that personal chore into a tactile pleasure. And watching Ernest's curious head tilt during the bidet's operation always brought what might pass for a smile on Phineas' impassive face. He'd installed the luxury appliance way back during the toilet paper hoarding of the COVID pandemic...before his affliction...when he could still use tools.

His wife helped him sit on the toilet and patiently waited for him to stand, her hands out and ready to catch him. He advanced the walker, shuffled, advanced the walker and shuffled until they reached their spacious walk-in closet where he sat on another stool that an occupational therapist had adjusted to a height optimal for dressing.

Ernest dutifully took his place seated in the back corner. When he'd first moved into the Mann household, he'd assisted his master with the chore of dressing. When the Parkinson's disease advanced closer to its current state, there was less that a service dog could do and more need to burden Iris for almost everything.

While the family described Ernest's expressions as sphinxlike, Phineas regularly read disappointment in the dog's face and body language. Ernest was trained to be the star in the team's starting lineup. Sitting on the dugout bench had to smother his spirit. Ernest had become a pet, a friend, and a confidant—all valuable positions—but positions that had to be perceived as demotions to one with his abilities.

Iris held up a light blue dress shirt. "Still want the clothes you picked out last night?"

"I...was thinking...maybe a tux...this time." Phineas watched for her reaction out of the corner of his eye. He hadn't retrieved his formalwear from their cedar closet since their son Jacob's marriage to Marie three years ago.

She wrinkled her forehead and pulled in her chin for a second then smiled. "Now you're reminding me of Jacob or Martha getting ready for kindergarten, when they insisted on wearing this or that—which was usually pajamas."

"They weren't...kidding...I am...you know." He hadn't been there to dress their children for school. Back then, he'd had to leave early for the hospital every morning. These days she had to dress him, like he was five years old again. *They say an old man is twice a child.* Hamlet, he thought. Shakespeare must be watching and grinning.

"Blue shirt...is fine." He settled onto the seat of his walker, and she pulled shirt, pants, socks, and shoes onto him. Tie shoes for the public. He hadn't sunk to Velcro fasteners outside the house. Yet. She helped him stand, his hands clenching the walker's handles, and tucked his shirt into his pants then buckled his belt.

"Zipper...please."

She lifted an eyebrow.

"Ready to teach, Phineas?" She was inspecting him, feet to face. "Wait." She stepped back to the sink and returned with a moistened hand towel. "Toothpaste on your chin." She scrubbed it gently. "There. Looking good for your conference."

If only that were true. She knew his teaching days were numbered. He'd seen the tears slip down her pretty cheek before she could wipe them or turn away. She knew.

CHAPTER 2

June 30

During each trip to the medical center as Iris' passenger, Phineas noticed something new. Today, it was the muscular young man lifting weights behind his townhouse on Martin Luther King Boulevard. Always before, the weight bench had been vacant; now it was keeping someone from losing their precious strength. Strength. Taken for granted until it leaked away like juice from a collapsing Halloween pumpkin in November.

Iris pulled up to the hospital entrance and parked in the spot designated for unloading patients. *Unloading. Like cargo. Was that his word, or was it the hospital's official term?* He scanned the sidewalk for a sign to answer this question and found none.

He waited until she readied his walker before he pushed open the Prius passenger door and began the arduous process of pivoting his legs inch by inch, then lower and lower. It always felt like his legs were descending into a bottomless hole until his feet sensed the reassuring pavement's surface. He still hadn't gotten used to that unsettling bottomless hole sensation, and it was only getting worse.

When he gripped the walker's handles, the whole apparatus shook until his weight pressed it down. Some days, he tried to envision himself as an astronaut ready to embark on a moon walk. Today, Marie brought him back to Earth before he had the chance.

"Hi Phineas. Lend a hand?" Her appearance never failed to impress, tall and slender in a long white coat, her wavy dark brown hair was predictably secured by a favorite mother of pearl clip into a thick ponytail down her back. One extraordinary day four years ago, she'd transformed in Phineas' eyes from a collaborator into a modern-day warrior when she saved him from a beating. That image of her was burned into his brain. It might one day be among his last surviving memories.

"Thanks...I got this." He pushed the walker forward a step and concentrated. He needed to keep his balance. A fall could mean a painful detour next door to the emergency room for stitches—or worse.

Marie sidled up next to Phineas. "I see you do, and I see you left Ernest at home." She kept her eyes trained on him and asked Iris, "How are *you* doing?"

"Phineas didn't want Ernest to be a distraction, and the conference room should be crowded for the fellows' first conference." Iris closed the passenger door. "We're making out okay. And you, Jacob, and the boys?"

"I'm sure you remember the chaos of getting two little ones ready at the same time."

A year after Marie married their son Jacob, they'd been gifted with identical twin boys, Iris and Phineas' second and third grandsons. The first twin out was christened Phineas, and he'd been honored to tears. Still was. The second born, Vincent, honored their elderly detective friend weeks before he passed away. Phin and Vin. Double trouble, especially after they gained their land legs.

"So, I'll see you again in an hour and a half?" Marie asked.

"I promise." Iris crossed her heart. "I'll run some errands and be back on schedule."

A uniformed security guard that Phineas had never seen before gestured with the back of his hand toward the asphalt in front of Iris' car. The guard's face was weathered and his hair sun-bleached and in need of a trim.

She hustled into her seat. "They need me to move," she said with a wave and drove away.

Though he needed to focus his attention on each step, Phineas still felt obliged to make conversation. "Your boys...all over...their colds?" Daycare sniffles, once a cause for panic, were less frightening now that a universal COVID vaccine was given routinely at six months of age.

"Still two snotty noses but improving. We'll wait till they're all better before we bring them over." She pressed the elevator button. Escalators were no longer an option. "Don't want to get you and Iris sick." With her arm fully extended, Marie kept the doors from closing on him.

He leaned into the far corner. "Be glad...to see them." Two dings later the door opened to the third floor. "How's Ruby?"

"Mellowing with age—finally!"

Four years ago, Jacob's post doc hadn't reclaimed her spirited beagle, Ruby, after he'd taken care of the dog during the woman's year of research abroad. Either that young scientist couldn't find her way back to North Carolina, or Jacob had become attached to Ruby and offered to keep her. Anyway, the dog became family and now kept a close watch on the two toddlers, herding them away from trouble on a regular basis. And Ruby loved Ernest. When she visited, she did her utmost to distract him from his service dog vigilance. When he refused to budge from Phineas' side, she'd curl up against one of his muscular haunches, sigh, and close her eyes.

Phineas recognized members of his division gathering down the hallway outside the conference room. "And Jacob's...book?"

Breath and Mercy was the true story of Hurricane Jezebel and Phineas Mann's 1985 arrest for murder. It had launched last month and spent its first weeks as an Amazon bestseller. Local bookstores promoted it on their websites and in their windows. Phineas no longer cared if his colleagues, friends, and neighbors knew the truth about the darkness in his ancient history. He had enough to worry about in his current daily existence.

"Doing *too* well. They want Jacob to go on a book tour. We're trying to postpone it. Too much craziness currently—plus he's trying to wrap up the big varroa mite study." Jacob, not only an author, but also an entomologist, was on faculty at North Carolina State University and researched honey bees and their afflictions.

Marie began studying her cell phone. "Text from Iris. She says Chelsea's all upset and is coming to your house. Says Chelsea got a call from her doctor that a surgeon wants to cut out part of her lung." Chelsea was an old friend, a retired WRAL newscaster, and the widow of one of Phineas' closest friends ever, Ron Bullock.

"Tell her...I'll look...at her info...as soon as...I can." Lung surgery in a septuagenarian should not be undertaken lightly. Too high a chance for complications. "Ask Iris to text...her medical...record number. ...I can look...at images...while we're here." He waited for Marie to tap the message into her phone. "If you have...time, Marie."

"I'll make time." Marie was also a close friend of Chelsea's.

Phineas felt a hand on his shoulder. Dr. Gabriella Morales-Villalobos came around the side of his walker to greet him face to face. His long-ago former pulmonary fellow, and now a faculty colleague and friend, Gabby had been drafted into the role of acting division chief while the department searched for a replacement. She'd quickly ironed out division difficulties and advanced the careers of young faculty members. Phineas hoped she'd be the one chosen for the permanent position, but currently the odds appeared to be stacked against her. Her load of clinical responsibilities kept her from logging the hundreds of publications her competitors for the position claimed. During her brief time in charge, the first white hairs had snuck in among the sleek, black ones she coiled into her work bun.

"It's good of you to come, Phineas. We have a great crop of new fellows for you to look over. Glad you'll be sharing your wisdom with them."

Before he could respond, a woman's amplified voice penetrated the hallway from the conference room door. "Welcome, everyone, to the first fellows' conference of the academic year. Please take your seats, so we can begin. We have two interesting cases for you to puzzle over."

Gabby grinned at Phineas, like she was anticipating an enjoyable diversion from her usual burdens. "Duty calls. See you later." She approached the young woman, a third-year fellow, at the podium.

Marie helped settle Phineas into an aisle seat in the back of the conference room. She folded his walker and secured the hinged desktop over his lap where he arranged two index cards and a pen, laboriously extracted from his shirt pocket. His system allowed him to give input without unleashing his humiliating voice onto an audience.

Gabby dramatically swept her arm toward the crowd. "Let's welcome our new fellows. Please stand." Four young doctors, two women and two men, in bright white coats popped up from the seated audience. Each nodded or waved as their chief announced their names. Trainees looked so much younger to Phineas with each passing year.

"Okay, fasten your seatbelts and let's hear the cases." Gabby took a seat in the middle of the front row.

While probably in her early thirties, the third-year fellow at the podium still struck Phineas as youthful for the weighty clinical responsibilities she carried. She began presenting with, "Our first patient is a 72-year-old retired dentist referred for abnormal chest imaging caught on an abdominal CT scan performed for borderline abnormal liver tests that were found when a blood panel was ordered for an annual physical." She continued with PowerPoint slides illustrating blood test results and pulmonary function studies.

The radiologist joined her at the podium and described the unusual finding of very dense linear structures scattered through both lungs—and, ironically, a normal appearing liver. Phineas had seen CT scans with similar densities several times and had been following two patients with this unique radiographic pattern when he'd phased out of clinic work. He suspected the current case may have been plucked from his pre-retirement patient panel. His other patient with the condition was an orthopedist.

Interesting how ectopic boney barrier islands had formed in the lungs of two who'd sawed and drilled bone during their careers, although the literature he'd found hadn't suggested an association with occupational exposure to powdered human bone.

"The tradition is for the first-year fellows to have the first crack at making the correct diagnosis," the senior fellow announced.

Each first-year fellow offered searching comments about the case. It was clear to Phineas that none of them recognized the condition. It was a rare enough condition that they might never see a case of dendriform pulmonary ossification outside of a conference or journal article.

Phineas gripped his pen in his right fist, leaned over the desktop, and fought to pin an index card in place with his wildly tremoring left hand. He pressed his lips together and forced himself to print big. Otherwise, the Parkinson's would shrink his letters to scratchings too tiny to read. Micrographia was the name of that frequent clinical sign of his affliction.

in turn passed it again until it reached the senior fellow at the podium. She glanced at it and winked at Phineas then held the index card aloft and announced, "Dr. Mann sent me this and, as usual, he has correctly identified dendriform pulmonary ossification." She proceeded to discuss the condition in detail. A first year fellow squirmed. Another looked down and slowly shook his head. The fellowship's first lesson in humility.

The senior fellow advanced the PowerPoint slide. "Is everyone ready for the second case?" Hopeful nods all around. Maybe this one would be easier. "This patient is a 58-year-old non-smoking woman with shortness of breath and multiple pulmonary nodules." She displayed slides with the patient's past medical history, physical exam, and labs. Breathing tests documented severe physiologic airways obstruction. The radiologist sauntered to the podium and displayed CT scans that revealed numerous nodules of varying size scattered throughout both lungs, as well as varying lung densities at the lobular level, a patchwork of centimeter trapezoids. He called it a "mosaic pattern".

Only one diagnosis fit, so Phineas, wishing for a shorter acronym, began laboriously scribbling on the second card. Marie folded it and passed it forward before he could try to add to the jumble.

The first-year fellows gave the case's differential diagnosis their best efforts. One guessed that it was the pulmonary manifestation of a rheumatologic condition. *Not a bad guess.* Another raised several chronic infections. Gabby let the audience go on until they'd run out of ideas then suggested diffuse intrapulmonary neuroendocrine cell hyperplasia, or DIPNECH, the correct diagnosis. She explained her reasoning while Phineas smiled his approval at her astute deduction. He'd helped train her—so very many years ago.

The next PowerPoint image was of a lung biopsy. Phineas' elderly pathologist friend, Dr. Henry Postum, with his rarely purposed tie askew, rose from his front row seat and described the microscopic features of DIPNECH. A muffled groan escaped from the second row where the first-year fellows sat.

The senior fellow held up Phineas' index card and announced his perfect record. Two for two. The first-year fellows turned as one to inspect him in a new light. As their year progressed, he'd find out which of them had the temerity or desperation to consult a hunched and wizened mystery man on puzzling cases. He wished his performance today felt like a victory. He was too much of a physical mess for triumphs, an old warrior so mortally wounded that there were no more true victories.

"Shall we...make our...way to radiology?" He wanted to see Chelsea's images and get home before he had to use the bathroom, and he didn't want Iris to have to wait for them in front of the hospital.

"Sure. Let's." She unfolded his walker and made sure its brakes were on while he stood. Rolling walkers tended to roll at the worst times.

Most of the crowd had exited the conference room, but now chatted and formed a loose gauntlet watching Phineas' sluggish progress. He scanned them for his friend Henry and couldn't find him. Must have a stack of tissue specimens in his subbasement office waiting for him to interpret. Perhaps another time soon. It had been too long since they'd caught up.

Phineas alternated forcing his meager excuse for a smile, the effort of a word here and there, and checking on the positions of his feet. Falling on his face would be an event no one could forget, and then he'd have to stop coming. Thank God Marie had a strong hand under his upper arm as he shuffled. Those new fellows had to be wondering who the young woman was who attached herself to such an elderly wreck. They'd learn soon enough when she, in her position as a leader of the inpatient hospitalist service, called on them for pulmonary consults.

Thankfully, the teaching conference room was only two doors from the radiology reading room. As he and Marie entered, Phineas spotted his favorite radiologist, Dr. Lacey Gray. They'd pored over thousands of images over the years. Not that much younger than he, she'd aged much more gracefully. Lucky for her.

Wait...Lacey wasn't wearing her wedding ring, and in the past, she'd worn it without fail. Had he somehow missed her husband's death? He and Siri would have to search the obituaries during the interval since he'd last consulted her. Then he'd send his too-late condolences. As he approached, sadness for her loss draped over his shoulders.

The sound of his walker made her look up at them from her bank of screens. "Hi Marie. And Phineas! To what do I owe this honor?" He'd always admired her perfect diction during their conversations and when he'd read her reports.

"I…I was hoping…you could…help us…review a friend's…images, Lacey."

Marie held her cell phone so Lacey could see Chelsea's medical record number. Several keystrokes, and a new set of images surrounded them on the panoramic monitors. Phineas had disciplined himself over the years to study images systematically. Avoid going straight for the lungs, or you'll miss something important in the other structures. Chelsea's bones appeared free of fractures and lesions, with only the first hints of osteoporosis. Coronary arteries were free of calcium, suggesting a lack of atherosclerosis. Soft tissues surrounding her thorax also looked normal. Okay, now he could inspect her lung slices and their 3-D reconstructions.

There it was. Behind the heart and near the spine. A choice place for a nodule to hide on routine x-rays. Without uttering a word, Lacey applied the computer's digital calipers to it.

"Twelve by thirteen millimeters, Phineas." Not a size reassuring for benignity. "Its borders don't look too terrible. It's not what I'd call spiculated." If it were, needle-like extensions would be a worrisome sign of an invading cancer. She expanded the culprit and varied the penetration. "No calcium in it." In certain patterns, calcium could reassure against cancer. She moved the images around to focus on more central thoracic structures. "Lymph nodes are unremarkable." Lacey clicked on another item in Chelsea's image menu. "Let's correlate her PET scan." The nuclear scan where 'hot' metabolically active areas would suggest inflammation or malignancy. 'Cold' structures suggested scar and reassured against a sinister nature—but only if a lesion was of adequate size to get valid metabolic measurements that confirmed benignity. Twelve by thirteen millimeters was usually adequate size.

Lacey lined the PET scan up beside the CT images then overlaid one on the other. She used another computer tool to take a quantitative metabolic measurement. "Sorry, Phineas, it's indeterminate." The grey zone. Neither clearly a threat nor a benign incidental finding. She spun her chair ninety degrees to look into Phineas' eyes and asked, "Are they planning to resect it?"

"Not if...we can find...old images that...show it's been...there for years." He leaned closer and squinted at the monitor. "Got any?"

Lacey scrolled through Chelsea's short list of images. Mammograms, an ultrasound or two, but nothing inside the chest. The nodule had shown up when an abdominal CT was ordered for a recent episode of abdominal pain. 'Rule out appendicitis' was that order. Chelsea's appendix looked fine, but the CT's slices reached into the chest just far enough to reveal that nodule. Was finding it a fortunate serendipitous event, the life-saving discovery of an early cancer, or would this septuagenarian now be subjected to the risks of thoracic surgery, only to prove a decades-old scar rested in her lung?

Lacey offered a shrug. "Sorry, Phineas. Maybe she can think of some study she had outside of all the health system records we have access to."

Finding outside images would be a long shot. Few healthcare facilities had failed to join the banks of medical records and images accessible to hospitals through the Internet.

Phineas dreaded breaking the news to Chelsea that her nodule could be cancer, and that statistically, her age made the odds of malignancy substantial, odds not to be ignored. If it were cancer, would it grow at a rate that would threaten her life? Some lung cancers grew agonizingly slowly. Others galloped without pause. Delaying resection too long could lead to a deadly outcome for his good friend.

As far as he knew, she was in good health and likely could have decades of life ahead. He had no way to reassure her she could safely forgo surgical resection. Unless... He would push her to remember every single time she'd crossed paths with any medical provider, whether in a rural emergency room, an urgent care clinic, an orthopedist, or even a chiropractor. Some facilities still warehoused old films collected in manila folders, but most recycled them for the one-time payout from their silver content.

"Thank you, Lacey...I'll talk...with Chelsea."

Marie glanced at her cell phone. "Iris should be here soon."

Phineas leaned on his walker and pivoted toward the door. He advanced the walker and stepped.

Lacey called out, "Come back and see us, Phineas."

He offered her a nod and as much of a smile his face could produce then murmured to Marie, "Not looking...forward to...telling Chelsea."

Marie responded, "I don't envy you that. Let me know if I can help look for old images."

Chelsea, Marie, and Iris had bonded before the 2024 elections. They'd teamed up to help Martha, Phineas and Iris' daughter, defeat the incumbent Republican for a U. S. House seat. Together, the four women had formed a formidable force. Chelsea, a charismatic former news anchor, had made impassioned television ads, while Marie and Iris donated countless hours of mental energy and legwork.

Near the hospital lobby's main entrance, Phineas used his walker to part the waves of arriving patients and their families. Iris waited on the sidewalk beyond the double glass door and appeared to be in a lively discussion with the security guard who was gesturing at her Prius. When Phineas and Marie approached, Iris pointed at them with apparent relief.

"I *told* you they'd be right here," she muttered at the guard. He retreated and began waving at the next car in line. She held open the Prius' right front door. "Chelsea's already waiting at our house. Hope you've got good news for her."

"Need to ask...her questions." He turned his walker ninety degrees, locked its brakes, then carefully lowered himself onto the passenger seat. He mumbled, "Thanks, Marie." Iris opened the hatchback, folded the walker, and slid it into the back.

"So, Iris, we'll plan to see you on the Fourth?" Marie asked, still holding the car door open. "Jacob and Felipe are grilling ribs and brats." Then she chuckled. "By brats, I don't mean the twins."

"Looking forward to it. Text me what I should bring." Iris had been talking for weeks about how excited she was that their daughter Martha, son-in-law Felipe, and their oldest and spunkiest grandson, six-year-old Mateo, would be visiting from Washington.

"Just bring Phineas—and tell Chelsea I'm looking forward to seeing her too." Marie carefully closed the passenger side door and waved good-bye to Phineas through its window.

"Will do. She could use the company. And thanks." Iris gestured with her head toward Phineas. She glanced at his shaking attempts to insert the metal clip of the seatbelt and shoulder harness then leaned across and guided his hand the last few inches. Click. "All secure. Let's get you home for your second cup of coffee." She buckled her own seatbelt, closed her door, and waved to Marie.

The security guard stared uneasily at Iris' car from the sidewalk where Marie frowned while addressing him. His brow was creased in obvious worry. Phineas surmised that she might be drifting into being overly protective of her in-laws and hadn't notice the guard's work shoes. One of the soles flapped rhythmically while he tapped it on the sidewalk. A strip of duct tape wrapped the toe of the other shoe. The man is new at this job—and to Phineas—and was trying not to allow a mistake to threaten his position. The poor fellow hasn't banked enough paychecks to buy decent shoes. Had he been homeless recently? His weathered face and shaggy hair suggested he had. Phineas made a mental note to introduce himself the next time, if the same man was lucky enough to still be employed.

Iris pushed the hybrid car's power on button and began pulling away. "I bet Marie's telling him he should focus on helping people. When he sees the title on her badge, he'll pay attention."

And fear for his economic security. Iris must have also missed his shoes while fussing over her needy husband.

"So, Chelsea's...waiting at...the house?"

"She said she'd bring maple-glazed donuts."

His favorite. "Wish I...had good news." Confirming that Chelsea might need thoracic surgery was the opposite of good news, and she was never a woman who kept her feelings inside. He used to keep his emotions sealed under a locked lid. Then he lost Chelsea's husband, his best friend, to COVID, ...and the accumulation of so many others' sufferings and his own miserable straits finally crowbarred that lid off and toppled his emotional walls. He might cry along with her.

CHAPTER 3

June 30

A surge of dread filled Phineas' core when he spotted Chelsea sitting planted on the Manns' front steps, her chin in her hands and elbows on her knees, staring at the ground. She must have abruptly detected the stealthy approach of Iris' hybrid car, for she glanced up as if startled, her face expressing a fear similar to the one she'd shown Phineas on December 1, 2020. On that somber day, he'd broken the news to her that her husband's COVID infection had progressed to such a severity that he required a ventilator's life support. ECMO, an invasive and desperate measure to provide supplemental oxygen, soon followed. Phineas had never felt so helpless or so broken when, despite all efforts, he watched his close friend die.

Two weeks later the first COVID vaccine became available to medical personnel.

Chelsea bounced off the stoop and hurried to the passenger door where Iris was readying Phineas' walker. The two women hugged. Chelsea's usually maintained appearance had been neglected. Over the decades, her hair had evolved from brassy blonde to platinum to snow-white, and each color had looked as stunning on her as the last. But this morning she hadn't brushed out all of the tangles, and her lips lacked their usual bright red coating. Several years ago, she'd once admitted to having her face "tightened a tad" to preserve her youthful looks for the television audience, and today traces of that procedure amplified a startled, frightened expression.

Chelsea broke from her hug. "Finman, I need you to get me out of a mess." Her lips pinched together and paled while she waited for his answer.

The nickname only his friends used both warmed and saddened him. He wished he could rescue her from the scalpel by parrying its blade with a unique Finman solution. Maybe if he could distract her for an instant, lighten the gravity pulling her down, she might think more clearly and help him to help her.

"I heard...you have...donuts."

Iris did a double take. "Jesus, Phineas!"

"My brain...needs sugar...to work." He pushed himself up and over the walker.

Chelsea's face relaxed and the beginning of a smile emerged. "You men! Always thinking of your stomachs."

Ernest waited patiently behind the front door with his soft eyes locked on his master, then he heeled beside Phineas' walker to the kitchen. Phineas commanded, "under," and Ernest took up a position scrunched beneath Phineas' chair and out of the way of traffic.

The three humans took silent places around the small table, each with a steaming mug of coffee, and Phineas with a maple-glazed donut on a paper napkin. He wrapped both hands around his mug and guided it through a wobbly path to his mouth. A few drops trickled onto his chin whiskers. *Too hot still.* He settled the mug back on the table and purposed his wildly shaking left hand to press another napkin to his face. Finally, he lifted his donut in his right hand and bit into maple frosting and airy pastry, savoring the flavor that always sent him back to his Vermont childhood.

Iris glanced from him to the ceiling. "Are you ready *now*, Phineas?"

He tucked his chin and carefully swallowed. "Yes...thank you...Chelsea." He gestured his appreciation with his donut.

She fidgeted and leaned forward. "Dammit, Finman. Get to the point. You saw my x-rays, right?"

He nodded that he had.

"Well, I'm too old to have a knife stuck into this chest." She hoisted a breast in each hand, to emphasize her point. "So, how are you going to get me out of this?" She narrowed her eyes and stared into his.

"I wish...I could...tell you..." His lurching speech pattern was creating suspense he wished he could avoid. "...that the images...suggest...it's only a scar."

With each of his involuntary pauses, her eyes opened a fraction wider. "So, it's cancer?" She blinked, and a single tear trickled across her cheek into the corner of her mouth.

There was only one path to escape. "Maybe not... If we can find...an old image...that shows it. ...Sometimes...infections can...leave a scar. ...Even dog...heartworm." He tilted his head forward and tried to lift a reluctant eyebrow. "Got any?"

"Heartworms? I don't think so." She glared at Ernest who tilted his head as if puzzled by her attention. Then she said, "But if you mean chest x-rays. I haven't been getting them—and I don't suspect mammograms would show it." She crossed her hands protectively over her breasts this time.

"No...they don't."

"Can't it be biopsied—maybe with a needle?" A fleeting look of hope.

"It's in a...tough place to...reach." Then there was the other conundrum. "And if a...biopsy did show...cancer, ...you'd need...that surgery."

"But what if the biopsy was negative?"

He gave her time to think through the question she'd posed. "Would... you believe...they hadn't...missed it?"

Her shoulders sagged; eyes closed.

Iris' hands were wrapped around a mug she still hadn't sipped from. She eyed her husband, imploring him to find an out for their close friend.

Could he find an out? There were a couple of desperate possibilities he'd purposed over his many years, ones the other doctors hadn't considered. "Chelsea...have you been...to a chiropractor?"

She shook her head.

"Had...an MRI...for back pain?"

Chelsea startled, like he'd poked her. "Once. In Sweden. Before the pandemic when Ron and I were on a tour there. I slipped on a forest trail and landed hard on my bottom." She shifted in her seat as if remembering her injury to that part. "You'd think I have enough padding down there, but my back hurt like hell right after. Right here." She pointed at a spot between her shoulder blades. "So the tour director took me to a hospital in a small town, and they did an MRI. Said nothing was broken."

Iris released her mug. "Chelsea, where exactly did you get that MRI?"

Chelsea pulled her cell phone from her jeans' back pocket. "Let me look at my pictures from the trip. They'll have a date and location."

Phineas wanted to feel relief, but knew the MRI was still a long shot for preventing surgery. They'd have to locate and acquire the images, and it would have to show an identical nodule the Swedish radiologist missed while focusing attention on Chelsea's back bones. A long shot. Swedish radiologists were good.

"Chelsea, when...did they schedule...your surgery?"

"Said they'd pencil me in for a couple of weeks from now. Told me to make arrangements for the help I'll need after."

"So, we have...a couple...of weeks."

The kitchen clock's emphatic ticking filled the silence that followed. The handsome timepiece was manufactured by New England Clock Company and set in a dark cherry stained wood frame. It had been passed down through generations in Phineas' family and required weekly winding. It hung prominently on the wall opposite the kitchen table, but Phineas and Iris had learned to ignore its brass pendulum's swing and ever-present pulse—except during tense and quiet moments.

Iris broke their silence with, "I'll help you start on this today." As a retired social worker, she'd be well versed in finding medical records. She tasted her coffee. It was surely past tepid by now, but she seemed to like it anyway, since she raised the mug in salute.

Chelsea raised her own mug in return. "Soon as I finish my cup...and have one of those delicious donuts." She placed one on a napkin and slid it in front of Iris. "I bought enough for all of us, and you better have one. You're looking a little pekid. You lost weight lately, Girlfriend?"

"Maybe later. I already had breakfast." Iris slid the donut back to Chelsea.

"Suit yourself—but Honey—you were skinny to start with."

So, I'm not the only one to notice Iris' weight. He resolved to get up the nerve to ask her about it when they were alone.

⌒

The two women located the phone number to the rural overseas hospital, but immediately heard only incomprehensible Swedish voices on Iris' cell's speakerphone.

"With the time...difference...you may have...reached...an afterhours service," Phineas guessed.

Undaunted, Iris called Marie who said she'd be glad to help Chelsea access UNC Hospital's translation service at a time when the Swedish hospital's radiology department was at full strength.

CHAPTER 4
July 1

"Siri...open my...emails." Seated at the kitchen window, Phineas strained to raise his voice over the background noise of Iris' living room vacuuming, a chore he'd once relished performing for her as understood foreplay to be banked for later withdrawal. This ritual began long ago during his internal medicine residency. After being up all night on call, he'd vacuumed their tiny rental in a desperate effort to stay awake until she came home from after-work grocery shopping. She'd been so pleased with him, that her affectionate thank you culminated in bed. Over the decades that followed, he'd repeatedly sought opportunities to relive that pleasurable ritual—until last year, when they determined that vacuuming while holding onto a walker was too cumbersome—and likely hazardous.

Iris had settled him earlier in his favorite window seat with his open laptop, and Ernest had tucked tightly under his master's chair at the first loud blasts of the hated vacuum cleaner. Phineas started with the email at the top, a probing advertisement for an expensive, newly released pulmonary fibrosis drug.

"Siri...unsubscribe." She obliged. "Siri...delete." The ad disappeared.

What's this? The next email had a Duke address. "Siri...open."

Dr. Mann,

Thank you for your interest in our Phase 1 Parkinson's disease study. We are currently enrolling selected referred patients. If, after reading the attached protocol, you would like to be evaluated for entry as a study subject, please have your physicians forward all of your pertinent notes and studies for our investigators' review.

I encourage you to accomplish this promptly, as we plan to close the study to new subjects in the next few weeks.

Respectfully,

Annabella Sanchez PA

Study Co-Ordinator

"Siri...open attachment."

A colorful title page appeared. Two elderly men faced each other. The frail appearing man on the left stooped over a walker and peered up at a more erect, robust version of himself on the right. The words "The Reprogram PD Study" headlined the image. A dozen thumbnails lined the left of the screen.

"Siri...next page."

Phineas pored over the study information and found it similar to what he'd expected from his PubMed review of the Duke group's publications of preliminary animal studies and their NIH grant proposal for this Phase 1 trial. Only subjects with severe and progressive Parkinson's disease would be enrolled, and they couldn't be so debilitated that they wouldn't be likely to survive the next six months. Investigators needed to be able to monitor results of the intervention at least that long.

He was in that exact 'sweet spot' *(hah! such an ironic phrase!)* in his Parkinson's course for now and would likely be for those "next few weeks". He had to tell Iris about the trial. He'd spared her so far, because of her lifelong squeamishness and the intense and gruesome nature of the study's intervention. It involved way more than only taking a new medication.

If he were accepted into Duke's study, they'd harvest his bone marrow. A team of hematologists and geneticists would isolate his stem cells and program them using CRISPR technology, inserting genetic code that would induce those cells to manufacture dopamine, the substance the basal ganglia area of his brain now lacked. Neurosurgeons would drill a hole in his skull to install a port under his scalp that connected to a thin catheter directed deep into a precise location near his brain's basal ganglia, next to the substantia nigra, the site that should be producing his dopamine. Over subsequent weeks, doses of his programmed stem cells would be injected into the port, titrating for a beneficial effect or for complications. If benefit occurred, the port would be removed once improvement reached a plateau.

The Duke team's ideas made sense to Phineas. In his constant scanning of the literature, he'd seen nothing more hopeful. He was willing to take the risks, to roll his personal pair of dice, but now he had to sell the study to Iris. Caring for his surgical site would frighten her. Her lifelong squeamishness might even make her retch. Maybe Marie could help with that part of postop care. And Iris might argue that she didn't want to chance losing what was left of the quality time they still had together by spending it in Duke's clinics and operating rooms—or if procedural complications doomed him before his Parkinson's disease.

"Siri...close attachment." Annabella's email reappeared. *Such a nice name, Annabella.* "Siri...forward email...to Dr. Wahlstrom." He waited for the swooshing sound to indicate task completion. He'd explain it to their internist, Dr. Wahlstrom, and she'd arrange the records transfer. "Siri...close emails...then shut down." He closed his laptop and glanced out the window.

Next to the woods, a devil squirrel wrestled with one of the birdfeeder lids, trying to pry it off. Weeks ago, one of the rodents had succeeded— and then plunged headlong inside the plexiglass tube. It gorged itself on sunflower seeds, then, newly bloated and upside down, found itself stuck. After an hour of watching its hind legs flailing out the top and unable to gain enough purchase to effect escape, Iris put on gloves and heavy boots and dumped the terrified beast onto the ground. It scurried to a nearby rock and scolded her. *Thankless rodent!* Iris now made sure the feeder lids were twisted tight after she filled them. Today's squirrel would have to settle for seeds knocked to the ground by sloppy cardinals and bluebirds.

He reached down to pat Ernest, thinking, "I know you're bored and sometimes frustrated, my friend, but it could be worse. At least you're well fed and loved."

The vacuum cleaner's moan ceased and was replaced by the rattle of it being dragged and closeted. Ernest came out from under his master's chair and stretched. Iris appeared at the kitchen door.

Phineas offered a wistful half-smile. "Wish I...could still...do that... and *more*...for you."

Her eyes glistened as she parted his knees and leaned close for a kiss full on his lips. "Come on you." She playfully caressed his groin. "Get yourself up. This part of vacuuming doesn't have to stop." She arranged his walker in front of him and boosted him from his chair. Ernest heeled at his master's side.

"Stay, Ernest. ...Lie down." The dog promptly obeyed, with disappointment evidenced by his ears flattening back followed by a heavy sigh.

Phineas' ambulation to the bedroom, her helping him out of his clothes and onto the bed, and then her disrobing passed like a fever dream. When she straddled him, her ribs appeared more prominent than he remembered, her breasts and upper arm skin looser. She *has* lost weight. And isn't she paler? This worry needed to be addressed—right away—after.

They lay side by side, arms draped over each other, warm chest and abdomen flesh pressed together. She whispered, "That was nice."

He hated to ruin the mood. Tried to wait for passion to fully melt away. Couldn't stop himself. "Iris...I'm worried...about you."

"Me! You've got enough to worry about without worrying about me." She pushed away enough to probe into his eyes and his thoughts with her penetrating glacial blue stare.

"You've...you've...lost weight."

"You're not cooking anymore." She was trying to deflect his concern. "You used to keep me well fed."

What he'd expected. "You're eating less...not finishing meals."

"My cooking isn't as tasty as yours."

"Please see...Dr. Wahlstrom...soon." He hoped his stubborn Parkinson's face was demonstrating enough of his intense feelings. "For me...please." Inside he was alarmed. And he'd just ruined as perfect an afternoon as they'd had in months. The whites of Iris' eyes now fully encircled the blue. His concern had also alarmed her. She knew how his colleagues respected his clinical observations.

A lifetime seemed to pass in the moments before she replied, "If you insist. I'll call Dr. Wahlstrom for an appointment." Her tone was one of defeat mixed with fear. More than anything else, she'd always hated the thought of being a patient, and until now, hadn't needed to think about being one.

Phineas and Siri would compose a second email to Dr. Wahlstrom, alerting her of his concerns about Iris. If he worded it right, it might expedite his beloved spouse's evaluation.

And he'd wait to tell Iris about Duke—spare her until he knew more—and then only if they invited him to be a subject in their groundbreaking study.

CHAPTER 5

July 4

As Mateo raced from his Uncle Jacob and Aunt Marie's front door toward Iris' car, Phineas felt certain that this Fourth of July was going to be even more sweltering than the last. And since Phineas last saw Mateo several months ago, their grandson must have grown at least two inches. Prior to his family's move to Washington, D. C. three years ago, Mateo had spent countless days and nights at his grandparents' Chapel Hill home. Now they saw him infrequently, and they sorely missed his energy and honest love.

"Waylo!"

Mateo's infant pronunciations of abuelo, Spanish for grandfather, still stuck. "Waylo" had brought guffaws from family members when toddler Mateo first tagged Phineas with it, but Phineas wore the handle proudly. Today, "Way-Low" described his decline and the mental state he fought to overcome at this treasured family celebration.

Phineas pushed himself onto his walker on frustrating unsteady legs, and Mateo stopped short, suddenly quiet, his brown eyes wide and staring. "Waylo?"

If the walker and interval decline in his grandfather's appearance gave the boy pause, how would he react when he heard his Waylo's sorry voice? Phineas rested his less shaky right hand on Mateo's shoulder and bestowed a gentle squeeze.

"You're getting...tall, Mateo."

"And you're getting..." Words seemed to elude the boy.

The honesty of the child, while painful, at least refreshed. Phineas knew what he looked like. "What are we...having to eat?... I'm hungry." The faint fragrance of searing pork promised savory sustenance and a much-needed rescue.

Iris came back around her car and hugged Mateo. As she bent toward him, her light summer slacks seemed baggier around her thighs, and she looked ever closer to her grandson's size. Would the family notice her weight loss, or would they be distracted from that observation by their patriarch's undeniable decline?

"We brought Ernest, Mateo." She opened the car's back door and Ernest tumbled out. He accepted excited pats from the boy then dutifully took his service dog's place at his master's side. Mateo had been fascinated by the dog's steady obedience and vigilance from the first days his four feet had padded through the Mann household. The boy often sat next to Ernest and watched him as if absorbing the virtues of duty and self-control.

"Daddy!" Martha burst through the front doorway, latched onto her father's elbow with a tenacious grip, and planted a kiss on his cheek. "I've missed you, Daddy." She gave him a fleeting up-and-down inspection, then disguised concern with a photogenic smile, the all-purpose tool of a seasoned politician. Her azure eyes still sparkled with the gold flecks she'd flashed since infancy. "Let me get you settled out back with the other cooks. I'm sure they'll want your input." Martha winked at her mother to let her know that she could relax her spousal vigilance.

"How's my...little girl?" Phineas asked.

"Fine, Daddy." She looked fit in jeans, UNC t-shirt, and running shoes. "Staying busy trying to preserve the democracy." Since she'd departed

North Carolina, the U. S. Congress had dappled her chestnut brown hair with threads of silver. A small price for democracy, and maturation looked good on her. *A daughter with graying hair. Wow!* One more sign of her father's advanced age.

"Glad...someone is...trying to...clean up...our government." News outlets were beginning to suggest that she planned to run for a third term. She'd told family but not announced it. "Will you...start campaigning... again soon?"

"Probably, but we've still got four months, and I'm an incumbent with an established political machine. My district should be safe." She offered him a proud smile. "And I'd like to enjoy some of the summer with family. Felipe has been dropping a few not-so-subtle hints."

She began guiding her father past the features Jacob required for his sanity, space for a generous vegetable garden and a small three-hive apiary. While other North Carolina beekeepers struggled with invasions of ill-tempered Africanized honey bee colonies that global warming brought from more southern regions, Jacob carefully selected and bred gentle strains of productive honey bees for his yard. Being the father of two toddlers, he monitored his bees' behavior with a heightened vigilance.

Side by side by side, the bulky Labrador, the walker-assisted father, and his athletic daughter made their way around to the back of Jacob and Marie's sprawling house. There, a broad, partially roofed wooden deck merged into a patio floored with slate pavers. Felipe, his thick jet-black hair plastered to the back of his neck, faced a gas grill. Martha's husband and Mateo's father had sold his successful Raleigh French restaurant after her election to the U. S. House, and he now guest chef'd his way around high-end Washington establishments when those gigs fit into the family's hectic schedule. Today he was helping Jacob with the family's holiday feast. Although Phineas would rather be an active participant, he looked forward to observing a master chef at his craft.

Under Felipe's sweaty white tee shirt, the muscles in his broad upper back bunched oddly, and he kept his right upper arm pinned against his chest, using his lower arm to baste racks of baby-back ribs.

"Did you...hurt...your shoulder...Felipe?"

He pivoted to face Phineas. Felipe's dark brown eyes studied his father-in-law, Ernest, and the walker without a hint of pity, only his usual unwavering respect. "Yeah. I didn't think it was that obvious. Those Washington guest chef dinners I create don't provide me with kitchen help, so I have to do it all. I had a big one Saturday. Lots of chopping, sauteing, and stirring—and lifting heavy pots and pans."

"May be...bursitis...let me know...if it's not...getting better...and I'll... research help...for you."

The back door slid open, and Jacob exited his house, cradling a pile of bratwursts nestled in butcher's paper, ready to hand them off to Felipe. Phineas and Iris' six-foot-six-inch son had trimmed his dark brown lumberjack beard close after the twins reached an age fraught with painful grabbing and tugging. Jacob inspected his father with the briefest wince then offered him a welcoming smile. "I hope you're hungry, Dad."

"Famished. ...Smells amazing."

Felipe spun back around from the sizzling meat like he'd remembered something. "Happy Independence Day, Phineas!" His son-in-law had always proudly celebrated both his U. S. citizenship and his Mexican roots.

Independence. If only... Independence was something Phineas sorely missed.

Felipe lined up his tools on the grill's shelf. "Let's find you a comfortable seat where you can supervise." He gestured at an empty cushioned Adirondack deck chair and footrest two paces from the cooking action and next to the picnic table piled with reusable plastic plates, cups, and utensils. A large umbrella in a stand shaded the spot. Felipe accepted the sausages from Jacob who hovered over his father, helping him settle into the low seat, a spot clearly planned for his role as today's supervisor in title only. Ernest sniffed, his snout pointed skyward. He let out a contented sigh and settled next to his master.

"Want something to drink, Dad?"

"Got an…IPA?" Hopefully ice cold in this oppressive July heat. He hadn't tasted one in weeks.

Iris arrived on the scene in time to hear the request and catch Jacob's raised eyebrows, his silent ask for her "okay." She nodded her permission.

"Hi, Mom." They hugged, she a slender sapling in his bear arms.

She released her son and looked up at his face. "And where are my grandsons?"

"Marie's changing their clothes. They were coloring with markers and—well, you can probably imagine."

The sliding door opened again, and the sound of a four-footed toddler stampede vibrated off the wooden planks. Phin and Vin, in matching red NC State t-shirts and shorts bounded toward Iris while Jacob blocked them from the grill. Streaks from the colored markers hadn't washed off their indistinguishable faces. *Was that Phin, whose were mostly blue, and Vin's mostly green?* Could be helpful for telling them apart on quick inspection, at least for today.

"Wayla!" Almost a perfect duet. Continuing the established grandparent nicknames had seemed simpler when the twins began talking.

Abuela Iris bent low and gathered one child in each arm. She whispered, "I brought cupcakes."

They stood at attention. The blue-faced twin stamped a foot. "Want it now." The green-faced one's head bobbed his enthusiastic support.

"Later. After your mother and father say you've eaten enough lunch." She stood and grasped the hand of each. "Come on. Show me what you've been coloring blue and green." Her gentle tug dissolved her grandsons' pouts, and they turned her, like a brace of spirited ponies poised to gallop back toward the air-conditioned house.

Seconds later, Marie, with a large, clear bowl of potato salad in her arms and a dish towel draped over her shoulder, maneuvered through the door. Her thick, wavy mane was again corralled back in a fat ponytail, this time for efficient childcare and food preparation.

Their beagle, Ruby, trailed Marie. Ruby seemed focused on the food until she spotted Ernest. She made a beeline for him, wagged her entire back end, and sniffed the larger dog head to butt. When Ernest failed to acknowledge her affections, she enthusiastically licked his muzzle. A flicker of a smile appeared at the corners of his mouth. Finally, the beagle lay down, pushed her body against his, and let out a contented groan. The heads of both dogs settled, side by side on the slate pavers.

Iris murmured, "Well, those two dogs seem content. Marie, I've got the boys. You're free for now. Enjoy it."

Martha relieved Marie of her potato salad burden, and said, "I'll get this and go back for the slaw and bean salad. Go say 'hi' to Daddy."

As Marie approached Phineas, he rocked forward and tried unsuccessfully to transfer his weight from his low perch onto his walker. "I might... need another...pillow...under my butt."

"Don't get up, Phineas." She leaned in close for a hug. "I'll find you that pillow." Which she did.

He settled back into the cushions. "Kids look...good." Watching them from his low perch was enough for now. He'd connect with them later, after they settled down some.

Jacob came to Marie's side with a pint glass of golden ale brimming with foam. Phineas leaned forward and clamped it between his shaking hands. "Thanks...I could...use this." A greedy sip produced a frothy mustache and a barking cough. Ale sloshed over his lap and onto Ernest. Jacob rescued the pint glass with the remainder of the ale while Marie gave Phineas her towel to blot the spillage. He was glad he'd worn black pants. He'd learned months ago that dark shades helped hide his spills.

Ruby pushed up from Ernest's side and dutifully licked Phineas' pant legs and what she could reach of Ernest tucked under the chair.

Phineas took several slow breaths and willed his cough to cease. "Sorry...Maybe one...of the twins' cups...would work better." The ones with lids and a spout he could corral between his lips.

Marie's eyebrows arched in obvious surprise. "You want your beer in a Sippy Cup?"

He'd suffered worse indignities. "Why not?" The old man becoming a child. Thank you again, Shakespeare. "Tasted...too good... to waste." He looked longingly at the frosty glass on the table next to him.

A woman's emphatic voice curled around the corner of the house. "Where do y'all want me to put this banana pudding?" Chelsea, in a bright pink blouse and white capris, stepped onto the deck. She shifted a royal blue ceramic bowl covered with aluminum foil high and away from Ruby's perpetually active nose. "Scoot, hound. Not for you." The fearless beagle rose up and pranced on its hind legs.

Marie relieved Chelsea of the bowl. "Hi, Chelsea. Let me put this in the fridge till we're ready for it. I need to get a cup for Phineas anyway." Ruby trailed Marie, close to her heels, ever vigilant and wagging her tail hopefully.

"Thanks, Honey." Chelsea pulled a deck chair over to face Phineas and plopped down. "I need to catch Finman up on things."

"Iris said...you and Marie...were going to...call Sweden."

Chelsea scrunched up her nose. "What an adventure *that* was. Seems no one speaks English in that town's hospital." She sighed and glanced at the clear blue sky. "Finally, with UNC's hospital translator service's help, we convinced someone there to look for my images. She said, if they still existed, they'd be on a disk, and she'd ship them, and then email me the info to trace them. I had to give her my credit card number."

"Maybe we'll...see them soon."

She began studying her clasped hands. "I've about decided to wait on surgery...to see if it grows first." Her raised eyebrows invited Phineas' response. "They mentioned that was an option—but they didn't recommend it."

"And just...hope it...doesn't grow?" Her proposed plans alarmed him. "Could lose...a chance at cure...if it's malignant."

"I might be better off if I'd never had that damned CT for my gas pains." Her voice expressed fear and frustration. "No more cabbage for this old girl's intestines."

"Let's not...give up yet...So, you...have the...email address...over there?"

"I'm hoping the one I have actually works."

Marie came up behind Chelsea. "I've got what you asked for, Phineas." The cup she offered was brilliant orange with a Kelly-green Tyrannosaurus Rex dinosaur baring pointed teeth.

Chelsea looked from Mr. Tyrannosaurus to the three-quarters full pint glass. "God, Finman. You must *really* want that beer."

By late afternoon the twins finally ran low on fuel and, to the immense relief of Marie and Iris, were napping. Mateo and the adult diners slouched in deck chairs and scraped at remnants of banana pudding in plastic soup bowls. Mateo let out a contented burp. Felipe chuckled as if oblivious to the stern look Martha shot at her men, then all got quiet and lazy again.

Mateo perked up and pointed to the back of the yard. "Uncle Jacob, what are they *doing*?" Dinner plate sized clumps of bees dangled off the landing platforms of Jacob's hives.

"They're cooling off on their front porches. It's called bearding because that's what it looks like. Want a closer look?"

"Yeah." Mateo bounded out of his chair, apparently eager for anything to relieve the boredom of drowsy adult company.

"Let's go." Jacob's knees creaked in protest when he stood, remnants of the athletic days of his youth. Soon the two were conversing out of earshot.

Marie dragged her chair across from Phineas and asked, "Mind if I tell you about a case?"

"Not if you...get me...a half of...a bratwurst." He'd enjoyed his first one and still had some of his second ale to wash more down.

Martha popped out of her chair and took three steps in pursuit of Mateo and Jacob then paused to declare, "If you two are going to talk medicine, I'm going to go look at bees." Felipe, Iris, and Chelsea rose and followed her toward the apiary, each saying, "me too" while hastily escaping a potential tale of medical misery. Ruby pursued them, apparently also eager for activity.

Phineas balanced the plate with the sausage and bun on his lap. "Looks like...you've cleared...the place, Marie." He took a healthy bite and listened.

Marie shrugged as she took note of the retreating backs. "Whoops. Not the first time I've done that with a medical case. Well anyway, I had a political VIP readmitted to my service. He's only forty-three and not a very nice guy. Refused to let any students, residents, or fellows see him. And he's mostly wanted to speak only with the pulmonary consult attending. Suits me, since I don't think much of his views. Guns, climate, voter suppression...about everything."

"And he...also has...a lung problem?" He took a second bite.

"Right. So, he has a mass near the hilum of his lung. Pulmonary did a bronchoscopy almost two weeks ago that started as an outpatient procedure, but that afternoon, before they could discharge him, he spiked a fever and had a shaking chill. So, they called our team to admit him overnight for observation. He was discharged the next morning to wait for results." She waited for Phineas to ask questions, and when he didn't, she continued. "Yesterday, he had more chills and a fever—and was readmitted. His cough was worse, and he was short of breath. Today, when I looked at his records online, I see his oxygen levels are considerably lower."

Phineas wanted to ask about x-ray changes but could produce no words, no helpful sounds. Nothing. He tried to cough but failed to suck in any breath, only emitting a fleeting weak honk. Air hunger and panic overwhelmed him. He clutched at his throat. His whole head pounded. His face was on fire. Everything in front of him dimmed. Ernest let out a distressed "yip." Darkness descended. Silence.

Oomph! A hard punch struck his guts. Whoosh!

Air!

He could inhale. His lights came back on, and he saw Marie's vacated chair across from him. Strong arms squeezed him from behind and hoisted him off his seat.

That murderous bite of bratwurst parked itself in his cheek.

"You okay now?" Marie asked as she released her tight embrace, eased him back into his chair, and came around to face him. She looked ready to pounce again.

He nodded and spat the bite of bratwurst onto his plate then took greedy breaths. Ernest sat, rested both front paws on his Phineas' knees, and probed his eyes. The dog's forehead was more deeply furrowed than his master had ever witnessed.

"You scared the hell out of me!" Marie raised her voice and eyelids.

"Me too...I owe you...once again." Would she ever fail to save him? He stared into her eyes and tried to look in control. "Please don't tell... *anyone*...about this," he whispered. Ernest settled down at his master's side but continued staring at him.

"But you could have died." Marie lowered her voice almost to his level.

"I'm trying to...get into...a trial...and I can't be...too far gone...or they won't...enter me." Pleading should have felt embarrassing, but desperation ruled. "Please Marie."

"Are you two done talking medicine yet?" Iris called out as she strode back from the hives.

He covered his plate and the partially chewed, nearly lethal, sausage remnant with his napkin.

"It's a complicated case," Marie answered. "I'll bend his ear more later. Come join us."

Iris pulled a chair close and reached for Phineas' shaky hand. If he'd been alone minutes ago, she might be finding his fresh corpse now. *Perhaps a blessing to all?* A quick and almost painless exit—and an unburdening for her. It would look like he'd suffered a cardiac arrest while celebrating his last holiday in the warm company of his family.

He glanced down at Ernest. *But you'd be without your master, my friend. What will your future be when that time comes?*

When he'd choked, Phineas experienced total darkness. There'd been none of the famous "light" people with near-death experiences speak of. Did that mean he hadn't ventured close enough to death, or that there was no light, no afterlife—at least not for him? His childhood religion had promised him one, a paradise, if he were to earn it in life. *Was there really an after...after?*

Yet, he still had work to finish. Marie's difficult VIP case. Chelsea's nodule. And he needed to know that no stealthy and sinister illness was stalking his wife. Of this, he needed to be more convinced than of anything in his entire life.

CHAPTER 6
July 5

Another morning, another pill. This one went down easily with Iris' meticulous help. She poured Phineas an aromatic mug of fresh-ground coffee and added his usual dollop of milk. He clutched it in both hands and brought it to his lips. Still stiff and shaking and waiting for his medication to kick in, he dribbled the hot liquid into his beard. The mug clattered when he tried to ease it back onto the kitchen table.

"Might be...better if...you put it...in that...Sippy Cup...Marie gave me."

Iris dabbed at his chin with her napkin. "Pragmatism trumps pride. Wow! I'm proud of you, Phineas." She kissed his forehead like he was a toddler who'd conquered a lesson.

"It's a...logical...solution."

She transferred his coffee into the orange cup with its green dinosaur, his new favorite animal. "Anything else, Sir?"

He took a sip and immediately bonded with that dinosaur. It was a game changer. Together he could have his morning coffee and use his computer without the danger of frying its circuits in a hot, wet spill. He reached down to scratch behind Ernest's ears. The dog groaned and sighed.

"How about...my laptop...too?"

She set it in front of him and opened the computer's lid then poured herself coffee and took the seat opposite him. She seemed content to sip her coffee and observe their bird and squirrel visitors in the front yard.

He listened to the musical boot up and pressed a shaky finger onto the password lens. "Siri...open emails." The message from Annabella Sanchez, the one he'd hoped for, was near the top. He clicked it open.

> Dear Dr. Mann,
>
> Thank you for arranging to have your records forwarded so promptly. Our clinicians have reviewed them in detail, and we are pleased to offer you the opportunity to be a subject in our Phase 1 trial, The Reprogram PD Study.
>
> Please arrive at Duke South Clinic 2E this Friday July 7th at 11 AM. It is highly desirable for your caregiver to accompany you then. Their active participation will be key to you completing all phases.
>
> We look forward to meeting the two of you.
>
> Warm regards,
>
> Anabella Sanchez PA
>
> Study Co-Ordinator

Phineas sipped coffee and reread the note. Now it was impossible to hide his previous covert actions. He inhaled a slow, deep breath. "Iris, I need...you to look...at an email." He turned his laptop to face her, his heartbeat pounding in his ears like synchronous tympani.

She put her cup down and stared, first at his screen, then at him. When her eyes probed into his, he sensed her apprehension merging into fear. "When were you going to tell me you were pursuing this?"

He shrank back into his chair. "I didn't think...I'd get in." When she remained silent, he added, "It's a chance...for me to...get better, ...the best one...I can find."

"Phineas Mann. It's a *Phase 1* trial." She sounded aghast that he asked to venture into uncharted medical territory. "Why on earth would you want to be the first to accept all the risks?"

"There's...nothing else...promising and...further along." Phase 1 was going to be hard to sell. "And Duke...is just...down the road."

"You're going to have to tell me what it involves and what my 'key active participation' means." She'd never gotten over the debilitating squeamishness she'd confessed to when he first met her. Over their fifty plus years together, they'd adapted, mostly by him protecting her from exposures that might trigger a queasy reaction.

"I'll have...two procedures...The first...will be a...bone marrow." He shrugged. "I'll just have...a Band-Aid."

"Why am I dreading hearing what the second one is?" She pushed her coffee away and sat back in her chair, crossed her arms, raised her defenses, and appeared to be circling her emotional wagons.

"Do you...want to... read the...description?" The images in the information guide might trouble her.

"Eventually. If you don't think it'll make me throw up." She pressed a fist over her mouth and muttered, "Oh, just tell me what it says."

What to tell her. "You remember...intravenous ports...for chemo...and drawing blood?" Nonfrightening devices hidden under healed skin. "I'd... have one." She wasn't reacting yet. "...that accesses...my brain."

Her face lost all color. She clamped her open hand over her mouth and stared as if, right before her eyes, his skull had opened up and a hideous gargoyle had flown out.

"The incision...will be small...Just need...dressing changes...and rides... to clinics."

A tear welled up in the corner of her eye, the left one.

"So, you'll...take me...Friday?"

"Why are you doing this, Phineas?" She sounded incredulous and angry. His care was already onerous for her without adding procedures and who knew how many clinic visits.

Why was he? "To get...better...for you...or at least...not worse." To be less of a burden would be a victory, a thrilling outcome. To really improve would be miraculous. Yet he'd stopped believing miracles happened decades ago when he saw countless cases that needed one—and one never came.

"There might be complications. You know that." She'd seen complications in her career as a medical social worker—and had done her best to help patients and families deal with the devastation that followed them.

"We can ask...about those." He'd skimmed over the fine print in the study's information guide. He needed to study it more completely. "If you don't...want to go, ...I can...ask Marie."

Iris shook her head. "Marie has a full-time job, a husband, and twin two-year-olds. She doesn't need to add your wild adventure to all her other obligations."

"Maybe Jacob...can help?" Daughter Martha was busy in Washington. Friend Chelsea had her own issues, including the threat of lung cancer.

"Jacob has a job, a wife, and those twins—not to mention a possible book tour they're pressuring him to take."

"Then what...are your...reservations?" Maybe her squeamishness and the extra care weren't the only issues.

She took a deep breath through flared nostrils. "We're doing okay now, Phineas. Sure, it's not perfect and we have our challenges, but we deal with them. We laugh. We have fun. We enjoy family." She focused on his eyes again, this time like she begged his support. "If something goes wrong, I don't want to lose all that—or lose you. I'm just not...not ready to lose you—and to be *alone*."

He should have known her answer. But every time he plotted his downward trajectory, he had to face that, without forms of life support or some novel treatment, Iris was going to lose him anyway—and soon. He hadn't assaulted her with that harsh reality. She might admit it if she wasn't in denial, and if her seeing him hour to hour hadn't made the speed of his decline less obvious. He was *not* going to burden her at those late and miserable stages. He'd documented his approval for palliative, and then terminal care in his advanced directives. She'd probably blocked those final instructions from her memory.

Early on, his neurologist had all but promised Iris that her husband would have ten to fifteen good years instead of the meager four he was granted before reaching his current late stage. Iris had brought up that incorrect prediction more than once, causing Phineas to remind her how variable medical conditions could be and how hard it was to make precise predictions. He'd been exposed to the worst of the spectrum of the Parkinson's disease patients in his pulmonary practice. Those patients suffered from complicating pneumonias after choking on food or soiling their lungs with the bacteria in their own saliva. He was as intellectually prepared for his rapid deterioration as any victim could be.

And since Iris had been promised many more good years with her husband than she got, she couldn't help feeling bitterness added onto her disappointment and sorrow. Bitterness slipped out from her during his low points despite her efforts to keep it buried. Bitterness at least told him how much she valued their marriage, how much she still loved him.

"At least...take me...Friday...Please, Iris."

She closed her eyes and massaged her temples. "All right. I'll take you. But I need to bring you home by 3:00. I have an appointment with *our* doctor at 4:00. She just now added me to her schedule. Nice of her. I didn't expect her to see me so soon."

His message to their doctor must have gotten the doctor's attention. "Good...I need you...to stay healthy." He regretted any implication that his wishes for her health were to serve him. "Sorry...you know...that I want...what's best...for you...that...I love you."

Ernest stood and rested his head on Phineas' thigh, probing his master's eyes for instructions. Hearing none, the dog studied Iris' face.

Phineas reached his less shaky right hand across the table.

She covered it with both of hers. "And I love you too, you crazy old man."

CHAPTER 7

July 7

Phineas fidgeted trying to find a comfortable position on the metal bench in front of Duke South while he watched Iris' Prius enter the parking deck beyond the clinic's traffic circle. She'd undoubtably have to circle the multiple levels waiting for a space to open while he simmered in the rising midmorning heat. At least they'd spared Ernest from baking in the sun under his thick, jet-black coat. Besides, the presence of a service dog might somehow unsettle Duke's investigators and sabotage entry in the trial. Ernest's sad eyes and flattened ears revealed his disappointment at once again being left behind, and the dog's sorrowful expression had dampened his master's feverish anticipation.

A tall, thin Black man in a royal blue vest approached. His nametag indicated that his name was Abraham, and that he was a Patient Ambassador.

"Sir, can I help you get somewhere?"

"My wife...is parking."

"At least let me bring you inside where it's air-conditioned and there are cushioned chairs."

"She has...my walker...I'd need...a wheelchair." Maybe they shouldn't have decided to rely on Duke wheelchairs for his appointment and kept his walker instead. He'd guessed that his struggling to walk through the clinic would take entirely too long, even if he didn't fall.

"Be right back." Abraham disappeared through the double-glass entrance doors.

"I'm not...going...anywhere," Phineas said to the heavy air and no one in particular.

Within minutes, his Patient Ambassador was back pushing a broad-seated wheelchair. There was room for two or three of Phineas' skinny butts on the blue cushioned seat. Abraham offered his arm for support. "This look okay to you?"

"Better...than okay...Thank you...Abraham."

Abraham wheeled him into the cavernous lobby buzzing with a wide spectrum of humanity and infirmities. A moon-faced woman wearing an oxygen cannula huddled in one of the overstuffed chairs. *End-stage lung disease or recent lung transplant recipient?* A balding and ghostly young man behind an N-95 mask leaned against the wall and watched the entrance. *Bone marrow transplant? Leukemia? Both?* Subtract all the sickness, and the place reminded Phineas of an urban train station. He kept his eyes on the glass entrance, vigilant for Iris. She might be concerned at his absence from the bench where she'd deposited him.

"Which clinic are you visiting?" Abraham asked.

"2E...I hope...I'm where...I'm supposed...to be."

"Yes, Sir." Abraham pointed at a hallway to the right. "The desk is about fifty yards that way. I can take you there now if you'd like." He'd pointed with his left index finger. A thick callus covered its distant tuft like the ones on Phineas' first pulmonary division chief's fingers. His chief was a violinist.

"I'd better...wait here...for my wife...She'll be...looking for me."

"Can I get you anything? A bottle of water?"

Heavens no. "Thanks, no...I'm fine." Phineas hoped to not have to use a restroom, and he didn't want a spill on his trousers. "Which instruments... do you play...Abraham?"

Abraham's face brightened. "I'm known for bass fiddle in a jazz band." He glanced around the room. "But I can't get enough of my cello recently. It's my secret project, maybe for my church orchestra." He'd lowered his voice almost to a whisper. "How'd you know?"

Phineas held up his left hand. It shook so, he couldn't imagine his fingers accurately pressing on cello strings. "Your calluses."

"Impressive observation. No one else notices them. You play?"

"My old boss...did...long time ago." Forty plus years ago, that boss, Phineas' first pulmonary chief, rescued a grateful Phineas by hiring him from a storm-ravaged New Orleans as soon as the murder charges were finally dropped. "He played...the violin. ...Chamber music...every Sunday."

"Another fine instrument." Abraham stared at his sizable hands. "These fingers fit a larger instrument better. Maybe someday I'll also get to play in a chamber music quartet." He flashed bright teeth in a broad smile. "Well Sir, as much as I've enjoyed chatting with you, I should go help someone else. Good luck with everything. I'll pray for you."

Iris burst into the lobby and scanned the crowd, like she was the law looking for a fugitive. She stood out without trying, dressed like she was back at work in a white silk blouse and navy slacks, and her long silver hair loose down her back. Phineas held up his left hand. It waved itself. She glided across the marble floor and stood in front of him. "Did you think you could escape me, Phineas?"

Abraham studied her then Phineas. For an instant, his expression suggested surprise. He had to be wondering what Phineas once looked like to be with such an elegant woman. Phineas was used to that reaction.

Abraham cleared his throat. "I brought your Phineas in out of the heat, Ma'am."

She studied his Duke nametag. "Thank you, Abraham. May we keep this wheelchair for his visit?"

"Yes, Ma'am. Can I get you a bottle of water?"

"No, thank you. We just need to find Clinic 2E."

Phineas pointed down the hall. "It's that...way, Iris." Abraham bowed at the waist, turned, and slipped out through the double entrance doors.

Iris pressed all the shape out of her lips, like she did before she undertook a dreaded chore. She'd been silent about the Phase 1 trial since he secured her agreement to accompany him, and he had to have alarmed her when he suggested she see their primary care doctor. Two new worries on top of the formidable everyday stresses he provided. She latched onto the wheelchair's handles and pushed it forward.

"Can I help you?" The woman behind the desk wore a patch-covered denim jacket, a statement not only against regimentation but to ward off the clinic's frigid air conditioning. The denim and a long blond ponytail gave her the look of a high school student. *Young people just look so...young these days.*

"I'm Phineas Mann...We have an...appointment with...Annabella Sanchez."

"I'll let her know you're here." She tapped on her cell phone screen. "Have you filled out your new patient forms?"

"Online." Siri and he'd completed that onerous task right away. He knew *that* drill.

"Great. Ms. Sanchez will be here as soon as she can." She gestured at the only empty chair in the far corner and looked up at Iris. "Please have a seat."

Once they'd settled in the space, Phineas stole glances at the other patients in the waiting area, mostly frail elderly men accompanied by uniformed caregivers or tired-looking, plump well-dressed women. The men's faces were blank masks, flat without the facial muscle activity that displayed emotions. Another curse of Parkinson's, one that Phineas now realized also afflicted himself. *Damn! That's my face!* The transformation had occurred so gradually that he'd managed to ignore it in his bathroom mirror—until now. A curse, insidious enough that Iris might not realize what troubled her about his constant detached expression. She'd never mentioned it. *Kind of her.*

A man with a bandaged head arrived at the check-in desk and within seconds was wheeled into the back clinic area. When Iris spotted the gauze wrap, she quickly redirected her focus to her lap.

"Phineas Mann?" A diminutive, mid-thirties olive-skinned woman scanned the room. Her shoulder-length black hair shone under the LED lights, and her white coat almost touched the floor.

He raised his hand as he had in grammar school when he thought he knew the answer—or had to go to the bathroom. "Over here."

She glided across the floor in royal blue running shoes. Her only visible jewelry was a delicate gold bracelet that glimmered around her slim right ankle. She held out her hand. "I'm Anabella Sanchez. It's such a pleasure to meet you."

His right hand steadied itself in her warm grasp. Hints of coffee and peanut butter trailed her and reminded him of his earlier meal. This dedicated and busy young woman must have come to work early today and consumed her breakfast between duties, and they shared morning food preferences. Points in her favor. At least Phineas hadn't lost his treasured sense of smell—yet. He'd read that others with Parkinson's disease did.

"I'm Phineas...and this...is Iris." Best to use his first name and not his title. He was a patient/subject now. He tried to stand but rocked back onto the wheelchair.

"You don't need to get up now, Phineas. I'll take you two to the back where we can talk." Annabella released his hand, turned to face Iris, and gave her hand a confident shake. Iris still wore a wary expression. Annabella released the wheelchair's brakes and grasped its handles. "Please follow me, Iris."

They paused in the clinic's back hallway only long enough to stand Phineas on a digital scale and to measure his height.

"Five feet nine inches and 160 pounds. Is that your usual?" Annabella asked.

"Down a...few pounds...and an inch...or two shorter." The Parkinson's had hunched his shoulders enough that his and Iris' eyes had begun approaching the same level a year ago. Could the trial's therapy gain him back his height?

"Well, don't lose any more. We need our study subjects to stay well-nourished."

"Phineas always loved doing the cooking," Iris murmured and shifted her gaze from the scale's readout to the ceiling. "I'm not much in the kitchen."

"Then I'll bet he can coach you to make some tasty meals." Annabella helped him settle onto the wheelchair. Her size belied a hidden strength.

Down a hallway perpendicular to them, the man with the bandaged head was taking halting steps, free of a walker. A muscular male nurse or physical therapist hovered vigilantly at his side. A tall Black woman in a long white coat stood at the far end and concentrated on each of the man's steps. As the stiff man ambulated, his arms did not swing. That normal part of ambulation hadn't yet recovered in this study subject, but he had to be just getting started. The telltale scalp bandage suggested they were collecting baseline data for the Reprogram PD study. Phineas had once tried to remember to swing his arms during the years before he depended on his walker for every step, lest he resemble a movie zombie fighting rigor mortis.

Annabella led them to a spacious examination room that easily accommodated the wide wheelchair. She pressed a button to lower the exam table to a level that allowed him to pivot onto it, then offered Iris the chair against the wall. Annabella sat at the corner desk where a computer hung from the ceiling on a hinged arm. She clicked it on. The study's website image of the stooped 'before' and upright 'after' elderly man appeared on the screen.

"Our study's Principal Investigator, Dr. Grace, and I have read your UNC record. We invited you here because you fit into our entry criteria." She looked from him to Iris while maintaining her constant smile. "Can I answer any procedural questions for you now? I'll let you ask Dr. Grace the medical questions."

Iris fidgeted in her chair. "How often will Phineas need to come here? Will there be overnight stays? Will I need help at home?" Her questions came out in a torrent, like water pouring through a breached levee.

Annabella clicked to the image of a flow chart. "Here's the standard schedule." She turned the screen toward Iris. "We'll fill in dates after you enter the study. Today will be for your exam and baseline labs. Next week will be imaging and a bone marrow aspirate."

"I've read...Dr. Grace's...publications and...the NIH...grant proposal. ...I know...the protocol." His words were too soft. He'd make an extra effort to speak up next time. He wanted Annabella to know that he, a medical professional, had researched, then enlisted *them* to help him. At least she was considerate enough to let him finish his comments without interruption, and her relaxed face reflected her patience. She was used to the slow and labored speech of Parkinson's disease patients.

Iris concentrated on the screen, her brow with its familiar gentle furrows, like she was trying to memorize the details.

"I'll print all the pages for you before you leave today," said Annabella. "Each procedure is scheduled for an outpatient visit. It's not likely there'll be a need for an overnight stay, and at home, it's just dressing changes."

Iris bowed her head and grimaced. "I'm really squeamish."

Phineas raised his less shaky right hand. "We have...help." Iris' queasiness was going to be a hurdle, but less than her fear of him suffering life-threatening complications. He couldn't let these worries keep him out of the study. It was his only chance.

Three soft knocks preceded the door inching open. The Black woman who eased into the room stood over six feet tall. Her white coat gleamed, and her thick black hair was restrained behind her shoulders as she studied Phineas' face. A gold band suggested she was married, and a neurologist's oversized reflex hammer protruded from one front pocket and a stethoscope from the other. The photo nametag clipped to the coat's lapel read: Dr. Wilhelmina Grace MD PhD.

Annabella stood and backed away from the desk. "Iris and Phineas, this is Dr. Grace."

Phineas tilted his head and torso back to meet the doctor's gaze. "Dr.

Grace, ...happy to...meet you." He'd seen her Duke headshots on the internet but had no idea she'd be this tall. She seemed to be mentally measuring him, gauging his tremor, registering his Parkinson's masked face. He offered his less shaky right hand. She pressed it warmly between hers.

"Dr. Mann, it's been a long time." Her husky voice touched a deep spot in his brain. He struggled to bring the image out.

"I'm sorry...Dr. Grace...I'm drawing a...blank." He prided himself on remembering people, and his memory hadn't begun failing—or had it?

She retrieved a pair of glasses from her breast coat pocket. Their frame was thick powder blue plastic. When she put them on, his recollection of her remained out of reach. She grinned like she was enjoying his bewilderment. "These are for after hours when I take out my contacts. I wore glasses when I was a medical student on the UNC Pulmonary Consult Service. Let's see, that was...eighteen years ago. I was on elective from Howard."

"I must have...failed somehow...You didn't...go into pulmonary." He chuckled at his tired attempt to make a medical professor's joke. "Dr. Grace, ...can I...buy a vowel?" His next feeble attempt at levity.

"Hah! Same dry sense of humor. Maybe you remember that we saw an amazing case of miliary TB together."

He couldn't pinpoint that particular case of a rare clinical presentation of a once common infection. Rare or not, he had seen several of those unusual presentations over his lengthy career.

Iris clenched and unclenched her hand. Her patience for the visit and Dr. Grace's game appeared to be wearing thin.

Dr. Grace probed his eyes for recognition. "Final clue..." She must have noticed Iris. "My name was William back then."

There it is. 2010. The slender young man with an Obama haircut and unique eyewear. Phineas recalled him as enthusiastic, intellectually curious, and appropriately reserved as a medical student. "I hope you... were satisfied...with your...student evaluation." Being in her good graces now might help him.

A hearty laugh escaped her. "Don't worry. Your kind words helped me get the residency match I wanted." A serious look replaced her mirth. "Your records suggest that you've had a difficult and rapidly progressive course. Now I want to help *you*." She stepped to the desk next to Annabella, whose head didn't quite reach Dr. Grace's shoulder.

A superhero team, he hoped. Batwoman and Robin in white coats.

Iris' frown softened. She relaxed back into her seat and crossed her ankles. Dr. Grace's journey probably interrupted Iris' tension over her husband, but did these two superheroes in white coats have the necessary powers to gain her support?

As if reading his mind, Dr. Grace addressed Iris. Her willing consent was vital, and the doctor obviously knew it. "Sorry about that, Iris. I couldn't resist. I recalled that your husband always enjoyed solving a good puzzle." Dr. Grace settled into the desk chair and tapped the keyboard. "I've already reviewed all of your records, Dr. Mann—read them thoroughly as soon as I saw your name."

She summarized his medical history, confirming key points with Iris and him, then rose to examine him. This started with his walking, Dr. Grace taking one arm and Annabella the other for a few of his halting steps. Then the doctor checked each muscle group's strength and tone, calling out number scores to Annabella, who entered each one into the computer. Sensation testing and reflexes followed. Finally, with the neurological exam complete, she checked his lungs, heart, and abdomen.

"I have to admit I felt a little humble listening to a lung doctor's lungs, Dr. Mann."

"I trust you...found them...in perfect shape." He didn't think he was aspirating into them yet. Only the one bite of an assassination-minded bratwurst. "That part...of me...still works."

"Yes, indeed, thankfully. It needs to for our study."

He'd been right about keeping his choking episode a secret. It might have excluded him.

Anabella vacated the desk seat, and Dr. Grace took it, each shift a practiced ballet in the confined space. "As you know, the first step is your brain imaging. We've scheduled it for Monday. If there are no surprises there or with your blood studies, we move on to a bone marrow aspirate to harvest your stem cells. We want to proceed expeditiously, since it takes more than a week for the stem cell cultures and their programming. We don't want you to have any complicating medical issues that intervene and sabotage your participation and follow-up."

He'd had brain imaging at UNC years ago when his diagnosis was established. There'd be no surprises there.

And he'd performed bone marrow aspirates as a resident. A local anesthetic for skin and covering tissues, then a quick pain when suction was applied into the closed marrow space. A "kick in the ass," he remembered one patient calling it. Worth it to him now, that kick in the ass.

Iris' eyes, now narrowed, were pegged on Dr. Grace. *Concentrating? Silently freaking out?* Phineas needed his wife and presumed medical assistant to hear something reassuring about the steps in which his brain would be invaded. Something factual, not too watered down, yet encouraging.

Hopefully, Dr. Grace was up to the challenge.

Phineas took a breath. "Let's talk about...the brain catheter...and the... stem cells." That had to be what was on Iris' worried mind.

Iris winced at the phrase "brain catheter."

"Glad you asked, Dr. Mann. As you know, Phase One trials are generally small, for subject safety and dose adjustment. Yours would be the eighth marrow harvested." She glanced at Annabella, who nodded at "eighth". "We've completed cultures and programmed stem cells from five subjects so far and infused initial doses in three of those subjects as of today."

"What about the brain catheter?" Iris planted her feet like she was bracing for the worst. "How often are there complications?"

Dr. Grace seemed prepared for worried spouses and offered her a confident smile. "Well first, you should know that our neurosurgeons and interventional radiologists performed the procedure on organ donors who were clinically brain dead before we entered any study subjects."

Iris grimaced as she asked, "Wouldn't it be hard to tell if there was a problem if they were brain dead?"

"Good question, Iris. What we were able to do was document perfect catheter placement, then perform subsequent spinal fluid analysis and brain autopsies looking for complications. We did all that before we entered *any* subjects." She spun the desk chair around to face Iris directly. "All five of our Parkinson's subjects have tolerated their catheters well, with only the expected mild local scalp discomfort."

Only five subjects so far? Phase 1 trials are typically small. Phineas was glad for Iris' sake that, for once, he could hide *his* fears behind his Parkinson's disease mask.

He might not be taking man's first steps on Mars, but this was clearly a pioneering study being led by a bold young investigator. He wanted to be part of it now more than ever. Nothing else had worked yet for someone in his condition. A new *proven* treatment would take way too much *time*, and he didn't have the luxury of that much time. Could Dr. Grace or anyone else make Iris understand that crucial fact?

He needed to have his wife's support, yet he'd need to shepherd her through the whole gruesome process.

CHAPTER 8

July 7

Iris prepped her husband for her absence in silence, as though her thoughts were on something else. First, he'd taken his preventive trip to the toilet, then she'd stationed him at his usual kitchen table chair by the window. With him settled, she'd reluctantly departed for her appointment with their internist.

A squirrel climbed onto the birdfeeder for one of a series of unsuccessful attempts to violate it. This time it was attempting to bite a hole in the impervious metal cap. Maybe a neurosurgeon could drill a hole so the beast could reach the good stuff, the high protein contents inside, like the Duke surgeons would through his skull.

Ernest extracted himself from under Phineas' chair and sat up between his master and the window. To most observers, the dog would now resemble a frozen British soldier guarding the palace, but Phineas knew Ernest was also dutifully monitoring the squirrel in his peripheral vision. *After all, Ernest is a dog.* An extraordinarily trained dog that Phineas felt privileged to have—a guilty privilege from the beginning, an entitlement. Through Martha's numerous connections in her district, she discovered the unique and costly program to provide service dogs to a few fortunate patients. (Scholarships *did* help some less affluent patients overcome the high financial hurdles.) Ernest had done so much for Phineas in the first years, but now, since his master's needs were so great, the dog was less an assistant and more a trusted confidant.

"And what...is your opinion...of Duke's...Phase 1 trial, ...Ernest?"

An ear cocked and Ernest stared at his master. His lips quivered as if to say, "I trust you to make the right decision, Phineas."

"But if I...get better...or die, where...will you go, my friend?"

The slightest mouth twitch repeated, "I trust you."

Marie's text said she wanted to drop by to show Phineas "the case." By this, she meant the troubling medical case she'd been poised to tell him about when he choked on the 4th of July. So far, she'd kept her word and told no one about his mishap with that brat. Today's message said her schedule allowed a half hour before she had to leave him and pick up the twins at daycare.

"I'm in your driveway," Marie's text read. She knew to let herself in.

"Oh Phineas...where art thou?" drifted from the front door.

"Back in...the kitchen." Despite his efforts to yell, his words would barely be loud enough to reach her.

She came around the corner in running shoes and jeans. Her thick, wavy hair fell loose past her shoulders. "Glad you're free today." Ernest turned his head to monitor her movements. "And hello, Ernest."

"My schedule is...always...so packed." No need to explain the earlier trip to Duke, yet.

She extracted a laptop from her shoulder bag and opened it in front of Phineas. The familiar chimes of it booting up followed as she pulled the other chair around the table to perch next to him. "Can I get you anything before we start?"

He shook his head and glanced at her shoes. "They have...casual Fridays... now?"

"Today was mostly administrative. I did look in on the patient I tried to tell you about though. He's worse, and they don't have any answers yet. The ICU team had to put him on a ventilator because his oxygen levels were low." She logged into the UNC Health system and pulled up a chest x-ray.

"Sorry I...interrupted you...on the Fourth." He tried to make his wooden face display a contrite smile, but after seeing so many other Parkinson's patients at Duke, doubted it worked.

She tilted her head and stared at him with an "I can't believe you just said that" look before she returned her focus to today's mission.

"Remember, this is the 43-year-old VIP congressman I started to tell you about...and this is the chest x-ray before his bronchoscopy." An asymmetric swelling in the central portion of one lung suggested a mass. She switched images. "And here's his CT scan from then." The images confirmed the mass and added the information that the surrounding thoracic lymph nodes were moderately enlarged. "At bronchoscopy, they saw nothing in his bronchi, so they needle aspirated the mass and the lymph nodes for samples using ultrasound guidance; then they washed the lobe. All negative. But then he ran a high fever, so they decided to keep him in the hospital overnight. He was discharged the next day when his temperature returned to normal."

Nothing was diagnostic on these images. So, his question had to be, "sarcoidosis, malignant, or...infection?" *Wait. I've seen these images.* "Was he...discussed in...teaching conference?"

"He was in one before the new fellows started, anonymously and without much background because of his VIP status. They showed these images and the needle aspirates. The pathologist saw a few poorly formed areas that suggested probable granulomatous inflammation."

"And the...conclusions were...?"

"A young nonsmoker with those findings—most likely sarcoidosis, since it's so common. Based on that working diagnosis and his symptoms, he was started on a moderate dose of prednisone and scheduled back in clinic follow-up."

"And I...agreed?" *I have a bad feeling about this.*

"You shrugged as if you had little to add."

She clicked further down the list of daily images, to the one with today's date. The mass had enlarged and contained a pea-sized area of low density, suggesting that portion was necrotic. Both lungs had exploded from top to bottom with innumerable soft-edged nodules of nearly uniform size. The screen's caliper read three to four millimeters for most of them. A plastic endotracheal tube was now in the patient's trachea for mechanical ventilation.

Jesus. Sarcoidosis shouldn't do this on prednisone.

Phineas tried to remember his impressions during that conference. Was he fully engaged and paying attention? Had he let the temptation of a common diagnosis bias him and shut down broader thinking? Sarcoidosis did fit the VIP's initial presentation. A condition without a known cause, but a well worked out and straight forward treatment plan. But this couldn't be sarcoidosis. It should have gotten better.

Were his physical troubles distracting him that day, so that he hadn't considered all of the diagnostic possibilities? Was he beginning to lose the expert edge he'd cultivated over half a century? Was the Parkinson's finally also affecting his cognitive abilities? Or was he giving up on helping others and selfishly withdrawing into his own crumbling shell?

Calm yourself, Mann. You need to help make this right. Focus on the information you have now.

"Impressive changes...you've sent...at least three...specimens for TB?"

"Started suctioning for specimens as soon as the endotracheal tube went in...and for fungi."

He reminded her that some infectious agents might be hard to see under the microscope among the mess of inflammatory debris. He reached across to her computer's touch pad and scrolled through slices from different views. "Tell me...his history." Phineas recognized the patient's name from news items, stories detailing the man's political positions, which happened to be diametrically opposed to his.

She wrinkled her nose in a display of frustration. "Like I said. He's a

VIP—an elected representative who lives most of the year in Washington. His party doesn't want anyone to know he's sick. They probably don't want him to look weak, or maybe in case he has something they might find embarrassing. So, they snuck him into Outpatient Surgery where the senior Interventional Pulmonary attending met him right before the bronchoscopy. The attending had only a few minutes to check the patient and his images, and to get informed consent."

He asked about when the VIP patient was admitted to the hospital the first time. "What history... did they get?"

"'they' was the after-hours on call hospitalist who had seven other admissions at the same time, all of which she had to see and discuss with medical students, interns, and residents. Our VIP patient didn't allow any students or trainees to see him, so he only saw the hospitalist, who was told to just 'Tuck the VIP in.', and that he'd probably go home in the morning."

"So, no one did...a complete history...the kind...an intern or...med student does."

"And now he's readmitted and sedated with a tube down his throat. It's his handlers. They hamstrung us from ever getting to know him." The colorful verb from Marie's rural upbringing slipped out.

"VIP medicine...Hmph." The 'special' VIP treatment the rich and famous often receive sometimes leads to extra tests and the risks and red herrings those tests create. In this case, it was the opposite, a government official, now deteriorating in an ICU free-fall, had insisted on excessive privacy—and consequently his physicians never got to know him.

Phineas was reminded of an old adage that went, "Professors make diagnoses from the patient's history, residents from an examination, and students from laboratory studies." Nowadays, it seemed everyone on the team made their diagnosis from an ever-expanding buffet of laboratory test panels. Everyone's in a hurry. Pressure for documentation to allow maximum charges and an accumulation of a doctor's Relative Value Units, bean counters' and administrators' scorecards of a clinician's worth. Phineas had felt those pressures before his retirement, but he'd resisted them and still taught trainees to pursue complete histories for their patients.

"At least tell me…someone's done his…HIV, TB skin, and…Quantiferon tests." If all were negative, pneumocystis and tuberculosis would be unlikely in the congressman.

"We did manage to order those, and they're negative or pending. We told his POA that they were essential, and he reluctantly agreed to let us order them."

"Who *is* his…power of…attorney?"

Marie lifted her eyebrows—twice—suggesting intrigue. "Now there's an interesting question. Our middle-aged patient is single and never married." She paused, apparently for dramatic effect. "His POA is a handsome, perfectly groomed, and stylish younger man who rarely leaves the waiting room. He says they're good friends, but the contact information in the records indicates they have the same address."

"How is that…so interesting?"

"It's interesting because our VIP represents a rural district in the mountains that is blue-collar and extremely conservative." She closed the UNC website and shut down her laptop. "So, I looked the guy up. His public image is rough and tumble to keep his voters—and he has supported discriminatory anti-LGBTQ legislation through his entire political career."

"I see. …We should…talk to his POA…soon."

"Can I pick you up tomorrow morning? Jacob can watch the boys on a Saturday."

"Works…for me." An outing, and he needed to prove useful. He now owed the congressman his full attention, this time without bias. Owed the patient a careful consultation that might provide new diagnostic insights, insights proving this seasoned consultant's thinking still functioned at a high level, even as his body crumbled.

"Good. Thanks for your help, Phineas. I'll text Iris in the morning before I leave home." She hoisted her bag on her shoulder and rose from the table.

He pushed himself up onto his walker. They'd once been about the same height. He now had to look up to meet her eyes. "I'll show you out." At the entrance, she gave him a quick hug then gently closed the door.

On the way back to his post at the kitchen window, he detoured to the study where he could scan the backyard with its fruit trees and the raised beds that had once produced a bounty of fresh vegetables. Without proper pruning, weeding, and mulching, the yield from his berry patches had steadily declined. A neighbor friend dropped by to harvest that scant offering each spring. At least the low-maintenance fig and persimmon trees still provided respectable late summer and fall treats, enough to share with anyone interested in picking the fruit. Apples remained an elusive quest, one he would never see succeed. He was a naïve gardener when he'd embarked on his journey with apples so many years ago. Without regular pesticide applications, destructive fungi and insects claimed most of them. And a beekeeper couldn't be spraying insecticides in his yard. Then there were those larcenous squirrels.

Jacob and Marie had visited in late April and shown the twins how to plant zinnias, sunflowers, and squashes in the vegetable beds. The flowers were sure things, and left to their own devices, outcompeted most of the weeds. Native bees and bright yellow swallowtail butterflies now flitted from one vivid blossom to the next. The butternut squash vines provided ground cover to lessen water requirements, weed growth, and a low-maintenance fall harvest.

Years ago, at this time of summer, he spent evenings after hospital rounds on his knees harvesting fresh black-eyed peas, snap beans, and summer squash. Now, the Parkinson's at least allowed him, actually seemed to encourage him, to fantasize, to relive the smell of fresh soil when he'd pulled a weed. To feel the tickle of sweat rivulets down his temples and into the corners of his mouth. To recall the steady background buzzing of his healthy honey bees as they searched for sustenance wherever they could forage it during the scalding July nectar dearths.

If he were to kneel now and pay homage to this once-hallowed garden space, he wouldn't be able to rise back up. He'd have to settle in there, and his dust could eventually dwell in perpetuity among his vegetable beds and fruit trees as he became one with them.

CHAPTER 9
July 7

The jarring sound from the slammed front door announced that it was shut with emotion. Ernest came out from under Phineas' chair and sat next to his master, his ears tilted forward in concern. Iris trudged into the kitchen and plopped into a chair, her complexion considerably paler than the healthy hue her New Orleans Babineaux family roots had bequeathed her at birth. "Glad that's over. I just hate it when they take my blood." She rested her head on crossed forearms. If not for the barrier the table imposed, she might have lowered her head between her knees. "They made me lie down—and I still almost passed out."

Phineas stretched his hand out to rub the tight muscles between her shoulder blades. "Sorry for that…What did she…tell you?"

"That I looked pale, and I've lost weight. I told her I'm not much of a cook and I don't go outside much anymore." Both undeniable facts, but was there more?

"She find anything…on your exam?"

Iris lifted her head, and a crease formed between her eyebrows. "She said she could feel my organs easier with the weight loss—even my spleen tip. What does *that* mean?"

Phineas had rarely felt a spleen tip in a healthy patient, even a very slender one. Did Iris have splenomegaly? *That* was a worrisome sign, suggesting the possibility of a malignancy. Lymphoma? Leukemia? Just the word "leukemia" made Phineas' blood freeze into ice and creep from his neck down both sides of his spine. Acute leukemias meant toxic and hazardous therapies that must start immediately. And those treatments would be devastating to Iris physically and traumatic to her spirit. She hated needles in all forms, and there'd be an endless parade of them unless her doctors inserted a disconcerting port in her chest for blood draws and intravenous treatments. A port, like the one the Duke Phase One investigators wanted to place in his head. Of course, he'd have to drop out of that study—if Iris needed him. He'd give up on his Parkinson's disease ever getting any better. He'd exit life as gracefully as his clumsy self could.

"What tests...did she order?" Maybe her tests would suggest a more chronic condition, like a more indolent chronic leukemia that could respond to a single oral medication.

"Lots of tubes of blood...and she scheduled a CT of my abdomen at the hospital next week." Iris held up her arm to display a Band-Aid over the crease inside her elbow.

The abdominal CT meant that she'd have to spend an hour hanging around the radiology department while drinking a nasty-tasting and nauseating oral contrast solution; and then she'd suffer another needle stick, this one for the injection of intravenous contrast material. Someone would have to be there for her. Someone might have to drive her home. Phineas would make Marie aware, complicating her busy life. She'd want to know, but they probably shouldn't worry Martha just yet.

During this first pause in conversation, Ernest settled his chest and belly onto the floor but watched Iris as if concerned she might also need to lean on his broad shoulders.

"Do you want...to check on...your blood tests...in your medical record?" Phineas always wanted to know his patients' results as soon as they became available, to be vigilant and ready to take the next needed action to address abnormalities. That was how he'd always functioned during his career.

"Not really. She'll let me know if there's a problem. Can't we just relax tonight?" She seemed almost to be pleading.

"Why not?" With the weekend, even if the labs were abnormal, there'd likely be no progress on sorting out her condition until Monday. There'd only be two extra days for her to fret without any action on the findings. Two extra days for her to carry an extra burden. He'd fret for her and try not to let it show. At such a time, his Parkinson's masked face might just be a good thing.

She sighed. "I don't feel much like cooking. How about I order a delivery pizza?"

"Sounds good." His appetite had evaporated with the words "spleen tip."

"I'll schedule delivery for seven, and after I call, I'd like to lie down and nap for a bit."

He also felt an urge to lie down, but he doubted he'd be able to nap.

CHAPTER 10

July 8

When morning arrived, Iris had the now familiar sheen on her forehead. Phineas studied her until she opened her eyes and stared back at him. "I guess we need to get up and get you ready," she murmured.

"You sweat...again...last night."

"It's called glowing when a woman does it, Phineas. Horses sweat." She sat on the side of the bed and stretched her arms over her head.

"You should...take your...temperature."

When Iris looked over her shoulder at him, her expression suggested a mix of frustration and alarm. She disappeared into the bathroom and reappeared with a digital thermometer and a frown. "It's dead, Phineas. Hasn't been used in years."

"Please get...a new one...soon."

"Next time I shop. Now, we need to get you ready for Marie." Iris seemed eager to abandon her own worries.

Phineas shared little about the case he was to consult on today, only that it troubled Marie enough that on an off-duty Saturday morning she was going to hand the twins over to Jacob and make a special trip into the hospital.

Phineas' usual coffee and bagel went down as expeditiously as he could manage. Only one cup. No restroom visits or distressful leaking.

Marie's gentle knocking barely reached the kitchen but caused the fur along Ernest's spine to rise more than a few millimeters. He kept his steady perch with the front half of his torso tucked under Phineas' chair and out of traffic.

"She's on time, as usual." Iris set her coffee mug on the table next to her cell phone.

Marie plopped into the chair next to Iris to happily share an update on Phin and Vin. "Our first tries at potty training have been hilarious. This morning I had to wipe pee off the walls and floor. How old does a male have to be before he can aim that thing?"

Phineas wished he could still aim a steady stream. He was certain Marie hadn't considered *his* difficulties when she reported on his grandsons. Why should she think *that* way about her father-in-law?

"Iris, didn't we...put a Cheerio...in the toilet...for a target?"

"That did help your husband learn, Marie." She chuckled at the memory he'd revived. It was her first smile in more than a day.

On the table between them, Iris' cell phone began playing *Carolina On My Mind*, her ringtone. Phineas made out the name, "Dr. Wahlstrom" on the screen. His wife's eyes became those of a frightened deer—if a deer could have glacial blue irises. She froze for a moment then touched the green dot answer icon before it could go to voicemail.

She pressed it to her ear. "Hello, Dr. Wahlstrom?" She blinked several times in rapid succession, a sign appearing in recent years when she stressed over her husband. "Dr. Wahlstrom, can I put you on speaker? I'm with Phineas and with Dr. Marie Porter, our daughter-in-law. I'm guessing you two have met." She set the phone back on the table and switched the audio setting to speaker.

"Hello, Dr. Mann and Dr. Porter." Dr. Wahlstrom, often a bit too formal, now sounded relieved, like she was glad Iris wasn't alone. "I certainly do know Dr. Porter. She admits my clinic patients to the hospital when they need it. How are the two of you?"

Marie looked like she was waiting for Phineas to respond, so he did, "You know...how I am...Dr. Wahlstrom." She knew his challenges.

"I saw that your records were sent to Duke, Dr. Mann. Do you want to tell me about that now or later?"

"How about...later?" He wanted to get straight to the reason for a Saturday morning call to Iris, but he looked to Marie for her turn to respond to Dr. Wahlstrom's greeting.

Knowing nothing about either of their dramas, Marie appeared puzzled. She first stared at Iris then at him, before she answered, "I'm fine Dr. Wahlstrom. Should I let you people talk in private?"

Iris shook her head vigorously. "No. Please stay. You're family and a doctor." She leaned over her phone. "What did you call about, Dr. Wahlstrom?"

They waited an uncomfortable interval for Dr. Wahlstrom's response while Phineas stared at the cell as if it might be a ticking bomb.

"I have some of your tests back...and I think we should do some more tests to explain the abnormalities."

Abnormalities. The word made Phineas feel the increasingly familiar sensation of ice forming along his spine.

"Iris, your blood counts are low."

Phineas leaned closer to the cell. "Which ones? ...And how low?" Maybe it was only an anemia and not leukemia. But there was the matter of Iris' spleen.

"Well...they're all low, white cells, hemoglobin, and platelets...They're not so low yet that a transfusion is indicated, but we need to get to the bottom of this right away. I don't want them going lower without a plan."

Marie put her arm over Iris' shoulders. Phineas wished he could get up and do the same, as much to give her what strength he could spare as to absorb her fear.

Dr. Wahlstrom broke the silence. "Are you still there?"

"Still here," Marie answered.

"Iris, your hemoglobin is usually around 14 grams. Now it's just a bit under 10 grams."

No wonder she looks pale.

"And your white count is down to 3500."

A lower white count would put her at high risk for infections.

"Platelets are 55,000."

A platelet count much lower and she'd risk spontaneous bleeding, possibly even into her brain.

Marie's mouth fell open for a moment as she took her eyes off Iris and stared at Phineas, the unspoken communication between two worried physicians.

Iris must have noticed the nonverbal exchange. Her hands began shaking in a fine pattern distinct from Phineas' coarse tremor. She asked, "Dr. Wahlstrom, how bad is it—and what's causing it?" She pressed one hand onto the other to smother their trembling, a feat her husband couldn't accomplish on himself no matter how hard he tried.

"I need to be honest with you, Iris. Your counts are low enough that if they go much lower, we'd have to consider transfusions to prevent complications."

Transfusions. Iris flinched at the word. To her, transfusions would mean more dreaded needle sticks, and these in order to receive *someone else's* blood. Years ago, as a hospital social worker, she'd been unable to avoid the sight of blood trickling through tubing into terribly ill patients. She'd told Phineas back then how she'd learned to concentrate on staring at the patients' faces to not look at the blood, because seeing it always made her queasy and sometimes even "all swimmy-headed." Despite those frequent exposures, she never reported getting used to it.

She'd gone on to get her PhD, so she could do research and teach, and be spared most of those dreaded clinical sights. Her aversion to blood changed her career path. Now her aversion was resurfacing to torment her.

Despite Marie's sturdy support, Iris' posture was crumbling at the nightmare news, inch by inch, moment by moment.

"Iris?" Dr. Wahlstrom's voice.

"We're still here," Marie answered before Phineas could salvage his voice.

"We need to get to the bottom of this right away. We need to know what's causing your low counts. I've contacted a hematologist, Dr. Moro, and he will see you Tuesday."

Three more days to fret. Phineas knew what was coming next, and he was certain Marie knew. The muscles around her chin tensed, and she kept her protective arm around Iris.

"Iris?" the cell again.

"I'm here, Doctor." A voice depleted of its prior strength.

"Dr. Moro wants you to expect a bone marrow test. Your husband can explain what that involves." Dr. Wahlstrom had to be relieved that she didn't have to explain the details of the procedure, that she could pass off *that* challenging chore to Iris' doctor husband.

Phineas couldn't help feeling a little disappointed that their main doctor wanted to hand off that task. But maybe as an outpatient primary care doctor, she felt less qualified. He understood.

"Do you have questions for me, Iris?" Dr. Wahlstrom again.

Iris took a deep breath. "What do you think the cause is?" After her question, her swallow seemed to stick in her throat. She coughed.

Dr. Wahlstrom let a moment pass. "Learning the cause is what the bone marrow is for. There's a broad range of possibilities for what is termed pancytopenia, which means all the blood counts are low. Some causes can be as simple as a vitamin deficiency. Others could require more complicated treatments." A child's voice squealed in the background then a pause, probably for Dr. Wahlstrom to cover the phone and respond. "Let's wait until we have results and a diagnosis, okay?"

"Okay, Doctor." Barely more than a whisper.

"Let's talk some more after Tuesday," Dr. Wahlstrom suggested. "I'm glad you have your husband and Marie to help explain things. If you don't have any more questions, I'm going to say goodbye now." She probably expected that Iris hadn't yet formulated more questions, guessing she was paralyzed in fear.

He might be disappointed in Wahlstrom for not lingering longer on the phone with Iris, but he couldn't help wanting to cut their doctor some slack. She'd always been good to them. Maybe she's on the way to her kid's tee ball game on a Saturday morning. Maybe her husband is upset that she's working again on a so-called day off. Maybe she's just dead tired after a hard week. He knew all of *those* feelings.

"Good-bye, Doctor. Thank you for calling." Iris rallied to be polite, but fright seemed to intensify her pallor as she stared at Phineas. Was she now measuring him as an asset or a burden to her frightening future?

"I should...c-c-cancel...my tests...at Duke." A new stammer on top of the voice tremor.

"No." Iris' voice strengthened, and she shook her head slowly to emphasize her answer. "You should go ahead, in case I just need a vitamin or some other easy treatment." Her hope for an easy path and denial of other threats were acceptable coping mechanisms for the moment. "You said this was your one chance. You need to take it."

But her enlarged spleen indicated that taking vitamins or some other easy path wasn't likely to be her future.

"My procedures...c-c-could conflict...with your needs." And he depended on her to repeatedly transport him to the Duke clinic in addition to all the care she provided for him at home.

Marie took her arm off Iris' shoulders and made a "T" time-out signal with her hands. "So, do you want to share any of what you're up to, Phineas, or is that top secret?"

What to share. The tangle of his and Iris' coming days swirled through his brain. His brain. Would it soon be invaded—or was that now an opportunity lost?

"Marie, it's...complicated. ...Want coffee?"

Marie *had* signaled a time-out. He could use one.

"I've had my quota already, Phineas." She leaned toward him over the table. "Now, do you want to tell me what *you're* up to?"

"I signed up...for a...Phase 1 trial." *There. No longer a secret.*

"Jesus, Phineas. Phase 1?" Marie studied him like she was certain he'd lost his mind. She'd once worked for a major drug company and was well-versed in the hazards of early trials.

"I've been…combing the…literature. …It's the best…option I've seen. … And Duke…is just…down the road."

"Please tell me it's for a drug already safety tested for some other condition." She glanced from him to Iris as if Iris might reveal more.

She did. "Marie, my previously sensible husband has signed up to have a port placed in his brain, so they can inject stem cells into it. They're going to drill a hole in his skull. Maybe that will let his insanity escape along with a demon or two."

Marie's mouth gaped open, but her hand quickly covered it, and no sounds came out. She looked horrified and astonished. She'd once fiercely wanted to be part of his family, believing her mother's deathbed lie that Phineas unknowingly was Marie's father. When DNA proved he wasn't, she and Jacob became a couple, then spouses, then parents. So now Phineas was the patriarch of the large family he knew she'd always dreamed of having—moreover, she had *recently saved his life* from a lethal piece of meat. She must be wondering if he was about to throw that life away on a futile and dangerous quest?

"Phineas, are you that desperate?" Marie must know he was. She'd dragged him back from the abyss.

"Yes." He offered his furiously shaking hands as evidence. "You know… where I'm headed. …if nothing intervenes."

Iris bolted from her chair and pivoted to face him. "I can't listen to any more of this."

Phineas understood all too well. Her worrisome news piled onto his drama demanded her temporary escape—and she hadn't even learned of his recent brush with death. Was this the time to tell his wife he'd almost died? Maybe that knowledge would help convince her that his decision to enter the trial had been correct. Not now. Better to hold his choking episode in reserve.

"I'm going to lie down, and with any luck, sleep. You two have work waiting for you at the hospital." Iris waved the back of her hand toward them like she was shooing away bothersome pets. "Go on. I'll see you two later."

Undeterred, Marie wrapped Iris in her arms, and the two hugged, shoulders heaving just enough for Phineas to detect their sobbing. Over the years, Iris and he had suffered through traumatic days, but mostly on *his* account. Today, Iris was threatened, and that made this day worse than any in their past.

He rocked from his seat onto his walker and hoisted himself onto leaden feet.

Ernest pushed himself out from under the chair, stood up, and stared into Phineas' eyes, as if asking to help. Their loyal service dog would be disappointed yet again.

CHAPTER 11

July 8

Marie had shown up for their trip to the hospital driving her husband's NC State red beast of a pickup truck. On any other day, Phineas would have relished a ride in the beast. Its front seat lifted its passenger high enough to allow inspection of deeper swaths of the roadside than Iris' compact Prius did. But instead of letting her father-in-law sink into the cushiony leather seat and enjoy the scenery in contemplative silence, Marie peppered him the whole trip with questions about Duke's Phase 1 study. And worse than the peppered questions was his daughter-in-law's palpable effort to remain patient as she waited for each of his sluggish and fragmented responses. Finally, mercifully, she ended her interrogation, deposited him on a bench at the hospital entrance and called out, "That study sounds like a science fiction movie, Phineas. I'm calling Jacob, and I'm going to tell him he should call Martha. It's time for a *family meeting* about Iris and you." With that declaration, she left him and drove away to park.

Family. Marie must sense its pending dissolution and be desperate to preserve it. She'd once longed for a family, having grown up knowing only her single mother, who'd then died of cancer and left Marie alone in the world.

She now seemed duty-bound to protect them as though Iris and he were becoming helpless—and Marie's words announced a coming intervention. He'd wanted to spare the extended family as long as he could but knowing now that Iris' and his news had escaped, a sense of relief washed over him. Marie, the archetypal scout in a B Western, bore the news that the cavalry would gallop to the rescue—as if Iris and he could be rescued from the sinister outlaws who threatened them.

God bless her for trying.

Even for a July morning, the sun beat down on his scalp hotter than usual.

"Can I help you, Sir?" The security guard who'd previously endured his flapping and duct-taped shoes while absorbing a stern lecture from Marie approached from the hospital entrance's shadows. Had he gone into hiding when he spotted Marie? He must have received a paycheck since he now sported a fresh haircut and new work shoes. Perspiration darkened the collar and armpits of his light blue short-sleeved shirt.

"Thank you. ...My escort will...be right back," *Iris has her appointment here on Tuesday. I should introduce myself.* "I'm Dr. Mann...kind Sir. ... What's your name?"

"Leon." The guard had looked surprised for an instant at Phineas' title. "I'm still getting to know the doctors here."

"Welcome to UNC...There are a...lot to remember."

"It was good to meet you, Sir. I'll be sure to remember you." Leon picked up a discarded candy bar wrapper and then suddenly retreated in the direction he'd come from as if he'd been spooked.

Marie bore down on Phineas, calling out, "Was he hassling you, Phineas?"

"Oh no...on the contrary...he was offering...to help me." Phineas shifted on the bench and grasped his walker. "Nice man, Leon...Just started... working here...I'll introduce you...next time."

Marie's concerned expression melted. Perhaps she even felt contrite. "Well, I just got off the phone. Jacob's going to call Martha then text Iris and me to say when he's going to make a group FaceTime call." She steadied his walker and waited for him to haul himself to his feet. "I told him I'd have you home around noon."

"Sorry to…complicate…your busy life. …Didn't want to." He willed his feet to begin their trudge into the hospital.

"Phineas! It's what families do."

Having hers threatened had clearly hit Marie broadside. Each time he glanced at her, she was watching him, as if he might dissolve into air.

"So I'm…learning." Way back, his parents had always helped him when needed, and in recent years, so had Marie and Jacob when Iris needed extra hands to care for her handicapped husband. He hadn't thought much about being so dependent on them until now.

"Should we start…in Radiology?" Time to return to the task at hand.

When Phineas shuffled into the dark domain of the reading room, the only radiologist present on a Saturday morning was a young man who looked up at the intruder and his walker with a puzzled expression. Marie's introduction of Phineas seemed to satisfy the radiologist enough that he hurried to arrange the sick congressman's images across the wall of screens. Not much change from those Marie had shown Phineas on her laptop.

The list of radiology studies offered one Marie hadn't previously shown Phineas—a PET scan—a study designed to light up areas of metabolic activity like cancer or active infection. It had been performed with the first CT, the one made before the patient's bronchoscopy and subsequent clinical crash.

"I'd like to see… the PET scan…please."

The radiologist brought it up on the bank of screens and arranged it next to the corresponding CT images. The original mass appeared bright or 'hot' in radiology parlance. "Before his condition worsened, it seemed the only activity was here in the tumor and surrounding lymph nodes." The radiologist pointed. Illumination from the screens made his face appear ghostly as he spoke.

"What about his...prostate?" Phineas asked. Being a chest specialist, he couldn't recall how that organ should look on a PET scan but wondered about its intense radioactive tracer uptake on this patient's study.

"It's more than usual, but that could just be some prostatitis, since he's too young for it to be prostate cancer." The young man offered, "It's probably unrelated to his pulmonary problem. So, what's the working diagnosis?"

Marie answered, "It *was* sarcoidosis."

"Sure. Seems rapid for that though. Did he get worse before treatment was started?"

"After." Her response hung between them.

"Hmm. Surprising." He began drumming his fingers on his desk. "Anything else I can show you?" He seemed eager to get back to his assigned weekend tasks.

Phineas had seen unusual cases of prostate cancer explode through patients' lungs, but in considerably older men. He mulled over the radiologist's point about the VIP's prostate. Ordinarily, the radiologist's assessment was likely correct, but this case wasn't ordinary. "Thank you, Sir. ...It's been nice...to meet you."

"Yes. Thank you." Marie nodded her appreciation. "Shall we go take a history, Phineas?"

"It's where one...starts to solve...a puzzle." He'd read about the patient online and found most of the critically ill VIP's political policies objectionable to his way of thinking—the representative's promotion of concealed and open carry of firearms, his demand for a whitewashed version of history to be taught to schoolchildren, and his fiery (and possibly hypocritical) attacks on alternative lifestyles. Phineas taught medical students and residents that doctors must treat all patients equally, regardless of how offensive the doctors found their views. Doctors must demonstrate empathy and concern, even when the patient hasn't—especially when the patient hasn't. Teach by example. A way to change minds.

And always make up for one's mistakes, especially the one that Phineas made because he'd been passive and allowed a bias toward a common disease to influence his diagnostic effort. The result of this bias then led to the congressman receiving the wrong treatment.

They rode the elevator to the seventh floor where the hospital's hallways were still quiet before weekend visiting hours. A solitary groomed and handsome young man occupied one of the low, cushioned ICU waiting room chairs, like he was stationed in his appointed place. His sculpted hair, tweed jacket, and form-fitting jeans reminded Phineas of a male model in an advertisement for men's clothes. The young man shot to his feet when he saw Marie. Concern spread over his face.

"Dr. Porter, do you have news for me?"

"I haven't heard of any change from yesterday, Michael." She gestured toward Phineas. "This is Dr. Phineas Mann, a pulmonologist. I've asked him to review Quentin's case for his thoughts."

As he took in Phineas from head to toe, Michael's eyes opened wider. "Nice to meet you, Dr. Mann." Was he thinking the team was now desperate, or was he glad to have someone on the case who'd obviously seen *a lot* of sickness? Phineas offered his shaky hand.

Michael's palm was cool and moist. He wore a gold ring with a polished onyx stone. "Michael, please tell...me about Quentin. ...When he first... got sick, ...everything. ...Please sit." Phineas gestured at the chair Michael had occupied then set his walker in front of the chair next to it. Michael needed to feel unhurried, to let his mind offer clues. The young man retook his seat, and Marie pulled another chair close to listen.

Phineas learned that a few weeks ago Quentin Tate's cough led to a course of antibiotic capsules from an urgent care facility near The Capitol. When the cough didn't resolve, an x-ray revealed a worrisome pulmonary lesion. Hoping to keep his illness under wraps and out of Washington media, Quentin's team arranged the hurried, covert diagnostic bronchoscopy back in his home state. His rapid descent to a critical condition caught everyone off-guard. The press was beginning to wonder about his absence from the legislature. He was usually a highly visible and vocal critic of any actions or bills from Democrats, making almost daily efforts to keep his face on social media.

Although Quentin and Michael's friendship hadn't made the news, Michael must have felt obliged (or was he instructed?) to come and go from the hospital unnoticed during hours free from other visitors.

Michael shared Quentin's past medical history, yet it yielded no clues to his rapid, severe illness. The more personal side of his life might.

"So, you know...Quentin well?" Phineas chose his verb to be open-ended.

"Friends since I was his legislative page while I was still in college." Michael offered a half smile and appeared ready to defend.

"Does he have...hobbies?"

"The job keeps him pretty busy. You know. Washington and public appearances for the party." An evasive, coached answer.

"How about when...he's back in...North Carolina?" Might be time to try another direction.

"Well, he hunts. He took a nice buck last fall." Michael offered up the manly hobby then brightened with a wider smile. "And we manufacture designer knives in the offseason when he's back home and we can work in the shop."

"Knives? You...make knives?" Another manly hobby. Maybe this line of questioning was also going to be unproductive.

"Oh yes. We make handcrafted knives—works of art. I do the metal-working, and he does the handles." He leaned back to extract his cell phone from a tight front pants pocket. "Want to see some?" For an instant, pride was replacing worry. "We sell them on our website."

"Sure." Phineas humored the young man. Perhaps he'd open up more after his personal art show.

Michael's cell screen revealed their names, an address, and a phone number over a lineup of knives artistically displayed on a black cloth background. The first featured a polished turquoise handle. The next one had a grip made from dark exotic wood with a twisting grain pattern. The third handle appeared to be fashioned from an antler. A strategically placed display light's reflections made the knives' blades look frighten-ingly sharp. And the prices! Was Congressman Tate selling them as art at those inflated prices to constituents who wanted to buy influence in legislative matters?

"Impressive." Grinding minerals could affect lungs, but not cause Quentin's acute illness. "Is the antler handle...from his buck?"

"You know, I'm not sure. Possibly, or from one of the antlers our buyers or his constituents drop by our house." Michael shrugged like he was embarrassed. "We get more than he has time to use, and some may even come from roadkill. His people love his work and want to please him."

Michael had said, "Our house."

"So, he cuts...and grinds...them himself?"

"Of course. He wouldn't let anyone else." Michael seemed surprised that Phineas would ask such a silly question.

"Does he wear...an N-95 mask?"

"Oh, he's too macho for that." Michael blushed. "I try to get him to wear one, but he says masks are for sissies."

"Of course. ...Maybe...a silly question." Quentin wouldn't be a mask wearer. *Maybe a clue, but time to move on to other questions.* "How about...travel?"

"He had to go to Asia several weeks ago for a trade mission. He's trying to bring industry to our district."

Asia. He probably hadn't mingled with the masses, a chance to get infected with tuberculosis. Maybe exotic cuisine was foisted on him by his hosts. "Did he eat...any raw seafood...while he was there?" Paragonimiasis parasites from uncooked snails could make their way from human intestines into the lungs.

"Ewww." Michael looked horrified for a moment then chuckled. "He calls that bait—or chum."

Not likely paragonimiasis, then. Phineas hadn't seen a case in years, and apparently this wouldn't be one. Also, the radiology images didn't exactly fit that infestation. He moved on to ask about Quentin's family's history (unremarkable) then labored through a thorough review of symptoms the VIP could have had.

Cough and scant blood spitting had preceded a fever, sweats, then shortness of breath—no other specific clues. At least now someone had taken as complete a history as possible under the circumstances, what should have happened on his arrival, if Quentin and his handlers had allowed it.

"Thank you, Michael...I'd like to...examine Quentin now." With Marie's and the nurse's help. Positioning a patient was now beyond Phineas' physical abilities.

"Dr. Mann, do you have any new ideas?" Michael asked with a desperate, pleading expression.

"Possibly. ...I still need to...see all of...the information." His new idea was a long shot, but a condition he'd seen a couple of times over his lengthy career. "We'll do...our best...for Quentin." Maybe today's consultation could make up for his earlier lapse. At that point in time when a critical clinical decision was made, he'd been lax, passive, and now a man was fighting for his life.

Marie raised an eyebrow enough for Phineas to catch it as they said their goodbyes to Michael. When they entered the ICU, the familiar smells of disinfectant and stool greeted them. She asked, "*Do* you have a new idea?"

"Maybe. Help me...examine him and...we'll talk more."

He accepted the standard gowning, gloving, and masking before Marie and Quentin's veteran nurse patiently assisted Phineas' examination of the heavily sedated patient. As he'd anticipated, his inspection yielded no specific or diagnostic findings, only a fit-appearing fortysomething-year-old with several days growth of salt and pepper whiskers. Quentin's lungs sounded damaged with soft crackles throughout, but his skin remained intact. No diagnostic clues there. Now at least Phineas had satisfied his compulsive nature, and his stiff excuse for a smile was concealed beneath his face mask. The nurse helped him shuck his protective coverings at the room's door.

When Marie and he took seats at the nursing station, the ICU team approached. This Saturday, his old friend Gabby Morales-Villalobos was on call and leading the team. At least she'd listen to him and not be threatened by an old man encroaching on her territory.

"Hola, Gabby." He waved as she drew near.

"Que pasa, Phineas? What brings you here."

"Marie...wanted me to...have a look...at your congressman."

"Well, if you have an answer for us, we'll be in your debt. Seems his condition got ahead of the answers, and we're in the dark." She pulled up a rolling chair and perched on the front of its seat, like she didn't want to miss any of his soft-spoken words. The team of young doctors and students in scrubs lined up behind her and examined Phineas like he was a circus sideshow curiosity. Gabby said, "Everyone, meet Dr. Phineas Mann, my mentor since I began my career at UNC."

Phineas basked for a moment in her kind words and hoped to not disappoint. He responded, "maybe a clue ...that could lead...to an answer. ...Maybe...a long shot. ...We just talked to...his friend." He held up his right hand for a moment as if he could silence the beeps, alarms, and conversations saturating the ICU. At least the staff voices around him paused.

"You once said 'tissue is the issue' when you trained me a long time ago, but he's too unstable for any more biopsy procedures. So, what would *you* do next?" Gabby seemed to genuinely want his thoughts, or she was ready for a short break from the hectic ICU workflow.

"Get a specimen...from...his prostate." He strained his obstinate vocal cords to be loud enough that all the team members would be sure to process his unexpected words.

Gabby's lips pressed together as she leaned forward to hear more. The crowd behind her stood frozen in their places like they expected to witness magic or embarrassment.

"Take out his...bladder catheter...massage his prostate...vigorously... then place a...condom catheter...and catch his...prostate secretions." When the youthful team members exchanged puzzled expressions, Phineas tried to make sure his masked Parkinson's face didn't allow an involuntary grin to surface. "Then take it...to the lab...for fungal culture...a KOH wet prep... and a silver stain." *If those tests are positive, this young team will have new respect for an old man who materialized out of nowhere. If the tests are negative, at least he won't be around to face their smirks.*

Gabby leaned back in her chair and smiled at him. "Well, that shouldn't do him in, and if you're right, I owe you and Iris a bottle of very good wine. By the way, we sent urine fungal antigen studies to the reference lab, but they won't be back for several days." *She had to know he was thinking of an exceedingly rare condition and probably betting she wouldn't be making an expensive wine purchase.*

"Who on this team knows how to do a prostate massage?" she asked. *Blank looks all around. Would they take time from their intensive care chores to actually* do *one, or would they decide they had more pressing matters and later chuckle about a silly old man speaking nonsense?*

A laugh burst out from the patient's nurse before she said, "I used to work in Urology where we had to do them for prostatitis. Time for you *young doctors* to learn a *new procedure.*" She held up her arm and mimicked pulling on a long glove from her fingertips to her elbow. Then she thrust her index finger into the air and rotated it. "And while I'm demonstrating it, I'll whisper in his ear and remind him about the nasty comments he made toward us healthcare providers during the COVID pandemic." A malevolent expression replaced her grin.

Phineas rocked himself forward from the rolling chair, gripped his walker, and pushed himself upright. "Time to...face the music...at home, Marie."

Gabby offered him a puzzled look. "Anything I can help with, Phineas?"

"I'll let you know...if there is. ...Adios." He trudged toward the ICU entrance as the students and residents on the ICU team whispered among themselves.

Marie overtook him with easy strides. "Fungal cultures. Which fungus do you suspect, Phineas?"

"Grinding deer antlers...a central lung mass...that abruptly becomes...a systemic process... Could be blastomycosis. ...That fungus can...spread to... prostate." He hoped Gabby would make sure the KOH smear was done correctly, that a sudden crisis didn't pull her away from what was a task rare for a doctor nowadays.

If his suspicion was correct, they'd see broad-based budding yeasts under the high-power lens. A fungus normally found in nature but capable of finding a portal to invade a previously healthy human and become a potentially severe condition, one that Phineas had seen two or three times over his many years. A diagnosis so obscure that the standard ICU computer care path algorithms wouldn't likely offer it. A diagnosis that might have come up for discussion if the congressman's handlers hadn't demanded caregivers cut corners because their Very Important Person was just so important.

And a treatable condition. Now, maybe the appropriate treatment could save the congressman from his doctors' earlier bias and their misdiagnosis.

CHAPTER 12

July 8

When Marie and Phineas arrived back at the Mann's house from the hospital, Jacob and his twins seemed poised for an ambush. Ruby reached Phineas first, wagging her tail and whining as she sniffed his walker and his pantlegs for the medical scents she'd always found intriguing. Ernest was right behind her and took up his usual post at his master's side. Phin and Vin, perched on either side of Iris on the sofa, scrambled to welcome their trailing mother and would have stampeded over their unsteady grandfather, if not for the protection of his walker and Ernest's bulk.

Jacob rose from a living room chair and silently embraced Marie then his father. Jacob's somber expression was a sure sign that Iris had shared news and her fears. Phineas could only guess how much Marie had explained to Jacob during her earlier phone call from the hospital's parking deck. Probably medical projections beyond what Iris could bear to consider, much less share with their son.

Phineas broke the adults' silences. "What a treat...to have visitors...on a Saturday." At least two toddlers and two dogs might keep the anticipated proceedings from being *too* solemn.

"Dad, Martha said we can FaceTime whenever you're ready." The family troops were poised to assemble. Jacob's tone was somber but gentle, as though he considered his parents' states fragile.

"Let me use...the bathroom...then...we can...talk." Iris and he could have a private moment there before the proposed family summit. "I guess lunch...will wait." He might digest better anyway after worries were aired and plans made.

Without a word to inquire about his foray to the hospital or the unscheduled arrival of their visitors, Iris assisted him to the toilet, waited, and helped him wash up. As she went through those motions, her silence and efficiency confirmed her shell-shocked state and the fears racing through her brain. Ernest's probing eyes pleaded in vain to allow him to assist his distressed people in any way possible.

"What does...Jacob know?" Phineas asked.

"That I'm scheduled for a hematology consult and bone marrow test," Iris answered weakly. "I told him I may need extra vitamins or something."

Hope. A coping mechanism he wouldn't tear down. Frailty now replaced the lifelong vigor that had abandoned her like a foot soldier fleeing from the charge of an overwhelming enemy. The last time she needed more than basic health maintenance measures was when Martha was born, and then she, an experienced mother, was out of the hospital in less than 24 hours cuddling her precious bundle.

"And what does... he know...about me?"

"That you're signed up at Duke for a novel Phase 1 trial, and they're going to stick a catheter in your brain." She muttered it as if he were some crazed stranger in the news.

"No need to...sugarcoat it."

Jacob must be freaking out at the additional revelation of his father's bizarre quest. Fifty years ago, the day Phineas first met Iris while blocking the attack of a disheveled vagrant, Phineas had referred to himself as Don Quixote. Maybe now he really was tilting at windmills. Better than accepting the fate of circling life's drain.

"Shall we...face them?" He hoped for a reassuring sign of affection and support, but Iris, in her stunned and brooding silence, with her perpetually erect shoulders newly slumping, had withdrawn into a private shell.

He advanced his walker and took a step behind it, pausing to look over his shoulder at his wife. She gave her head a single vigorous shake as if she was clearing it of cobwebs she'd unexpectedly walked into, then trailed Ernest and him back to the living room.

From Marie's laptop propped up on the coffee table, Martha's voice greeted her parents' return. "Hi Mom. Hi Dad. How *are* you two?" Her image, except for a UNC t-shirt and worried expression, resembled one crafted for television interviews. She was sitting at an optimally illuminated desk just the right distance from the camera. Inspirational book titles lined shelves behind her: *The Giving Tree*, *The Prophet*, and *The Art of War* were propped with their covers facing forward in front of the fat bindings of autobiographies and history books.

Phineas lowered himself onto the edge of the sofa across from the computer, eager to partake of a view of their daughter. Iris took a seat next to him, sank into a back cushion, and muttered, "We've had a couple of surprises recently."

The twins clambered to the table and blocked the screen. Phin (or was it Vin?) reached for its keyboard.

Must be impossible to find babysitters on short notice these days.

Marie scooped him up before he could interrupt the connection, while Jacob gathered in his identical brother.

Vin (or was it Phin?) wailed, "Want to watch cartoons..."

"Sorry, Boys. We need this screen for a while," Aunt Martha said and waved from Washington. She offered them the patient smile of a mother. Marie herded her boys into the next room and flipped on the television. Hopefully, the treat of cartoons at low volume would keep them planted there and quiet for now.

"So, what's going on, Mom?" Martha asked.

"Your father signed up for a scary study at Duke. They're going to deposit his own re-programmed stem cells into his brain—after they stick a catheter in it," Iris blurted, "and I just heard that I have a problem with my blood cells and need to have a bone marrow biopsy." She waited for Martha to absorb her words. "Your grandmother used to say, 'when it rains, it pours.' Seems we've hit a stormy patch."

"Jacob and Marie filled me in on the general stuff before you got on, and we're ready to help. What's scheduled?"

Help from Washington? Phineas strained his vocal cords to be audible to the laptop's microphone. "Are you going...to send in...the National Guard?"

"The Governor would have to do that, Dad." She shook her head while offering him a smile. "I'll do better. I'm sending Felipe and Mateo until I can wrap up a few things here. Then, I'm coming." As if on cue, Martha's husband and son entered the screen from each side and offered concerned smiles. They took up positions behind her and waved. Phineas held up his left hand and let it wave itself.

Felipe and Mateo. A chef and a spirited six-year-old. Reinforcements. Maybe Iris will find an appetite, and maybe Mateo will pry open her shell.

〜

As bedtime approached, Iris squirted a dot of toothpaste on his electric toothbrush and said, "Okay. Go ahead," as if she were impatient for her husband to press its 'on' button.

"Well, that...all happened...quickly today." He studied her reflection in the medicine cabinet's mirror. The dark circles under her eyes stood out against her pale cheeks.

"I'll be glad when they're here helping. I'm exhausted." She retrieved his dressing stool from the closet and sat on it while watching him in the bathroom mirror, waiting for him to continue with his bedtime preparations. She'd said little since the family FaceTime call ended.

Instead, Iris had put out towels, dusted, and vacuumed with nary an accompanying word. Ernest spent much of the afternoon with his rear half protruding from under his master's chair. He'd been predictably cowed by the roar of the vacuum cleaner that smothered most of Iris' terse grumblings at the corner collections of his shedding. Iris finally apologized to the beset dog when she presented him his dinner. Then she went online to order the delivery of human suppers.

More work for his besieged wife today before she'd have less. More work was not what she needed. If only her willing husband could do it for her. She was pushing herself despite an obvious dearth of stamina and a profound hit on her emotional reserves. He'd put a major burden on those reserves in recent years, and now her sickness was torpedoing what was left of them—broadside.

"Are you going to brush your teeth or stare at me?" She covered her face with both hands and bowed her head. "I'm really tired, Phineas."

He pressed the toothbrush's button. There'd be no pillow talk tonight before he strapped on his CPAP mask and was silenced. No reflective chatting after a day's major events, as they had in years past. There was the Wahlstrom call. The virtual family meeting. Her rushing around to prepare for guests—activity that at least distracted her from dwelling on her uncertain future. She wouldn't want to probe any of that now. There'd be time for that conversation later—he hoped. Time.

CHAPTER 13

July 9

Early Sunday afternoon from his seat at the kitchen window, Phineas and Siri combed the medical literature to refresh his memory on the subjects of splenomegaly and pancytopenia. Despite the rolling hills of Phineas' unusual quantity of voice commands, Siri obeyed him, having nimbly adapted to his speech patterns from the guts of his laptop.

Ernest's front half was scrunched, as usual, under his master's chair, head hidden, yet vigilant for commands. Iris had chosen an escape nap before Felipe and Mateo's anticipated arrival. She expressed a wish to put her worries aside and to dream of more cheerful times.

As Phineas had expected, Siri's searches turned up no surprises. While Iris might be clinging to a vitamin deficiency theory as her simple salvation, deficiency was an unlikely culprit. Even with her reluctant cooking, they ate reasonably well-balanced meals replete with vitamins. And sure, a deficiency *could* lead to pancytopenia, but it shouldn't enlarge a spleen. That required more serious pathology, like malignancies or an uncommon, smoldering systemic infection. A rheumatologic condition could rarely result in her combination of findings, but she had no signs or symptoms to suggest one of those. On Iris' arrival at her hematology appointment, she wasn't going to be blessed with her hoped-for gift of a low serum folate or vitamin B12 level. She would have to face trouble.

Back when Phineas took care of his own patients, his style was to be open and truthful with information to prepare them for what was coming. Today, he fought that customary urge, the compulsion to prepare this patient, his own wife, with all the facts, including the inevitable bone marrow invasion and its revelations. But he didn't have it in him to dash her hopeful fantasies with reality; her mental state was too fragile. Keeping his feelings buried wouldn't be as much of a challenge as it once was. He was still a terrible actor and a worse liar, but now, his Parkinson's emotionless face and halting speech was an ironic asset.

A tentative knock at the front door brought him back from future dramas. Ernest pushed himself out from under the chair and sat, staring at the kitchen doorway in anticipation. Phineas' Apple watch's screen displayed the text from Felipe that read, "We're here."

"Siri...shut down," Phineas commanded.

He pivoted to his walker and rocked forward to push himself to a standing position. If he hurried, he could get to the door before his son-in-law rang the doorbell and awakened Iris. Yet the moment he transferred his weight onto the walker's handles, his maddening and tremoring left hand slipped past the walker's rubber grip, and his entire weight shifted onto thin air. The next split second stretched into a drawn-out scene, a long-lost teenage memory of a refreshing plunge into a welcoming Vermont lake. Yet, this time an unwelcoming surface, one hard enough to shatter ceramic mugs, careened at him. He tumbled over and hit stone.

His walker, still clutched in his right hand, piled on top of Ernest and him. Poor Ernest must have attempted to insert his body under his master's to block the impending trauma, but gravity acted a split-second faster than dog and accelerated Phineas' descent onto unforgiving quarry tiles.

The first sign signaling his fall was the whooping alarm from his Apple watch. The second sign was a sharp pain near his left hip. He steeled himself to not cry out, as the cursed alarm ratcheted up its volume by the second. He had less than a minute to press the button on his watch and prevent the dispatch of an ambulance to his GPS location. His left hand and attached watch shook more than ever, making the watch's crown a moving target for his purposeful right index finger.

The doorbell rang, then rang again. More noise piled onto his futile effort to not disturb his sleeping wife. Ernest paced, looking like he was waiting for the command "Go fetch Iris." The watch was still whooping, the doorbell still ringing, the dog still pacing—primed to bark, and the pain, oh God, the hip pain was—

"Waylo? Wayla?" Mateo's angelic voice from the living room.

Phineas pinned his left arm to the floor with his right hand, slid his right hand's fingers to his left wrist, and pressed all four fingertips against the side of his watch. His middle finger found the crown and the timepiece's cacophony ended. *Phew!* No ambulance today—and maybe he'd switch back to a watch that simply announced the passage of time. Time, by itself, was a cruel enough master.

Now to disentangle himself from the aluminum bars of his traitorous walker and greet his kin before Iris awakens. Ernest gripped the metal bar directly over his master in his teeth and tenderly tugged.

"Waylo?" At the kitchen entry, Mateo froze, eyes wide.

"Phineas!" Felipe slipped past his son and rushed to kneel at Phineas' side.

"Phineas! What happened?" Iris hurried into the room with eyes a blend of sleep and fright. Her long silver hair hung in tangles, and her pale nightgown billowed behind her, a ghostly apparition that hugged the front of her spindly frame.

"Lost...my balance...trying...to not...wake you." The sharp pain above his left hip settled into a dull ache. "Seems I've...failed that." He shifted some of his weight onto Ernest's muscular shoulder. "Help me stand...please."

"That might not be a good idea, Phineas. You could have broken something." Felipe lifted the walker and set it upright. His usually smooth forehead was creased with worry.

"Well, let's...find out." Phineas ran his hand over his left upper leg and reached up and around his hip joint to locate a tender palm-sized spot on his buttock, his gluteus maximus. *Phew!* He carefully flexed and extended his left hip. No pain there. *Phew again!* No hip fracture this time. "I landed on...my butt...just a bruise."

"Are you sure?" Felipe's worry lines remained deep.

"Yup. Sure." Phineas put weight with his right hand on the walker's horizontal bar and pushed himself onto his knees. "See? Fine...except for the...likely bruise." He accepted Felipe's strong arm to rise to his feet and then shifted back to his chair. His weight on his buttock sent a convincing signal of tenderness along sensory fibers to his brain and confirmed that, yes, a bruise had indeed developed, a substantial muscle and tissue hematoma, a soon-to-be purple trophy to display tomorrow to the physician who would suck bone marrow from his pelvis. Shouldn't be an impediment to the procedure though. Hopefully nothing to alarm Dr. Grace and risk exclusion from the study. *Please no!*

Glad I'm not on that blood thinner.

"Should have...worn...hockey pants." Once before, he'd raised this padded solution for unsteady seniors as a half-serious joke, said it could be an investment opportunity in their retirement. Hockey pants in designer hues for senior citizens.

"Suit yourself." Iris responded. "And how about a matching helmet?" Phineas couldn't tell from her tone whether she was kidding or sincere.

Iris hugged Mateo and kissed his cheek. "Thank you for coming." She embraced Felipe then gestured toward the refrigerator. "You guys must be hungry after your drive." A startled then embarrassed look surfaced when she looked down and realized she was wearing an especially thin summer nightgown. "Whoops! I must look a fright. Let me get a robe." She slipped out the door.

Mateo sat beside Ernest on the floor and put his arm around the dog's thick neck. Ernest gave the boy's cheek a single lick, and Ernest's raised ears finally relaxed along the sides of his head. He let out a sigh of relief and contentment.

"You're welcome…to any food… you find. …Might not…be much though." An older couple didn't eat like a young man and a six-year-old.

"No worries, Phineas. No chef travels empty-handed. I stocked up on groceries before we left, and I'll get whatever else I might need with a quick trip to the store tomorrow. Would you prefer chicken or pork tonight? And I was thinking a nice porcini mushroom risotto on the side."

"Sounds great. …Glad…you didn't…bring sweetbreads." Phineas offered Mateo a reassuring smile. His grandson, snug next to Ernest, still wore his worried face and seemed hesitant to approach the shaky and fragile old man who, against everyone's wishes, had replaced his grandfather. "What do you…like best, Mateo?"

"Pollo, Waylo." He searched his father's impassive face for approval of his request for chicken. "With the lemon and caper sauce."

A chicken dish Phineas hadn't yet tried, and a chance to watch a master chef create it. "Spoken like…a chef's son."

If Duke's treatment of his affliction worked, he might one day prepare the same dish for Iris. Cooking was once such a pleasure for him. When forced to abandon it, that loss and the accompanying grief was more than he'd expected. He told himself that others had it worse, like a painter who's suffered a stroke or musicians who've lost their hearing. He at least still had his reasoning and a medical mystery or two to solve.

"Sounds like we have the beginnings of a menu for dinner," Felipe said. "Now, we'd better get the cooler and bags of groceries out of the car. Come on Mateo. I need your muscles to help me." Father and son marched out of the kitchen.

The vibration in Phineas' right pocket preceded his Rolling Stones ringtone, the choir stanzas from *You Can't Always Get What You Want.* As he extracted it, he fumbled, juggled, and dropped it onto the unforgiving quarry tile floor. Thankfully, its protective case allowed it to continue its song. He leaned from the edge of his chair and reached out. *Damn!* Just beyond his reach. He shifted much of his weight onto his walker's brace and inched closer.

"Get it!" Iris' command to Ernest startled Phineas; her yell almost dislodged him from his chair.

Ernest pounced toward the device and worked his mouth around it.

"Since you didn't break your hip the first time, are you trying to finish the job?" She grabbed her husband's arm and settled him back in his seat. The Rolling Stone's stanza ended as Ernest proudly presented the saliva-coated cell. Its screen indicated a missed call. Phineas unlocked it with his facial ID. Marie. Ahead of his shaking finger, Iris touched the icon to return the call.

"Hello, Phineas?" Marie's barely audible voice.

"It's Iris, Marie, answering for him. He's right here. Should I put it on speaker?"

"Speaker's okay. I won't mention the patient's name. Iris, how are you?"

"I'm okay. Just woke up from a nap." Iris put the phone on the table in front of Phineas.

"I'm here, Marie...Felipe and Mateo...just arrived. ...What's up?"

"That's great to hear. I'm *so* glad they came." Her tone sounded relieved but edged with excitement. "Phineas, I called to tell you more about the patient you saw with me."

"Like corn, ...I'm...all ears." He wished Mateo had heard his childish joke. The boy loved that kind of joke. Iris glanced at the ceiling and groaned.

"Ha ha Phineas. Listen to this. The most unusual specimen you suggested they obtain might contain the answer. They saw organisms consistent with your suspicion. The appearance was suspicious enough to start the appropriate treatment. Tomorrow, the Micro lab will examine the culture plates and we'll have Cytology do special stains to try to confirm the diagnosis."

"Let's hope...they do confirm...since...it's a treatable...infection." *And let's hope it's not too late.* A congressman's death would explode across the media. While Phineas wouldn't have to face any direct blame, he'd been physically present at the conference when Quentin's doctors decided to start steroids, but he'd been mentally absent and passive when he'd allowed the easy path of accepting the common diagnosis of sarcoidosis. Then the steroid treatment had suppressed the patient's immune system and allow the untreated infection to worsen. Since he'd been a spectator, Phineas probably didn't deserve to feel guilt over the misdiagnosis, but he couldn't help it.

"Gabby sends profuse thanks." Marie added. "The young doctors were still shaking their heads about your diagnosis when I left them this morning. Still wondering about the mystery consultant who unexpectedly appeared in their ICU, whispered instructions for them to complete an odd task—then vanished."

"Tell them...I was a ghost...from Medicine's past, ...and...to always take...a good history."

And beware of bias.

"We all need to be reminded of that valuable lesson. Well, I thought you'd want to know." A pause. "Remind me. What's the schedule this week? And how can we help?"

Mateo shuffled into the kitchen dragging two bulging cloth grocery bags. Felipe huffed behind him with a cooler big enough to hold a small person.

Iris leaned closer to the phone. "Tomorrow, we go to Duke for Phineas, and Tuesday I have my hematology appointment at UNC. Thank you for your offer, but I think we'll ask Felipe and Mateo to escort us. You're off the hook this time." She raised her eyebrows at Mateo then winked. Hearing his vital role, he stood an inch taller.

"But tonight...we eat...French cuisine," Phineas announced. "Care to join us?"

"Wow! Tempting, but Jacob and I have so much to do to get ready for the coming week—and we need to be caught up so we can help too."

"I'm sure there'll be plenty of chances to help, Marie." Iris responded promptly. "Thanks for giving Phineas something else to brighten his day. Talk to you soon." She winked at her cherished grandson a second time.

CHAPTER 14

July 10

On Monday morning Phineas felt his pulse and, thankfully, it was yet again in a regular rhythm. He wrestled with the CPAP harness and, with mask removed, his machine reported last night's sleep had been only a few minutes shy of his seven hours goal. Sunday's hearty supper, a half glass of Bordeaux, and poached pears for dessert had helped him fall asleep promptly despite the anticipated stress of a pivotal day ahead.

Ernest rested his furry block of a head on the bed's edge and whined softly to ask if he should fetch Iris. Her side of their bed was empty. A sweet smell of fresh-baked pastry permeated the bedroom and mingled with the expected enticing aromas of fresh-brewed coffee. For the briefest moment, Phineas contemplated trying to deal with the condom catheter on his own then thought better of it. The last thing they needed at the start of a very busy day was a urine-soaked king-sized bed. He lay still and listened.

"Chocolat, Papi?" Mateo's voice from somewhere outside the bedroom. The boy was testing the unusual circumstances for the bonus treat of his favorite hot drink.

Phineas hoped his feeble voice would reach the three in the kitchen. "Hello...Iris...I'm awake." He hedged his bet. "Ernest, go...get Iris."

Within a minute, the eager dog returned with Iris who hustled through the bedroom door, Mateo close on her heels. She put gentle hands on each of the boy's shoulders and spun him back around with the words, "Go help your father, Mateo. I'll help Waylo." She closed the door behind her grandson, sparing him the distasteful condom catheter ritual.

Her face had brightened overnight, the likely result of absorbing the many photons of Mateo's unbridled energy. Before the boy's engine had slowed enough to sleep, she'd had to read him at least three bedtime stories.

"Let's get you squared away, Phineas." She pulled back the sheet and, with practiced skill, disengaged him from the condom catheter. "Felipe baked blueberry muffins. Figured we could pack some for snacks if it's a long day. And he's waiting for your egg request." She disappeared into the bathroom with his urine bag and was soon back monitoring him with his walker.

With a few quick sniffs, Ernest's uptilted nose sampled the novel smells permeating the house. Then the dutiful dog took his place and marched at his master's side toward the kitchen.

"The fragrance...does give one...an appetite." But black coffee was all he was allowed until after his MRI scan. Since intravenous contrast was planned, solid food would have to wait. At least the test was scheduled for 9 AM, and he could have a muffin after. And he'd have them pack all the muffins in case Annabella Sanchez and Dr. Grace were hungry.

Once again, a disappointed Ernest will have to keep his lonely vigil at the house. At least when they return, Mateo would get a chance to brighten the dog's day.

The four humans paraded into Duke South, Mateo leading like the group's drum major. Iris and Felipe flanked Phineas, their eyes pegged to him, ready to steady him as he trudged behind his walker. When they reached the front desk, Iris rested a hand on each of Mateo's shoulders as if she were using him for her support—her own personal flesh and blood crutches.

"Phineas Mann checking in," Iris announced to the young woman seated in front of a keyboard and screen. She was the same receptionist they'd seen at his first appointment, but now she seemed more polished in a stylish blouse and carefully applied makeup. Her blond hair, released from its ponytail, cascaded over her shoulders. She glanced up at Phineas then returned her attention to the screen, but only after stealing a fleeting look at a modest-sized diamond on her left ring finger. And this time, she wore a visible nametag.

Phineas leaned toward her desk. "Congratulations, ...Michelle. ...Just get...engaged?"

"Thanks. ...How'd you guess?" Her blush framed a sheepish grin. "Saturday night. He caught me off guard. A *complete* surprise." She giggled, obviously pleased that Phineas had noticed her sparkling prize. Then she cleared her throat and returned her attention to her computer in case an ever-present supervisor happened to be scoring her performance. She pressed a button on the clinic intercom. "Mr. Mann. Here for an MRI followed by an appointment with Annabella Sanchez."

Mateo wore a puzzled look as he glanced over his shoulder at Iris. "Wayla, isn't he *Dr.* Mann?"

Iris patted his shoulder and smiled. "You're right, Mateo, but it's okay. Today he's a patient."

"Subject, ...Study subject." Phineas softly corrected.

"Well, *Dr.* Mann, you can have a seat, and they should call you shortly for your MRI." The young woman offered him a warm parting smile. From now on, she might remember that he was the one patient who'd noticed the glint from her diamond.

The busy waiting room lacked four seats together, so Iris and Phineas found two chairs in the corner, and Mateo and his father settled into two across the room. Iris' phone dinged. She extracted it from her compact purse and inspected the screen.

"An email from UNC." She touched her screen and studied it. "They want me to fill out forms for my appointment tomorrow."

"I can...help now...or we...can wait...till we're home." It would be easier if she could use her laptop.

"I'll see what I can get done now. It'll help pass the time while we're waiting." She began tapping and reading. "Really small print." She reached into her purse for her reading glasses. She touched the screen with two fingers and spread them apart. "At least they have all my demographics from Dr. Wahlstrom's records."

A vaguely familiar man shuffled behind a walker to the reception desk. Phineas fought the urge to stare as he tried to place him. The man pivoted slowly toward a waiting room chair, and a four-inch area of stubble became visible amid the longer hair on the side of his head. A quarter-sized, round bulge protruded from the bare spot. *A port. The guy with the gauze head bandage from before.*

Could this be me three weeks hence? Five weeks hence?

The study subject's face lacked expression. His motions still appeared stiff, and when he settled into a seat and released his grip on his walker handles, his hands tremored. Perhaps today would be the day he'd get his first dose of programmed stem cells. Perhaps he'd be fluid and expressive with steady hands the next time Phineas spotted him. Perhaps...

"Dr. Mann, we're ready for you." Annabella Sanchez waved from the door leading to the examination rooms. The Study Co-Ordinator wore a dress and matching high heels the orange color of a ripe persimmon. Phineas recalled that she'd sported royal blue athletic shoes at his last visit. Today must not be her running day.

Phineas rocked once, twice, three times before he succeeded in pushing himself into a standing position. *Why do they have such low chairs in this of all clinics?* When he started to wobble, Iris and Felipe gripped each of his upper arms. Mateo's small, steady hands cradled the team's Tupperware case of muffins and other snacks.

A bronze-skinned middle-aged man in scrubs trailed Annabella and pushed a wheelchair. "Mohammed will take you for your magnetic imaging, Dr. Mann." She turned to Iris. "We should have him back in a half hour or so. The snack bar is around that corner if you want coffee." She gestured down the hall and squatted to Mateo's height. "And they have hot chocolate there too." He shot a hopeful look at his father.

Phineas settled into the wheelchair. "Mateo...a magnetic...version of me...will return."

Mateo's mouth fell open. "You'll be magnetic?"

Iris groaned. "Your grandfather's trying to make another one of his silly jokes, Mateo."

Mohammed steered the chair into the lengthy glassed-in tunnel that connected the Duke South's clinics with Duke North's hospital wards and the Radiology Department. Through the tunnel's clear walls, the morning sun accented the nearby buildings, their manicured bushes, and emerald-green patches of lawn.

"Comfortable, Sir?" Mohammed's exotic voice pattern was barely detectable.

Phineas' stomach responded to the cue with a growl. "Just hungry. ... How...are you?"

"I couldn't be better, Sir. Grateful for every beautiful day here." They approached another reception desk. "I have Dr. Phineas Mann for his MRI, please."

A radiology technician in royal blue scrubs came around the desk. His closely cropped beard contained flecks of grey, and a faded tattoo that read 'U.S.M.C.' crept out from under his short sleeve onto a muscular arm. "Well, hey Mohammed. Dr. Mann, my name's Josh. I'll take you back and start an IV for your contrast infusion. Do you have any questions or need anything?"

"No, ...Josh. This...isn't my first...MRI."

Josh wheeled him to a room next to the MRI chamber where intravenous paraphernalia had been laid out. He found a receptive forearm vein on his first try, secured the catheter with tape, and attached the clear bag of contrast. The solution sent a cool stream up Phineas' arm until it reached his core. "This isn't…your first…IV either, Josh."

Josh chuckled. "We'll run this in while we make your images. Now, let's settle you in." He positioned Phineas next to the MRI chamber.

"Were you…a corpsman, …Josh?"

"Yessir, put in my twenty. Now I'm living the dream. Here. You'll want these, Sir." Josh helped him insert soft ear plugs. "Ready?" Josh's strength made the transfer into the MRI seem effortless.

"Thank you…for your service…Josh."

The MRI chamber was more comfortable than Phineas remembered, so comfortable that an urge to sleep enveloped him—until a realization startled him into full wakefulness. He wasn't wearing his CPAP. If he gave in to sleep, he might go into atrial fibrillation. Then he'd need the anticoagulant, and they'd probably postpone his bone marrow procedure and reassess his enrollment in the study. The disturbing thought that he could be excluded kept him at full alert until his worry was replaced by the jarring noise of someone repeatedly hitting an anvil with a sledgehammer, the sound of the powerful MRI making images of his brain. *Thank God for the earplugs.* A low-tech solution to a high-tech contraption's deafening noise. Better yet, the noise proved to him that this cozy chamber wasn't his soundproof coffin, no matter how comfortable he was in it.

"We're done, Mr. Mann." A soothing deep voice from speakers surrounded him, as if it found its way from his afterlife. "We'll have you out as soon as we review the images to make sure we have all we need. Should just take a minute."

An alarming discomfort replaced the earlier urge to sleep in the magnetic tomb.

"We're good. We'll get you out now." Back to the world of the living.

It wasn't a simple discomfort. He needed to pee. Really needed to go! Those IV fluids with the MRI contrast material. Should have skipped the coffee. Now was not the time for incontinence and soaking his embarrassing diaper—and possibly even his trousers. Not before the bone marrow procedure on his hip.

Finally, the MRI began extruding him from its guts like he was an oversized mammal skat on a forest trail. He focused on tightening the muscles to hold his urine and wished the machine's gears operated more quickly. Josh awaited him and replaced the IV catheter with a Band-Aid. "Best of luck to you, Sir."

Mohammed offered two confident arms to transfer him back to the wheelchair. Despite the deadpan mask of Phineas' Parkinson's disease, Mohammed must have sensed distress, since he whispered, "Do you need something, Sir?"

"Bathroom."

At the rapid pace of an emergency transport, Mohammed rolled him down the hall and into the nearest men's room, where the handicapped stall was magically vacant. *Phew!* He helped Phineas stand and waited nearby while observing Phineas' tremoring hands fumble with his belt.

"May I assist, Sir?"

"Yes. ...Thank you...Mohammed." Necessity trumped indignity.

Mohammed methodically unbuckled Phineas' belt, unzipped him, and slid pants and adult diaper down to shaking knees.

He's probably done this a thousand times.

He eased Phineas onto the toilet seat and stepped out of stall. "Let me know when you're finished, Sir."

Phineas let a sigh of relief escape and let the muscle relax that had required all his concentration to hold back the torrent now gushing into the toilet bowl's water. The release of his pent-up water rivaled all recent sensory pleasures, and the volume now draining from him seemed sufficient to deflate him into an empty husk.

When the flow finally ceased, he heard Mohammed clear his throat and murmur, "A remarkable offering, Sir. Shall I assist you now?"

"Yes. ...Thank you...Mohammed."

Clearly practiced and remarkably efficient, Mohammed had Phineas neatly dressed, in the wheelchair, hands washed, and on his way back to the waiting room—all while Phineas extracted the story of Mohammed's university education and his work in Afghanistan as a translator, then his family's harrowing escape as the Taliban wrested control of his troubled country. When the soft-spoken patient transporter concluded his dramatic tale, he revealed it was Josh whose tireless efforts saved Mohammed and his family. Phineas felt honored that Mohammed shared his remarkable story.

Mateo bounced to Phineas' side, his cheeks dotted with blueberry stains, and under his nose, a chocolate mustache.

"It appears you...found the...snack bar, Mateo." Phineas gestured with his hand at the evidence of his grandson's snacks. Felipe found a napkin and wiped his son's face clean.

"Would you like to keep this chair for the rest of your appointment, Sir?" Mohammed asked.

"Yes, thank you." Iris added a nod of approval to Mohammed's suggestion.

I'd rather walk while I still can. "You can keep it...Mohammed...I have... my walker. Please...help me into...a chair."

Iris rolled her eyes at the ceiling, making it clear she'd rather not have to worry over her husband's every step, but she didn't seem to want to argue in front of everyone watching the only activity in the crowded but otherwise silent waiting room.

"Mateo, do you...have a muffin...for Mohammed? ...He rescued me... from...a biblical flood."

Mateo's mouth fell open. "Like Noah, Waylo?" When the boy opened the container, the enticing smell of the just-baked muffins escaped.

Phineas' hunger pangs reawakened. "Sort of...like Noah, ...but quite local."

"You're too kind, Sir. Thank you." Mohammed held the pastry in two cupped hands as if it were a ceremonial gift. "May the rest of your day be pleasant and productive." He bowed and backed away, pulling the wheelchair behind him.

"Thank you...Mohammed...for all...your help."

Iris turned toward Phineas in the chair beside her. "Flood?"

"Dr. Mann." Annabella's voice. She held the entrance door to the clinic rooms open. "We're ready for you." She'd donned her white coat since his MRI and was fetching him before he could score a much-needed muffin.

This time, it was Felipe who hoisted Phineas to a standing position behind his walker. The four trudged toward Annabella, who smiled at Iris then spoke to Felipe. "Thank you for helping, but we only have room for one visitor, and we don't allow children in the patient area."

Iris glanced at Felipe with an expression suggesting she also needed his support to go on but said, "I'll go back there now, but you can take my place when he has his procedure." She clearly wanted to avoid witnessing it. Phineas had planned to remain stoic in front of her, hoping to allay her fears over her own bone marrow.

So much for that idea.

The three paused at the scales. "Have you gained any weight?"

"Looks like...two pounds. ...We have...a guest chef."

If only Iris would gain weight too.

They returned to the same examination room as before, while Annabella entered his vital signs in the computer. "So, tell me how you've been since your last visit."

"The same...but we...now have...reinforcements."

"Good. Good. I'll notify Dr. Grace that you're ready. She'll study your MRI, and we'll record today's exam. Then, we'll ask our hematologist to obtain your bone marrow. We might even be done by lunchtime."

"If you're hungry...we have muffins...in the...waiting—"

Dr. Grace strode into the room and offered her hand to Phineas. She held his longer than she might have in a casual greeting, seeming to absorb his tremor while she studied his face. "Good morning, Dr. Mann. I just reviewed your MRI and found no surprises. Since you've not had any change since last week, Annabella will record today's neurological exam. She'll then photograph your face for the record. I'm guessing you've never had a bone marrow." Her face was serious, all business. Each statement felt clipped, and their pace suggested she was in a hurry.

"Done several...as a resident. ...That was...a while ago." Phineas hoped the light-hearted Dr. Grace might re-emerge if he joked. Perhaps she was puzzling over her last patient, or maybe a hiccup had occurred in her research.

Please not in the study I've entered.

"Well, the procedure hasn't changed, except what we'll do with your cells. Do you have any questions thus far?" She looked over at Iris, who'd flattened herself into the back of the chair, as if she sought maximum distance from any medical actions. Iris shook her head slowly.

To keep the train rolling on its track, he answered, "No, Doctor...I'm all in."

"Great." Dr. Grace stepped toward the door. "Annabella will carry on, and I'll see you at your next visit." She slipped out.

"She seems...busy today," Phineas observed.

Annabella seemed only slightly less busy. "Mondays are always hectic. She has to follow-up on emergency cases admitted over the weekend." Annabella touched her cell phone screen and held it up. "I need your picture, first relaxed, then smiling." For the second shot, he tried to exaggerate a smile when instructed but wasn't sure he'd produced much difference. She loaded the images in the computer. At least those stone faces weren't public for all to see.

Next came the ritual neurologic exam with detailed strength and tone measurements. More recording. Then the shaky walk of shame in the hallway side by side with the clinic's sturdy physical therapist.

They had a new test waiting for him today, a timed stacking of blocks at the therapist's desk. Stacking blocks was an activity he'd barely been capable of performing with Jacob and Marie's twins as they passed their first birthdays. It was always a guess which of the three of them would be the first to knock the stacks over, him by tremor and them on purpose. Twice a child again, and today a truly humbled child, his clumsiness numerically scored and on full display.

Finally, mercifully, Phineas was returned to his seat on the examination table while Annabella left to fetch the hematologist. Iris leaned forward, her hands on her knees. She looked poised to bolt. He asked, "Would you...like to...make good...your escape?"

She appeared immediately relieved at his offer. "Felipe's probably tired of entertaining Mateo, so I'll take over for him." She stood and patted Phineas' hand. Her hands were clammy and again possessed an uncharacteristic fine tremor.

He composed himself when she closed the door. For the time being, he only needed to be concerned with himself. *Did Iris feel the same way?*

Within minutes, Felipe slipped into the seat she'd vacated. "This should be easier than keeping Mateo occupied. All I need to do is sit here, right Phineas?"

"Right...you can...even nap...if you want."

Annabella re-entered, this time trailed by a young Asian woman in black-rimmed glasses and a long white coat. She carried a tray wrapped in green towels and sealed in plastic. Annabella introduced her as Dr. Cheung, fellow in hematology, and part of the study team. She nodded without smiling. *Hematologists always look so serious.* Phineas introduced Felipe.

"Annabella said you've done bone marrows during your medical career, so I won't go through every step with you now, but I'll explain what I'm doing during the procedure. Is that okay with you?" Dr. Cheung asked. Still no smile.

"Perfect...I'm eager to...get lunch."

"Sounds good to me." A subtle grin emerged at his mention of lunch. She placed her tray on a small metal stand tucked in the room's corner and wheeled it next to him. "I need you on your left side with your trousers down to your hips and your shirt up halfway. You can have your knees bent up."

Felipe stood as if to help but was told he could sit. Annabella and Dr. Cheung assisted Phineas with his belt, positioning, and exposing his back. As they stood behind him, an abrupt and unexpected silence fell over the two. He waited for the sterile prepping and draping but felt only cool, gentle hands palpating his hip. The two young women were studying his backside.

"I didn't think...there was...anything...special about...my butt."

"When did you get this large bruise? From the color, it looks recent," asked Annabella, concern in her voice. "Do you have other bruises? We didn't find any clotting abnormalities in your bloodwork." She came around to the foot of the table where she could see his face. Her easy smile had been replaced; her mouth had hardened into a straight line.

"Oh that. ...My walker had...a mechanical problem...and gave way. ... All fixed now." Phineas winked at Felipe, enlisting him as a co-conspirator in the white lie.

"Yeah. We fixed his walker." Felipe was in. Good man. Iris would have exposed his mishap. Might have sabotaged his entry into the study.

"Well, okay. We'll keep going since it looks like we'll be closing the study in a few days, and you're one of the last patients enrolled." Annabella retrieved her cell from the desk. "I'll need to record this bruise's appearance, so I hope it's okay if I take a picture."

"Go ahead. ...Never had...a picture made of...my backside before." And by two young women. His butt in bytes for all of eternity. *Quite a day, so far.*

He recognized every step of the bone marrow procedure: the familiar snap of sterile nitrile gloves being pulled on by the operator, cold liquid swabbed over his lower back, the pungent smell of alcohol in a chlorhexidine prep solution. Towels being draped around the operative site. Glassware clinking—special containers for the specimen soon to be aspirated.

"I'm going to put the local in now." Dr. Cheung's voice. He felt a prick then a searing pain that dissipated quickly. "You should just be feeling pressure now." He did. "I'm putting the bone marrow needle in now."

So far, so good.

"Now, Dr. Mann, when I aspirate, you will feel it, since I can't put the anesthetic through bone to the inside of your marrow space. Are you ready?"

"As I'll...ever be." He balled his hands into fists and swallowed.

A hammer blow. The sudden negative pressure applied to the closed marrow space from the syringe's suction fired countless pain fibers. A single twitch of Felipe's cheek reflected the sudden pain Phineas had felt. Apparently, his Parkinson's mask hadn't hidden enough. Then the hammer blow dissipated to a dull ache. The pressure change inside his bone must be diminishing.

"We're getting a good return. Should have what we need shortly," Dr. Cheung reported in a matter-of-fact tone.

"I'm not...going anywhere...get all that...you need." He hoped they wouldn't have to repeat the procedure. Ever. But he'd feel that hammer again tomorrow through Iris' bones.

He felt one of the women press a Band-Aid onto to his backside, then they assisted him in pulling his clothes back together. "Would you like to lie for a bit or sit up?" Annabella asked.

"I can...sit."

The discomfort was almost gone, and he didn't feel that much worse for wear. They eased him into a sitting position. On the metal stand, specimen tubes of varying sizes now contained a rich, thick dark red liquid—his marrow and its precious stem cells—his hopes for a future. The two women gathered them into a plastic box and snapped the lid closed. Dr. Cheung gripped it in both hands.

"It was nice to meet you, Dr. Mann. I've heard about you from an older member of our division." Dr. Cheung offered another rationed smile. "He told me about you and a bee swarm that saved UNC's hospital."

"That was a...very...long time ago." Notoriety couldn't hurt now.

She held up the box. "Well, I'll make sure we get started right away on your stem cells. Bye." Annabella followed her out the door.

"Seems like...we're about done...Felipe...I guess we...should wait...to be discharged."

"Well, that was a first for me." Felipe leaned back into his chair, and his face relaxed. His wide-open eyes returned to their usual size. "We French chefs often cook with marrow, but we scoop it out of the bones."

"Let's not...have that...on your menu." Just *seeing* marrow was more than enough for Phineas.

Felipe laughed out loud—a hearty laugh and welcome sound that punctuated the tense morning.

A soft knock. The door eased open, and Dr. Grace re-entered. She appeared surprised when she saw Felipe. She approached him and held out her hand. "I'm Dr. Grace, and you're..."

"Felipe Hernandez. Son-in-law." When he stood, he still had to look up to meet her gaze. "My mother-in-law, Iris, preferred looking after my young son to observing a bone marrow being performed."

His explanation brought a ready smile from Dr. Grace. She must be recalling Iris' squeamishness. She released Felipe's hand and turned to face Phineas. "I wanted to apologize for my abruptness earlier. The weekend left me several Monday morning fires to extinguish."

"It's not...a problem, ...Dr. Grace." He'd also had those Monday mornings back when he was on clinical services.

"I want you to know how grateful I am that you put your trust in me and my novel study." She pulled the rolling stool in front of him and sat. "Since this work hasn't been done anywhere before, your participation shows me your courage—and your faith in me. That means a lot." Having a former teacher come to her for help had to boost her self-worth—but would also add pressure she must be feeling.

"I believe...in you." Phineas began explaining how he'd researched all the novel studies he could find and that hers was the one he'd concluded had the best chance of a major benefit. He'd also read her published work and her NIH grant proposal. She studied him and listened patiently to his uneven speech without once interrupting, as he labored to succinctly outline his journey through the Parkinson's disease literature.

He ended his monologue with, "then I...met you and...learned I'd...helped train you." He hoped his heartfelt emotions were evident. "That...clinched it."

"I can honestly say that my month with you as a medical student was one of my best, and your evaluation of me helped tremendously. I *so much* want to help you." Sincerity filled each word.

"You...already have." She'd at the least given him hope.

She stood and pressed his shaky left hand between hers, stilling his tremor. Would her novel medical treatment do the same for him?

"How's...*your* life?" His question bordered on nosy, but he couldn't help asking.

She appeared caught off guard, as if she hadn't considered that question in a long time, too long. "Full." Then she added, "Clinical work. This trial."

Her short answers suggested that if he waited silently and looked receptive, more would flow.

"And being a face of diversity. People want me to represent them, to share my story. You may remember me as being on the quiet side when I was a student. I still *am* quiet underneath." The beginnings of a smile formed. "And now we have a three-year-old daughter. Our treasure. Every spare moment is hers." She glanced at the space over Phineas' head then into his eyes. "If only there were more of those moments. There's just *never* enough time."

"No. There...never is. ...Time is...so precious."

"Thank you, Dr. Phineas Mann, for coming back to me." Her eyes shone under the bright ceiling lights. "May we enjoy better times together." The instant she released his hand, his tremor returned.

Felipe watched her close the door behind her. Then he sat back and stretched his legs out straight. "She's impressive, Phineas—and tall."

"She's all...of that, Felipe."

CHAPTER 15

July 10

By mid-afternoon, the four had made their way home, lunched, and begun to relax. Felipe busied himself cleaning up after the meal of sandwiches and fresh fruit, then took a thorough inventory of the sparse refrigerator, cabinets, and pantry contents. Iris produced a deck of playing cards and began explaining the game of Go Fish to Mateo as she and Phineas lingered at the kitchen table. She hunched over Mateo as his partner for the first contest to demonstrate how to fan the cards and to be sure he grasped the game's purpose and flow.

Phineas clamped his fingers onto his cards, doing his best to not drop any. "Got any...kings, Mateo?"

Iris pointed at one of Mateo's cards. "You need to give him this one with the K, Mateo." She shook her head to send her hair out of the way back behind her shoulders.

"You sure, Wayla?" The look he gave her suggested he didn't want to give up any of his cards, much less one with a sword and a crown. When she nodded, he placed the card on the table and watched his grandfather labor to pick it up and insert it into his shaking irregularly fanned cards.

"You got...any sixes, ...Mateo?" Phineas did his best to raise an eyebrow.

Mateo studied his cards then glanced at his grandmother while slowly shaking his head. She whispered, "You say, 'Go Fish' to him then you get to ask him if he has one of the cards you have."

"Go Fish, Waylo!" Mateo smiled triumphantly and sat tall.

Felipe held up a small pad of paper. "I've got my list. If it's okay with you two, I'll head to the store. Be back in an hour or two."

"We should...be able...to hold down...the fort...that long."

"You're sure you're okay after your procedure, Phineas?" Felipe asked.

"Fine. It...wasn't much." The soreness was almost gone, and he didn't want Iris to dread her coming appointment.

"Then I'm off." Felipe gathered his cloth grocery bags and slipped out of the kitchen.

"Got any threes, Waylo?" Mateo peered at his grandfather.

Phineas squeezed his cards with his cursed and tremoring left hand while trying to extract a three from the middle with his right. As the three came free, half his cards slipped from his grip and toppled face up onto the table. He eased the three toward Mateo and hastened to cover and reassemble his cards.

Mateo stared at the spilled cards then his own. "Got any eights, Waylo?" He knew his grandfather had an eight.

Merciless little card sharp.

Phineas handed over his eight. "So that's...how it's...gonna be, Eh?"

After the first two games, Mateo no longer needed his grandmother's help. She joined for the next two contests. Score Mateo 2, Wayla 1, Waylo 1. Phineas only fumbled once more. Practice was helping. He hadn't played cards in many months.

"Can we do something outside now?" Mateo abruptly asked. Either he'd had enough of cards or wanted to quit while he was ahead. When son Jacob was six, he'd hated losing and was usually ready to quit when leading. Learning to lose gracefully would have to be a necessary later lesson for Mateo as it had been for Jacob.

"What is it you want to do outside?" Iris sounded reluctant. The July day was easily in the mid-nineties and as humid as a salt marsh.

"Just walk around. I haven't seen everything here in a long time. And can Ernest come with us?" Mateo pleaded with the irresistible expression only a child could pull off.

"Maybe a short time," Iris answered. "Your father can go out longer with you later."

Phineas pushed himself up onto his walker's handles. Ernest stood and searched his master's face for a command. "Heel, Ernest."

Mateo shot ahead of them with Iris in close, hurried pursuit. "Wait for us, Mateo!" she hollered after him.

Mateo raced for the backyard, his pace exceeding anything his grandparents had attempted for months. Iris trailed him, and Phineas and Ernest lumbered behind.

It had been weeks since Phineas had surveyed in person what for him were once hallowed grounds. The extensive, verdant space that had been regularly purposed for food production was now mostly fallow. Honeysuckle vines smothered the former site of the apiary. A miserable, suffocating weed, by the name of Creeping Charlie, covered most of the ground under the fruit trees. Phineas had fought that weed to a stalemate when he'd been an able gardener. At least the fig and persimmon trees still bore fruit. But his poor berries. Without the laborious pruning, thinning, and mulching necessary for optimal blackberry and strawberry production, those harvests were slim shadows of their prior bounty. Once his debility blocked his constant efforts, chaos overwhelmed order.

At least the raised beds, once purposed solely for vegetables, exploded with color. Golden sunflowers towered above rainbow mounds of zinnias. Long fat squash vines trailed out of the beds and explored the pathways. Someone else's honey bee flitted from blossom to blossom. An iridescent blue mason bee rested in the center of a flaming red-orange zinnia bloom.

Mateo plucked a ripe fig and took a healthy bite. He swallowed and observed, "The ones with ants are the sweetest. You just need to brush them off."

Iris gingerly lowered herself onto the landscape timbers that formed a corner of one of the beds. Her face blanched and shone under the blazing sun. Beads of perspiration seeped from her hairline, trickled down her temples, and matted her hair onto her neck. She pursed her lips and panted. Her neck muscles stood taut from the angles of her jaw to her collarbones.

Ernest approached her and whined.

"Iris, ...are you... okay?" Phineas shuffled to her and pressed the back of his fingers to her forehead. "You're too hot. ...We should...go back... inside." He was also beginning to feel uncomfortable, beginning to soak his shirt across the chest and in his armpits.

Fright replaced Mateo's usual cheer. He stared at his grandmother with his mouth hanging open. "Wayla?"

"Give me...just a minute...to rest, you two." She, minutes earlier, had struggled to keep up with her grandson's eager explorations and now leaned forward, elbows on knees. "My stamina isn't what it used to be." Her breathing slowed. Phineas stared helplessly at her, waiting for signs of recovery or impending crisis. Finally, she said, "Look at you guys. You look like you saw a ghost." She appeared to force a smile. "I'm about ready now. Let's go back inside."

"You went too fast, Wayla. This time you need to go slower." Mateo placed her hand on his shoulder. "You can lean on me now."

Phineas turned his watch at an angle that made the screen light up. Tuesday 2:30 AM. He'd emptied his bladder into the catheter bag fifteen minutes ago hoping he'd soon fall back asleep. But the events of his visit to Duke Neurology, Iris' frightening near collapse in the zinnias, and his worry over her appointment today with the hematologist, Moro, had his eyes open and his brain churning. The silicone mask strapped tightly over his face and applying constant air pressure always became harder to ignore whenever rehashing a day's stresses replaced calming thoughts.

He needed calming thoughts. He cracked open his mental album labeled 'Calming Thoughts' and flipped through its pages then settled on images of Iris' and his last major adventure, the August trip four years ago to northern Italy, the last big trip before his Parkinson's disease anchored him to North Carolina. Weeks before they'd departed, he'd scheduled a honey tasting course in an Italian mountain village with plans to begin the process of becoming a honey sommelier—but then, scant weeks before their departure, all of his bees had succumbed to a pest control company's careless insecticide applications in a neighbor's yard. That horrible day now brought him none of the calming thoughts he was seeking. He pivoted his focus to the serene days in Italy.

He'd still enjoyed the honey tasting course and made plans to re-establish bee colonies the next spring, but by spring his tremor had intensified enough that his skills with a hive tool had deteriorated too much for him to be competent amid a frenzied 60,000-bee colony. He'd donated his equipment and became an occasional rapt spectator in Jacob's apiary.

Calming thoughts, Mann.

Iris had savored their vacation days in Italy, her first trip after retiring from the UNC faculty, and before she had to become her husband's caretaker. While he'd tasted numerous varieties of honey in a classroom of international beekeepers, she'd tossed back tiny cups of expresso, pampered herself with a spa treatment, and joined walking tours. Late afternoons, they'd meet at a sidewalk café and enjoy small plates of local fare and goblets of a crisp vinho verde wine. Then, since Italian suppers began after 8, they'd returned to their villa room for lovemaking and naps pressed against each other.

He missed her silky body against his. Every night. First his tremoring, then the condom catheter, and finally the CPAP, had distanced her to her side of the bed. Maybe if the Duke study's intervention worked, he could once again feel her pressed against him at night.

Her breathing. She wasn't struggling now as she did in the garden.

Hers was always so peaceful during sleep, so soft and regular. Soothing his tensions.

He slid his less tremoring right hand under the sheets to touch her smooth skin, gently so as to not disturb her. One touch to absorb her calm, and he'd settle himself enough to fall back asleep.

Yet her skin radiated intense heat, beyond any heat years ago during her time with menopause. Instead of silky, her skin was sticky with perspiration. He pulled his hand back when she let out a soft groan and rolled onto her side further from him.

His troubled tears welled up, and he closed his eyes and waited for the evasive escape of sleep.

CHAPTER 16

July 11

On Tuesday morning Iris lingered in her robe at the breakfast table sipping black coffee. Phineas, tired but still hungry, greedily enjoyed his portion of a mushroom and cheese omelet, being extra certain to tuck his chin and swallow carefully, so as not to choke and have these mushrooms turn into the lethal fungi of a timeless crime saga. These beauties were hand-picked Shitakes from Felipe's Washington, D. C. produce source, and the omelet bathed them in Gruyere cheese. Perfectly melted and served warm.

Mateo sat close to Iris and devoured bite after bite of cinnamon French toast dripping with maple syrup. Faithful Ernest stretched on his side between Phineas and Mateo's chairs. The only sound was the clinking of forks on plates. Iris' mouth was the only one that wasn't full, and she wasn't talking. Her instructions indicated that she could only have clear liquids before her CT scan, and she seemed cheerful and consumed with watching Mateo gobble forkful after forkful of his sweet treat.

Her composure surprised Phineas. She should be a bundle of anxiety in preparation for her appointment, and by now, she should be getting dressed and applying a hint of makeup. She looked like she wasn't going to budge.

His culinary duties complete, Felipe pulled up a chair and sampled portions of both offerings. He appeared satisfied. "So, Phineas, I'm thinking I'd thaw some grouper fillets for dinner. Sound good?"

Phineas offered a shaky 'thumbs up' and wished his impassive facial muscles would let him reward Felipe by showing his enthusiasm for the feast. He swallowed his last bite of egg. "Sounds great." He stared at Iris until she returned his gaze. He said, "We should be...getting dressed soon...so we're not...late."

"I'm not going." Her words were faint but firm. "As soon as the clinic opens, I'll call and cancel."

Did he hear her right? "But...your consult...and tests...are scheduled." And rescheduling everything anytime soon would be a monumental task, if even possible. Why was she doing this? He hadn't anticipated having to again convince her of the importance of an expeditious evaluation. Time was precious.

She tilted her head back. "I'm going to take vitamins." While she announced her escape plan, her tone was defiant. She was a strong-willed woman, even stubborn at times.

Feelings of helplessness and fear filled Phineas, a new trembling in his core, like when, as a young boy, he knew trouble was coming, and he could only watch and suffer the consequences.

"I read on the Internet that B12 and folate could help me," she said.

"They won't," he blurted. Her surprise proclamation had breached Phineas' defenses.

Was Iris so far from her academic career in medical social work that she grasped at random Internet chatter? He hadn't meant to assault her with his response; he couldn't imagine assaulting her in any way, ever. Those grim, stark words just slipped out.

"Why...why do you say that?" Softer. A hint of fear and uncertainty in her question.

"Your spleen." No one had assailed her yet with the hard truth that enlargement of that organ made a vitamin deficiency an unlikely explanation for her low blood counts.

Felipe stood and pushed his chair back. "Come on, Mateo. Let's go brush your teeth."

"Last piece, Papi. Ultimo." The three adults waited silently for him to chew and swallow his French toast, then drain his milk.

Phineas' throat constricted. He kept his gaze on his empty plate and concentrated on slowing his breathing.

"Okay, Papi." Father and son departed, and the crisp click of the guest bathroom door closing reached the kitchen.

Ernest rose to a sitting posture and probed Phineas for instructions. The dog looked like he was trying to suppress a yawn, but then it escaped, his mouth open wide with his tongue curled—a dog's sign, not of boredom, but of a stressful moment.

"What *about* my spleen?" Had she blocked out her doctor's words?

"Your doctor said…it was enlarged…Vitamin deficiency…doesn't do that."

"So, what does?"

Did she really want to know?

"Things we need…to diagnose to…determine…the right…next steps." He couldn't say the words leukemia or lymphoma to her. Her hematologist would have to. "We need to…keep today's…appointments. …Trust me… please, Iris. …Trust me…on this."

She slapped the table, and Ernest flinched and trembled.

"Damn it, Phineas! Why do you have to be such a buzz kill?" When she sniffed, her nostrils flared. "Then *tell* me what you know."

"That…your grandsons…need…their Wayla…to live." He needed to reach into that place that mattered most to her.

She stared at him then closed her eyes and bowed her head. "Okay." Almost a whisper. "I'll go."

〜

"You can do it, Wayla." Mateo proclaimed.

Iris held her nose and swallowed twice, gagged, then wiped the pink liquid from her lips with a tissue. "How much more of this foul stuff am I supposed to swallow?"

"Just...one more." The CT contrast material in the cup Phineas offered quivered in sync with his tremor. She rescued the last aliquot before any spilled.

"Okay, last one. Down the hatch." She choked it down then immediately covered her mouth and paced back and forth in the waiting area, appearing to will the pink stuff to stay down, the volcano to not erupt. The muscles under her jaw spasmed with a series of gags then slowly relaxed. "Now, how long before the CT?"

The receptionist looked up from her computer screen. "We wait long enough for it to reach your intestines. We'll call for you. Then they'll start your IV for the intravenous contrast."

"Good job, Wayla." Mateo, who'd been coaching throughout, nodded his approval. His words and expression mimicked the adults who'd coached *him*, and those grownup words made Iris smile. Mateo extracted an electronic tablet decorated with stickers from his backpack and carried it to her. He pointed to two empty seats in a quiet corner. "You sit over there, Wayla, and read this with me."

"Emergency! Coming through!" An exclamation from the hallway. Uniformed members of a team rolled a bright yellow stretcher to the receptionist's desk. The patient lay supine on a back board with their neck in a brace. A bloody bandage covered much of their head. One of the team squeezed a clear plastic manual resuscitator bag, sending breaths into an oral tube. The receptionist waved them through and paged a CT tech overhead.

Iris pointed at the tablet. "Mateo, let's start here." She'd raised her voice over the commotion.

⌒

Two hours later, in the hematology clinic's examination room, Iris and Phineas planted themselves against the wall on the two steel and vinyl chairs and awaited the eminent Dr. Moro's entrance. Five minutes. She scratched at the crook of her elbow where a Band-Aid now covered the CT's injection site. Ten minutes. Iris extracted her cell from her purse and scrolled. Fifteen minutes. Phineas rocked his weight onto his walker and stood. He leaned on the examination table in front of them and gave each stiff leg two shakes, hoping to ward off cramps. Twenty minutes. He retook his seat.

"What is *keeping* that man?" Iris muttered.

"Maybe he wanted...to go over your...CT scan...with a radiologist." Phineas had done that on occasion when something about images puzzled him, and he knew Dr. Moro's reputation as a knowledgeable clinician. But the man carried himself as if he lacked all warmth and had once been called a "cold fish" by one of Phineas' patients.

Phineas appreciated that Moro's specialty often required detached, emotionless objectivity when he was faced with gut-wrenching decisions for difficult to treat life-threatening diseases. Moro had to maintain a clear head to give his best advice. And in recent years, he had to deal with the constant burden of electronic medical records that his patients could access and question him about at all hours. Adding to those stresses, fewer medical trainees were choosing the specialty of hematology, even as the population aged and developed more hematological conditions. Dr. Moro must be seeing more patients than ever as *he* aged and probably was at significant risk for burnout. Burnout would make Moro even more detached and might even impair his judgment at times. Phineas needed to keep this insider information to himself. He dared not share it with Iris. She was plenty stressed already.

She tilted forward like she was thinking of bolting, like a sprinter before the starter's gun. "How much longer do we wait?"

The door cracked open, then abruptly closed. Muffled words. Was it Dr. Moro, ambushed by an emergency? A soft knock. Dr. Moro pushed the door open and strode through with a fleeting, forced-looking smile. Genetics and a career of stress had claimed every last hair on his head. Yet, his tanned scalp gleamed under the clinic lights as if it had been polished. He peered at Iris then Phineas over frameless reading glasses. His white coat lacked its lowest button, evidence that it had popped off when he'd once sat down in a hurry.

"Iris Mann? I'm Dr. Moro, and I'm running behind." He held out his hand. She accepted it for an instant then took hers back like she'd touched a slimy marine carcass on a frigid beach.

Phineas could understand her response. There was something different about this doctor's face that made him appear even more grim than Phineas remembered: the crease from Moro's nose to the corner of his mouth, the nasolabial fold. On him, these were not symmetric. The left was deeper, sharper. Dr. Moro tilted his head just enough to reveal that a subtle thread of a scar snaked its way up from the fold to under his eye and across his entire cheek, typical of a plastic surgeon's cancer resection and sizable skin flap repair.

It seemed the hematologist's fondness for sunshine had cost him once and likely would again. "Hello, ...Dr. Moro." Phineas' voice came out even squeakier and softer than he'd anticipated, adding to his usual embarrassment.

Moro turned from Iris to study Phineas and his walker. A surprised look of recognition replaced Moro's all business work mask. Apparently, he didn't know about Phineas' physical decline. He offered his hand. "LONG TIME." Almost a yell.

Not long enough. "My voice...is impaired. ...Not...my hearing." Instantly, Phineas regretted his hasty correction. Shouldn't antagonize Iris' doctor. Moro's only visible response was to turn away, pull the rolling stool over to the compact desk, and log onto the computer.

During Phineas' career, he'd hoped never to need Moro's services personally, to never have one of *his* diseases. Back in the ICU, Phineas had taken care of a biased sample of Moro's sickest patients—always when the medical teams struggled to try to save them during horrible complications of those diseases or their treatments. The moment he accepted those patients with accelerating blood disorders onto the critical care service, Phineas' attempts to intervene felt futile. Bleeding and infected, they were usually facing death. As for Moro, who'd directed their treatments all along, he would then soon step aside and turn over to Phineas—a late inserted stranger—the delicate end of life discussions and decisions with stressed out families.

"Thank you...for...seeing Iris."

"It's what I do."

How freaking noble of you.

Phineas resisted a sudden urge to suggest that he and Iris should seek help elsewhere. Time mattered. They'd have to tolerate Moro.

Moro turned from the computer to address Phineas. "Actually, it's good that you came when you did." He cast a knowing glance at Phineas, one physician signaling ominous news to another. *An asshole move.* "I just reviewed the CT. It confirmed significant splenic enlargement, and so are several lymph nodes near it."

Iris wilted for an instant then stiffened. "So, are you going to continue like this, Dr. Moro, only communicating with my husband, or can we get on with my evaluation?" She leveled her most probing stare at Moro.

Good woman. Made Phineas proud, but probably didn't endear her to her new doctor.

It was Moro's turn to stiffen. He tapped on the computer keyboard and scanned her medical record. "So, you've lost weight, and your blood counts are low. Had fevers or sweats?"

"Sweats."

So, she had paid attention to them.

"But doesn't everyone in July? With climate change, no one sets their air conditioner below 76 degrees anymore." A convenient rationalization for her sweats, but last year in the heat of July she hadn't had a shiny brow and damp sheets.

"Appetite?"

"I'm not much of a cook—and I fill up fast."

"That's from your enlarged spleen."

More frightening words—and delivered as though she wasn't sitting right next to him. *Asshole!...Calm yourself, Mann. You're tired and stressed out.* At least his blank Parkinson's face wouldn't be a window to his feelings.

"Well, your history's all in your note from Dr. Wahlstrom. Go ahead and climb up there and we'll do your exam." He gestured at the exam table with his head.

What? He's not going to take a history? He's going to make decisions from computer record, some labs, and a CT scan?

Phineas had never done that, no matter how far behind he was running. Moro didn't know anything about Iris' long and rich life—a life of sacrifice and achievement. And the man was about to stab a coring needle into her pelvic bone for a marrow biopsy.

Moro glanced at the computer record. "Vitals are fine. No fever today." He pulled a penlight from the breast pocket of his white coat. "Open." A three second look at her throat. She flinched when he ran his fingertips under her jaw, over her neck, and across her collarbones. "I need to check your armpits." She lifted her arms and stared defiantly at him as he probed through her blouse.

"Any respiratory symptoms?" Moro lifted a burgundy stethoscope from a side pocket. He didn't specify cough, shortness of breath, or any of the others.

Iris shook her head slowly. The look she sent Phineas suggested she wished he could somehow rally to rescue her from this doctor.

"Breathe deep." Moro lifted the back of her blouse and pressed the stethoscope's diaphragm to her back. She twitched from the instrument's obviously chilly surface then complied. "Lie back." Moro pulled out the table's leg extension. He slid the stethoscope under the front of her blouse long enough for a half dozen heartbeats. "Heart sounds fine. I saw that your recent breast exam and last mammogram were normal. Have you felt anything new there?" he asked.

"No." Her tone. As if he'd asked her if she abused children.

"Okay, then you can leave your bra on. I'm going to check your abdomen now. Unzip your pants." She complied silently. Using his middle finger as a bony hammer, Moro tapped out dull sounds from her right side. "Liver's borderline in size."

Borderline. Not what a scared patient wants to hear. Iris' jaw muscles clenched while she studied the ceiling tiles.

Moro began palpating her left side, sweeping his fingers from above her groin to up and under her ribs. She grimaced. On the second, deeper pass, he paused with his hand cupped below her ribs. "Spleen's down three, maybe four centimeters."

Clearly enlarged.

Two more deeper passes and Moro stepped back. "You can zip up your pants."

Her five-minute exam would be entered into a computer template as a complete physical. Another practice Phineas loathed. At least their primary care doctor, Dr. Wahlstrom, was thorough.

Moro squirted an acorn-sized dollop of sanitizing gel from a wall dispenser into his palm and rubbed his hands together. "I agree with Dr. Wahlstrom. Next step is a bone marrow. I'm sure your husband explained it to you. Questions?"

She shook her head slowly as if she was a victim of a hit-and-run accident trying to process the sudden, violent event. Then abruptly, she sat upright. "I want you to explain what you are doing while you are doing it. Will you do that for me?"

So, the fire in her, while trampled, wasn't extinguished.

Moro cleared his throat. "Okay. I can do that."

Had he understood her reprimand? And that thin, blue-eyed Iris could turn fiery when crossed?

"The nurse will bring you a consent form, and I'll be back with the procedure tray." He slipped out the door without documenting any of her history or examination on the computer. He was going to do that chore in the workstation, away from this patient and her reprimands.

"That could have…gone better. …Sorry for…his rudeness," Phineas muttered and tried to recall if Moro been less of a "cold fish" when they'd worked together earlier in his career, before the harsh realities of his field had hardened the man.

"Let's just get this over—"

The door flew open, and the nurse, Gladys, who'd checked Iris in earlier, held out a clipboard and blurted, "He'll need you to sign this by the 'X.'" She pointed at the attached paper. "It lists the risks here. Other than the discomfort, they're all pretty rare." She offered Iris a pen. "He does these all the time, you know."

Iris accepted the clipboard and began poring over it. "Give me a minute with this, Gladys. Haven't read a consent form in years."

Gladys shifted her weight from one foot to the other. Her attempt to hurry the process had been thwarted. She held the pen out, at the ready, pulled it back, and held it out again.

Iris accepted it and, with lips pressed tightly together, signed. "Will he be back soon?"

Gladys shrugged. "He's with another patient. Probably after that." She exited as abruptly as she'd arrived, clutching the clipboard triumphantly.

"In such a hurry. When did doctors and nurses start treating their patients like this?" Iris asked. "At least Wahlstrom hasn't yet."

"Wahlstrom's in an…outpatient clinic…off-site. …She can control…her schedule better. …Here, they…have to see…referrals…that can't wait." And Iris' condition couldn't wait. Phineas stretched his legs, trying to avoid the cramp he felt coming on. He hated to make excuses for Moro, but pressures could pile up and keep a clinician behind schedule.

Two soft knocks, and Moro was back. This time he displayed a thick tray wrapped in green cloth. Gladys followed with a rolling stainless-steel table, sterile gloves, and a bottle of sanitizing prep solution. Moro wore an almost cheerful half smile on his asymmetric face, like he was about to enjoy himself. A doctor more at ease stabbing someone than talking to them. Or was he recalling Iris' reprimand?

"I'll need you to unzip your pants again then lie on your side facing your husband." Iris followed his instructions, and the nurse pulled up Iris' blouse and lowered her slacks to expose her lower back and upper buttocks. Moro opened the outer wrap of his tray, pulled on sterile gloves, and arranged containers, syringes, and vials. He gestured at a metal bowl with his head, and the nurse poured the clear prep solution into it. He clamped gauze pads into a metal holder and dipped them into the liquid.

"This is going to feel cold." He swabbed Iris' skin in enlarging circles. Next—and without describing what he was doing—he applied sterile towels to create his operating field. From Phineas' seat on Iris' front side, he could tell that Moro was palpating Iris' bony posterior landmarks to identify the pelvis site for sampling—and still he explained nothing.

So much for his promise that he'd tell her what he was doing.

The hematologist then drew the local anesthetic into a syringe. Phineas looked away from the procedure and focused on Iris' so-far stoic face. He took her hand in his shaking but steadier right hand.

"I'm going to numb things up now." Moro finally remembered his promise.

A minor miracle.

"You'll feel a burning as the medicine goes in."

Iris grimaced, then her face relaxed back to stoic. "If that's the worst of it, I'm okay."

"I can't numb the inside, so you'll feel a quick pain when I aspirate cells. Sorry about this." His tone shifted as though he was trying to use the best soothing voice he possessed.

Iris looked mildly surprised at the unanticipated apology. Then her eyes flew wide open, and her leg straightened. "Yow!" She squeezed Phineas' fingers in a grip fierce enough that it contained the potential to damage his finger bones. She'd felt every bit of that "kick in the ass" he'd endured yesterday.

Her grip had begun to relax, and his fingers were beginning to recover when Moro announced, "I'm not getting anything when I aspirate. We'll need to perform a core biopsy in order to get an adequate sample. For this procedure, I'll need you to roll onto your stomach slowly." He held the towels in place as she turned over. The larger bore needle, the thickness of a decades-old meat thermometer, flashed under the bright clinic lights.

Phineas cringed at Moro's terrifying announcement. "Not getting anything" on aspirate. The dreaded 'dry tap'. He recalled that could mean the empty marrow of an aplastic anemia or a crowded marrow, jammed tight with diseased cells.

Iris clenched Phineas' fingers in anticipation of another wave of pain. Her eyes squeezed shut, and her upper body trembled.

"All done, and I got what we need that time." Moro sounded proud and triumphant. From the biopsy needle, he extruded then deposited a small fraction of the blood-streaked tannish, cylindrical biopsy specimen into a microbiology culture tube and the majority of it in a pathology fixative jar.

The pale color of her marrow sent a chill through Phineas. It wasn't the dark red of his normal marrow aspirated yesterday. Her biopsy *had* to contain serious pathology. It *had* to contain an answer.

Moro peeled off his gloves and tossed them in the biohazard trash. "Gladys will bandage you and let you recover." He came around the table to face Iris. "Then she'll make you an appointment with me for early next week. The results won't be available any earlier because the bone in the biopsy needs to demineralize then be sectioned and stained. All that takes a minimum of five or six days." He patted her hand. She didn't pull hers away this time. "And I'll want up-to-date blood counts the day of your visit, so you'll need to come in at least an hour before your appointment time." He withdrew his hand from hers. "You did well." Like a parent to a child.

Iris glanced up at him, and the beginning of a smirk appeared on her face. "You've never birthed a baby, Dr. Moro. That's worse pain—and it comes again and again and again for hours." She inhaled deeply. "A mother never forgets."

Moro gathered the specimen jars and stepped toward the door. "Obviously, I wouldn't know about that." He slipped out.

The tension that tugged up and down Phineas' spine began to ease. Impressive. Why had he worried so about his wife tolerating her procedure? She possessed a birth mother's fortitude. But if this brave woman could remain stoic with a large needle coring her bone, how much suffering was she hiding from her family? She was slipping away day by day. Paler. Thinner. Exhausted. The activities she'd previously done without effort had transformed into onerous chores. And he was the most taxing of those chores.

He pushed himself up on his walker and did his best to stand tall.

Please let today's biopsy reveal something treatable—and soon.

Fortitude carried Iris through the rest of the day, including indulgent sessions with Mateo, who drew and colored his ideas of what animals and family members looked like, including an impossibly thin representation of his father in a chef's tall hat, his mother's face centered in a television screen, and a bearded, hunched stick figure leaning on an upside-down 'U', his too-honest depiction of his Waylo. Phineas promised it would go straight to the front of the refrigerator. Ernest's portrait, at least, made the dog look sturdy as he flashed a toothy smile.

Mateo had powered through the last of the paper and the limits of Iris' endurance by the time Felipe announced that they'd reached the hour for Mateo's bedtime story. The boy leaned against his Wayla's shoulder on the soft living room sofa while she read from the first of the books that he carried to her. By the second book, his eyelids were drooping. During the third, they closed. Iris' voice softened to a whisper. She signaled to a vigilant Felipe, who hoisted his son against his shoulder and carried him to his bed. Iris' attentiveness to Mateo, after her grueling appointment with Moro, proved how much she'd missed her grandson's spark and warmth since his family's move to Washington.

"Good thing Mateo finally gave in," she told Phineas. "I'm running on fumes."

Phineas grappled with his walker to raise himself from their one living room chair firm enough that he could still escape it without help. "Ernest, time to...get busy." The signal to the dog to use his outdoor bathroom. The command sent Ernest hustling to the front door with Phineas shuffling two steps behind him.

"I'll let him out, Phineas." Iris boosted herself from the sofa and beat her husband to the door. "Why don't you start washing up. I'll catch up with you, and we can both get to sleep early."

He pivoted in installments back toward the hallway and trudged toward their bedroom. Before he could reach the adjoining bathroom, Iris slipped by him, squeezed toothpaste on his brush, and held it for him.

"Thank you. ...So, how's your...backside?" He grasped the toothbrush and waited for her answer.

"It's only sore if I bump it on something." She tapped his hand to urge him to start brushing. "I'll let Ernest in while you brush." Her heavy eyelids exposed only a fraction of the brilliant blue irises that had captivated him from their first meeting early one morning fifty years ago on a frozen Boston street.

Ernest padded into the bathroom and sat, poised for the next command. Iris followed, back in time to help her husband rinse the toothpaste, wash his face, and sit on the toilet. Then the three moved to the walk-in closet for his pajamas. Ernest took his usual place in the corner, out of the way.

Phineas perched on the dressing stool. "Care to...share your...thoughts?" He raised his arms over his head for her to peel off his shirt.

"My thoughts..." She slipped a short-sleeved button-up pajama top over one of his arms then the other. "I don't even want to share my thoughts with *myself*. Letting them out chokes me with fear. *You* know how I am." Her face, inches from his as she buttoned him up, transformed from warm grandmother and dutiful wife to displaced and terrified victim of a tsunami, exhausted and unsure of what miseries lay ahead.

If only he could reassure her that everything would be fine. She had to know her future would be stormy, so a placid present was where she wanted her thoughts to remain—as long as they could. He wished he'd kept quiet tonight, wished he hadn't again unlocked the vault in her brain where she confined her demons.

CHAPTER 17

July 12

Early Wednesday afternoon Phineas hunched over the kitchen table and tried again to gather as much insight into his wife's disorder as Siri offered. He could at least do that. PubMed, his preferred search engine for all topics medical, listed numerous articles that reviewed the spectrum of conditions capable of producing Iris' pancytopenia, the abnormal reduction of all her blood cell counts. Many of those disorders could also cause her enlarged spleen.

While Iris read books to Mateo in the living room, Felipe readied generous quantities of food for their supper then dusted, vacuumed, and mopped as if royalty would soon arrive. Ernest hunkered in his usual station half under Phineas' chair, as secure as he could be from the troublesome vacuum cleaner.

A car door closed, then another. No one had said they were expecting visitors. Maybe a pair of Jehovah's Witnesses had heard of their troubles and dropped by to salvage two more souls. The front door opened without any audible prayers or pitches to save anyone. Instead, Iris squealed in delight. Mateo's light and rhythmic footsteps reverberated on the living room's hardwood floor. Ernest pushed himself out from under the chair's rungs, stretched, and sat expectantly, his tail sweeping a steady arc.

"It's so good to be back with my men." Martha's voice. "Where's Daddy?"

"Where he usually is. The kitchen," Iris answered. "Next to his window."

Phineas sat up as straight as he could. When Martha spotted her father, she hesitated an instant at his appearance then continued her fluid entry into the kitchen. She'd almost mastered hiding her initial shock at his rapid decline. At least Iris' condition hadn't yet stolen *her* good looks and left *her* a rigid remnant.

Dressed in the casual day attire she preferred, a UNC t-shirt and jeans, Martha wrapped him in her arms and planted a kiss on his forehead, the kind a parent uses to screen the health of their child. "I snuck away early from Washington." She released him, petted an appreciative Ernest, and peered at her father's laptop screen. "Now, what are you up to, Daddy?"

"Trying to...make sure your...mother's doctor...thinks...of everything."

"Good. Keep him in line. She texted me that she wasn't thrilled with him on her first visit."

"He...may be an...acquired taste...like turnips." He offered her his best sluggish attempt at a grin.

She wrinkled her nose. He never could cook turnips to her liking. "And *your* visit, Daddy? Did you like *your* new doctor?" She pulled a chair next to him and settled into it.

"Oh yes. ...She...is impressive." And eager to help him, especially after he'd been good to her so many years ago.

"You're really going to let them stick a catheter in your brain?" Her tone sounded dubious, incredulous. She tilted her head, chin down, as if she were cross-examining a witness on the stand.

"I'm going to...*ask*...them to." The difference between letting and asking. "I believe...there's a good...chance...it'll help."

"Why?" She either wanted him to justify his decision, or she was poised to try to talk him out of it.

Phineas had Siri open a folder labeled 'Duke Study' on his computer's desktop, then a file with the title 'Adenovirus Study 2024'. He watched

Martha scan the abstract before he said, "This was…a Phase One…trial. I'll…be taking …the next step."

He laboriously explained how, in the 2024 study, genes that instructed dopamine synthesis were loaded into a nonpathogenic adenovirus, a strain deemed safe, and now re-purposed to be a biologic container delivering a genetic payload. The virus was then instilled, via a catheter, into the part of the brain where a dopamine deficiency results in the symptoms of Parkinson's disease. Those earlier Phase One study subjects' subsequent courses had suggested a transient, modest clinical benefit, but the subjects' immune systems' reactions to neutralize the virus had limited the duration of dopamine production and sabotaged any long-term success. Then there were the complications—the fevers, headache, and transient confusion that resulted from an inflammatory response to the virus in the brain.

"My own…stem cells…with those genes…shouldn't cause…an immune reaction." As he concluded his lengthy explanation, he could feel drops of spittle dribble from the corner of his mouth. His daughter would be watching him drool like an infant. He leaned forward so he could reach into his back pocket for his handkerchief and wiped at his chin whiskers, hoping he'd thoroughly cleaned his face. "And…those stem cells…might establish…themselves…to keep producing…dopamine."

There. It'd been a long time since he'd said that much in one uninterrupted monologue. Martha had listened patiently and resisted any hidden urges to interrupt him or finish his arduous sentences. It had taken him long enough for his laptop's screen to time out and darken, and for Ernest to lie flat on his side and sigh, as if he'd heard it all before.

"That was an impressive lecture, Finman." Chelsea stood leaning against the door frame wearing pressed black slacks and a scarlet blouse that matched her lipstick. Concentrating on Martha, he'd missed his friend's silent arrival. She'd likely witnessed him drooling too.

"You…look nice, …Chelsea." And she'd brushed her hair smooth this time.

"Martha thought she'd surprise you and Iris. I picked her up at the train station and earned an invitation to a gourmet dinner."

Ernest stood and took a step toward her, thought better of it and sat at attention. More than once in the past, she'd uttered the confusing command for him to "Scoot, Dog." She wasn't a dog person and *that* wasn't a command he'd learned in his training.

"Have a seat... And update...me on...your quest in...Sweden."

"Thought you'd never ask." Chelsea eased into another chair. "I'm watching the package with my CD's progress on the FedEx website. So far, it's made it from the small hospital to Stockholm. Now it has to make it across the pond."

"Any ETA...yet?"

"FedEx hasn't given one yet. Probably because it's international."

"Well...don't cancel...your surgery." Difficulties rescheduling might cause her to lose time and lessen the chance for a cure. If the nodule was malignant, time could be critical to her survival. Phineas recalled notable cases where surgery was unexpectedly delayed, and when finally performed, a cancer was tragically inoperable. The patient, their family, and Phineas couldn't help wondering, "What if?"

"Easy for you to say. No one's sticking a knife in *your* chest." Chelsea looked from him to Martha and back to him. Desperation crept into her voice, amplified with every word.

"You're right...about that." He shook his head slowly. *Only a hole through my skull—if all goes as planned.*

A horrific screeching drew their attention to the window facing the front yard. A red-shouldered hawk landed on the lawn and gripped a writhing prey with its golden talons—a baby grey squirrel. The frantic mother circled close, protesting. Ernest raced to the window and stared, his ears and hackles raised, the dog in him escaping the discipline of his training. Suddenly, with a series of powerful wing beats, the predator ascended into the tree canopy, and the helpless mother pursued the abductor and its precious cargo along the ground and out of sight.

In the silence that followed, the old kitchen clock inserted its steady pulse.

"Sure is quiet in here." Felipe glided into the kitchen and stationed himself at the counter next to the range. He looked surprised, probably anticipating that Chelsea and his wife would be engaged in their usual lively banter. "Mind if I start making a Bolognese sauce?"

"You go right ahead, Felipe. We're about done airing our worries." Chelsea turned from the window. "And thanks for letting this loud and lonely old lady join y'all."

"Glad to have you, Chelsea, and thank you for delivering my wife back to me." He looped his apron over his head and tied its straps in one smooth motion. "And we have more guests coming. I've got a fair bit of chopping ahead of me."

"More guests?" asked Phineas. Another surprise? Their house already resounded with more life than it had in many months.

"Jacob, Marie, and the twins should be here soon. I'll bake some brownies once I get the sauce going." Felipe lined up several onions on the counter. "Rigatonis work for you, Phineas?"

"Good choice...Spaghetti noodles...are like...I'm fighting...flailing demons...with cutlery." Phineas wiped his chin again. "Always look...like I've...done bloody battle."

Speaking of battles, Finman. I saw where patients with Parkinson's benefit from training for boxing." Chelsea peered at him like she was measuring his pugilistic potential.

"So, you...want me to...get punched?" He held up two shaky fists.

"No, *Silly*. It's just training. Agility, balance, endurance. You should check it out. The patients in the article raved about it helping them." Chelsea pushed her chair back. "And the gym manager in the picture was quite handsome. You go, and I'll drive you." She gave Phineas a wink then aimed her next words at Felipe. "Find me another apron, and I'll start chopping onions for you. Maybe they'll draw some much-needed tears out of my system."

Two car doors closed. A pause. Two more. The front door opened. "Waylaaaa!" A chorus from two toddlers reached them in the kitchen. "Mateo! Play games!" Their older cousin was a rock star to them.

"Where's Dad?" Jacob's deep voice.

"Holding court in the kitchen, as usual. He seems to be attracting a crowd in there," Iris' voice. And then, "Wait. Are you two going to leave me alone with these three wild boys?"

"I won't be long. Mateo will help you," Marie said. "Holler if you need reinforcements." She stepped into the kitchen, followed by Jacob. He pressed himself against the wall next to the antique clock in the nearly packed room. His wife exclaimed, "Chelsea and Martha! Great to see you." They took turns hugging. "And Felipe, thank you for including four more hungry mouths."

"Not a problem, Marie. Just add a bit more of this and that. Actually, quite a bit more for that husband of yours." He raised a horizontal hand high over his head and grinned. "He still growing?"

Jacob, waiting patiently for his turn to greet everyone, chuckled at Felipe's joke, then offered, "Can I help you too, Felipe?"

"Wow! Helpers. You guys are spoiling me. My shoulder just healed up from my last big solo guest chef gig." Felipe rotated his shoulder to demonstrate its return to health. "Jacob, you can sauté the sausage for the sauce." Jacob threaded his way through the women's spirited conversations and accepted the package of meat.

The pungent smell of chopped onions spread to fill the kitchen. Chelsea turned her face away from the bright white pile forming on the cutting board. Tears trickled down her cheek and splashed on the quarry tile floor. "Been a while since I cut this many." When the kitchen fell silent at her tears, she waved her knife like a conductor's baton and added, "Y'all carry on. I'm fine."

Marie settled into Chelsea's vacated chair and pulled it close to Phineas. "Phineas, I can't wait to give you a progress report on the patient you saw with me."

"So soon?"

"It's been what, five days?" She ticked off the days on her fingers. "Well, anyway, his fever is gone, and he's needing less oxygen. He may come off the ventilator tomorrow, and before you saw him, we were deciding whether or not to perform a tracheostomy. Hopefully, *that* won't be needed now."

Phineas' thoughts drifted from Iris to Marie's patient. It was always a relief to hear that a patient might not require the ventilator's support long enough for the ICU team to suggest the patient have a hole cut in their neck to relocate the breathing tube. The congressman might even escape his ordeal without any lasting scars.

"Any proof of...a diagnosis?"

"Cultures and send out labs are still pending, but those prostate secretion stains you suggested—those and his clinical response to the specific antifungal treatment—they both indicate that your diagnosis was correct."

Phineas couldn't help but feel a surge of pride. A rare disease, especially a diagnosis that had evaded the computer's analysis, coupled with a likely triumph would be a high for all physicians involved—and Marie sounded truly excited. Now they needed to escort the congressman safely across the finish line to the goal of fully healed. Then they could finally, collectively—and probably privately—let out sighs of relief that the VIP had escaped the early error in managing his case.

Chelsea paused her chopping and glanced over her shoulder; her nose wrinkled in apparent revulsion. "Ewww! Antifungal? *Prostate secretions?* What in God's name have you two been *up* to during all of *our* troubles?"

Her mention of "*our* troubles" jerked Phineas back from the hospital work to concern for Iris, who seemed to weaken day by day at a frightening pace. "One of...us should...relieve Iris...of all...those boys."

CHAPTER 18

July 13

$\mathbf{N}$ear dawn Thursday, Phineas again occupied his customary post next to the kitchen window. He glanced outside in time to witness a single flaming ray penetrate the early morning cloud cover for an instant. Minutes earlier, he'd coaxed his sleepy wife into pouring him coffee in the dinosaur Sippy cup and setting up his laptop for him. Then she'd escaped back to their bed to "pursue dreams of past joys." He let his thoughts wander to a place of his own "past joys."

When he was healthy, he often filled his early morning coffee mug and strolled past his backyard garden to his apiary. He'd sit on the weather-beaten cedar chair at that favorite post with its full view of the southeast-facing hive entrances. The rising sun heated his back and each hive's front, drawing his bees onto the landing platforms then launching them into the air on quests to forage nectar and pollen. Their beating wings filled his ears with buzzing, at first a soft hum, then at a level impossible to ignore. The seductive fragrance of warming honey blended with that of his coffee's steam. Soon his bees would return, and the pollen sacs on their hind legs bulged with yellow, orange, and sometimes even scarlet harvests. A straggler bee might settle on his knee or arm—drawn by a mystery smell in his soap perhaps? She'd land heavily there, weighted down by her nectar-filled stomach.

Ernest, bless his kind soul, broke Phineas' reverie. The dog was fresh from relieving himself and his daily sentry romp around the property. He stretched out across the floor tiles beside his master then let out a deep, contented sigh.

Back to work, Mann.

"Siri, open…PubMed." Phineas began to review the research he'd begun yesterday but had to tell Siri "never mind" when Martha and Chelsea arrived from the train station. He scrolled further down the lists of publications and scanned those that reported the more uncommon causes of pancytopenia and splenomegaly. Nothing new stood out to offer him a novel solution that could lead to his wife's salvation. He closed his eyes and began searching his own mental files for an answer, the more notable memories he'd accumulated over fifty years of patient care and study.

When Ernest abruptly boosted himself up to sit at attention and stare at the kitchen door, he brought Phineas back to the present. The dog had heard Martha's shuffling slippers. Her hair still pillow-tossed, she looked sleepy and then surprised at the unexpected sight of her father awake and at his computer. Her shuffling footsteps came to a halt, and she cinched the belt of her light blue robe one tug tighter with her free hand while clutching her laptop in the other.

"Morning, Dad." She headed straight to the coffee maker. "Working already?"

"Trying…to find a…miracle answer."

"For Mom?"

"Of course."

Martha set her coffee and laptop on the table, pulled out the chair next to him, and sat. Concern stretched across her face. "Where is she?" She patted Ernest, who responded with his version of a loose-lipped smile then settled back onto the floor.

"Back in bed. …Resting…and hoping…to dream."

"I've never seen her like this—so far from her usual energetic self. She just dropped into a chair when Mateo went to bed last night." Other than the family's frenetic Fourth of July barbecue, where Martha had focused her attention on her handicapped father, she hadn't been around to witness her mother's decline. Iris' rapid interval deterioration had to be a terrible shock.

Iris was no longer the woman who functioned beyond independent as she had from the first day Phineas met her. The woman who, after her father died unexpectedly, pulled her own mother, Sara Jane, out of a near terminal depression. The same woman who, while pregnant with Jacob, worked overtime as a hospital social worker to support her embattled husband as he prepared to stand trial for multiple murders. And later, with thirteen-year-old Jacob's help, she rescued Martha from a revenge-seeking kidnapper. Her life had been one challenge after another that she'd met with determination, including stepping up in recent years to care for her husband's increasing needs. But now, her biggest battles still lurked ahead, and she seemed to be withdrawing from the fray.

"She had so much energy four years ago when she worked on my campaign—before we moved to D. C." Martha held her mug in both hands and leaned over it to inhale the coffee vapors.

"Before she...had to become...my caretaker." The day of his diagnosis, they'd accepted the erroneous promise that he had "ten to fifteen good years" left. But then his "worse than expected" case accelerated into debility, and Iris had stepped into her caretaker role far better than he as care receiver.

"She's always been *everybody's* caretaker. She doesn't know how to let others care for her."

"She's never...been a burden...to anyone." He'd rebelled against being cared for early on. Still did—but tried not to let it show.

"She's been great since we got here, especially with Mateo."

"He brings out...her best, ...but she's...barely able...and getting... weaker." He dabbed at his eye with the back of his steadier right hand. "She tries...to hide...her exhaustion."

"Felipe and I will try to stay ahead of her tasks—before she gets to them. That should help." Martha stared out the window like she was trying to recall something. "I don't remember her ever being sick."

"She...hasn't been." But she'd felt others' suffering. Her strong empathy had been part of the challenge of being on the front lines of hospital social work. She'd shared the misery of others' infirmities but never experienced her own, and now hers were a constant presence.

"That's just...part of it," he added.

"What's the other part?"

"Being a...patient. ... Until now, ...She's only had...health screening."

"But you said she did well with her bone marrow biopsy."

"She did."

Iris' stoicism during the procedure had indeed surprised him, but later made him realize that she was keeping her constant malaise, weakness, and myriad discomforts more to herself than he'd appreciated. And she hadn't yet faced the actual frightening diagnosis and the toxic treatments it could indicate. Not to mention the future bone marrow biopsies Moro would ask for, so he could assess the effects of those treatments. She might draw the line at those, then at other interventions, stepwise, until she'd finally say, "Enough!"

Ernest rose to his feet and stretched, a downward dog stretch. His tail wagged as he stared at the kitchen doorway.

Mateo raced through it in unzipped shorts, an inside out tee shirt, and sneakers. "Can Ernest go outside and play with me?"

"You bet...Mateo. Go...have fun." Phineas smiled at Ernest's probing gaze. "Ernest...release." The command that tells a service dog they're off duty.

Felipe met Mateo and Ernest at the doorway and escorted them to the front door. He returned to the kitchen in time for the three of them to witness Ernest lifting his leg on a tree and Mateo following the dog's example.

Martha slapped her forehead with the heel of her hand. "Did you teach him that, Felipe?"

"Looks like Ernest did." Felipe poured himself a cup of coffee. "To a boy, most of the outdoors is a bathroom." He gave Phineas a knowing wink and asked, "So, what are you two plotting?"

"We're trying to figure out what Mom's going through and how we can help her."

"Why don't you just ask?" Iris voice caught Phineas by surprise.

Ernest, their official sentry and greeter, had left the mere humans on their own, and they'd failed to detect Iris' approach. She appeared in the kitchen doorway, dressed and apparently seeking caffeine like the rest of them. She couldn't have slept much, if at all, during her attempt at a nap. Couldn't have relived "past joys" in her dreams.

"What can I fix everyone for breakfast?" Felipe clearly hoped to redirect the conversation.

Martha preferred to face issues head on. "Okay, Mom. Please tell us what you're going through."

Iris poured herself a mug of coffee, inhaled its steam, and sat at the table. "What I'm going through...Let's see." She sipped and swallowed, looking thoughtful. "Phineas, what's a spleen for?"

"It's for...fighting infections. ...Kind of...like a large...lymph gland."

"And how big is mine?"

"Probably...several times...normal size." He never could lie, especially to her, and he'd have needed more time to come up with a less grim answer.

"So, whatever is enlarging my spleen is also affecting my bone marrow?"

He nodded. "Bone marrow...is more accessible... to biopsy."

"You want to know what I'm going through. ...Okay, here it is. I'm tired, short of breath, and having hot flashes worse than I ever imagined." She put her mug down and sat up straight. "And besides the frank discomfort I feel every time I eat, I feel like there's some vile organism gnawing at me from the inside. I feel it now more than last week and more than the week before, so whatever it is, it's growing, consuming me...one bite at a time." She looked from Felipe to Martha to her husband. "Now, does that answer your question?"

They sipped their coffees, and the only sounds came from the antique clock, which pulsed beat after beat after beat while Phineas' guts twisted in sympathy for his wife.

After lunch, learning Monopoly intrigued an eager Mateo but frustrated Phineas when his tremor scattered the tiny green plastic houses onto the floor. When Felipe suggested that he and Mateo should head outside for a catch, Mateo mercifully agreed to a break.

The two donned their baseball mitts and set up on the front lawn where Phineas could watch through his window. Felipe started out with gentle tosses then took steps back, one at a time, until Mateo was throwing hard, what Phineas and Jacob had once called "airing it out". The boy would have to learn accuracy next. Good thing Felipe was nimble and fielded most of the wild tosses. Mateo was beginning to get the hang of catching the ball, of locating his mitt in the right location at the right time.

Watching those two took Phineas back to Jacob's early days acquiring basic baseball skills. The two of them would stand in the same places Felipe and Mateo now stood, make the same tosses, and Phineas would offer the same suggestions and encouragements. Back then, his body would instantly react, stretch, and deftly glove Jacob's errant throws. There'd be a satisfying soft thud when solid baseball hit soft leather. The rich smell of Neatsfoot Oil they'd applied to their gloves days earlier for preserving them and taking any stiffness out. And at the end of a session, there'd been the gratifying ache in his muscles—and *those* muscles had always obeyed without hesitation when his brain commanded.

He closed his eyes and mouthed "thanks" for his stockpile of memories and his still vivid imagination. Would those strengths also soon abandon him?

CHAPTER 19
July 14

Marie's Friday morning invitation for Phineas to meet her grateful VIP patient was a surprise and a welcome diversion. Following Iris' sharing of her frightening sensations, they'd tried to fill Thursday with activities, but uncomfortable silences kept punctuating their waking hours. Today, Phineas welcomed a reason for him to escape for an outing, and he suspected Iris was glad to have a break from him.

From the living room and the seat of his rolling walker, Phineas watched the front door and willed it to deliver Marie. Despite Iris' ailments, she had him ready in plenty of time for his expedition. Ernest sat expectantly at his side, never giving up hope he'd be needed. His instincts had earlier sent him to fetch his bright red Eyes, Ears, Nose, and Paws service dog vest which he now proudly sported. Perhaps Marie would invite him to accompany them this time.

"Who's she taking you to see?" Iris asked. It had been a lazy morning and she, still in her robe, lingered near the hallway entrance. She'd paused there on her way back to the kitchen to sip more coffee and watch Mateo and Felipe finish off a batch of waffles. Martha had cloistered herself in a bedroom to work on her laptop. Phineas heard several voices coming from that room, suggesting she was attending at least one Zoom meeting.

"The patient...I consulted...on last week...wants...to meet me." He couldn't say much more. Patient confidentiality. "He's better...and he's let... his constituents...know his...diagnosis." That part was public knowledge at least. The congressman seemed to want the world to know he'd survived a deadly disease that rugged outdoorsmen risked catching. Blastomycosis. A manly disease. His publicist didn't admit that a deer's microscopic fungus had exacted revenge on the hunter/congressman.

And none of the doctors wanted it known that the patient's initial treatment accelerated his precipitous decline. No need to air that dicey detail to the press.

"I'm glad that you helped and that you're getting out," Iris said. "You've been even more fidgety than usual, and you're about to get on my last nerve." She offered him a half smile then slipped away to the kitchen.

Yesterday, he'd searched the Internet during the intervals when the house was quiet, and he'd found numerous entries on pancytopenia's common causes, but those all read as though the authors referenced the same original source reviews and studies. So, he moved on to reading case reports with unusual causes and focused on those entities with effective treatments. What good would it be to find a disease no one could do anything about? In some of those rare diseases, bone marrow or stem cell transplants only prolonged survival by a few months. Iris wouldn't accept transplantation if it meant going through anguish and misery while dragging her family along.

A gentle three beat knock on the door. Marie's. He knew one knock from another, even when he was hunkered down way back at his kitchen window. He rose from his walker seat and lurched toward the door, but before he was halfway there, Mateo streaked by him and heaved the heavy wooden door open.

"Well, hello Mateo! How's my nephew?" Marie appeared surprised by his enthusiastic greeting. Her black dress slacks and white silk blouse were nicer than her usual casual Friday wardrobe.

"I'm good. D'you bring the boys?" He peered past her, obviously hoping for a diversion from the house full of somber and boring adults.

"They're in daycare today, since it's a weekday."

Her nephew's shoulders slumped.

"Maybe we can bring them by over the weekend."

He rewarded her with a nod and a smile across the threshold.

"May I come in, Mateo?" Marie asked in the patient tone of a parent.

"Papi and I are having waffles." He stepped aside. "Want some?"

"Already had breakfast, but thanks. I bet those waffles are good."

"Sure are." With those words, he was gone. Back to warm waffles and maple syrup.

The boy's agility filled Phineas with envy. "I'm not...used to...having...a doorman. ...Ready?" Ernest took up a post next to Phineas' left leg, anticipating a command to heel.

"As soon as I let Iris know our schedule."

"Ernest would...like to...come along." The dog's ears perked up, and he turned his best hopeful expression from his master to Marie.

"Why not? We're just meeting in the visitors' lounge." Her smile at Ernest elicited cautious tail wagging. "Ernest, are you ready to help?"

Help was his default mode. He stood, ready to heel and serve.

Marie turned toward the kitchen and called out, "Iris? I'm stealing your husband."

"You can bring him back whenever you're done with him." Iris stood leaning against the wall at the end of the unlit hallway. Her pale robe and complexion made her appear almost transparent in the dim light, like she was giving in to her final transition several molecules at a time. (or, as she'd said, "one bite at a time.") "I'm not going anywhere." Those words sounded tired and were delivered with less certainty than her husband desired.

Iris' image and tone stayed with Phineas the entire duration of his ride to the hospital despite Marie quizzing him about Iris' symptoms, his Duke study, and Chelsea's worrisome nodule. Marie's medical instincts and dedication to family clearly demanded that she stay up to speed about every family member's problems. It wasn't until she deposited him at the usual bench near the hospital entrance while she parked her SUV, that the interrogation ceased, and he could finally feel relief. His walker stood at the ready in front of him, and Ernest gingerly took up his seated post on the sunbaked concrete beside his master.

"Hey, Dr. Mann. How's it going?" Security Guard Leon, in pressed short-sleeved shirt and polished work shoes, approached from the shady alcove he inhabited while waiting for arrivals.

"Fine, Leon. ...Can't seem...to stay retired." Phineas scooched over inch by inch and patted the seat next to him. "Take a...load off."

"I'd better not. Might look like I'm not working." Leon kept his eyes on Ernest. "That's a mighty fine-looking dog. What's his name?"

"Ernest."

Ernest turned his head to stare at his master and wait for instructions.

"Good name for a service dog." Leon's smile faded when he glanced toward the parking deck. His expression shifted to one of prey spotting predator. Marie approached with long strides.

"Let me...introduce you...to another...Dr. Mann." Phineas gestured toward Marie. "Leon, this is...Dr. Marie Mann. ...Marie, this...is my... good friend...Leon."

Leon seemed to gather courage with Phineas' welcoming words but looked puzzled when he heard her name. "Pleased to meet you, Ma'am." He held out a leathery hand.

"Pleased to meet you, Leon." She accepted his overture. "It seems you know my father-in-law."

As if he'd think my wife would be so young. "Marie, Leon's...been good... to me...as long as...I've known him."

"Please let me know whenever I can help *you*, Ma'am." Leon stood taller.

"I will. But Leon, 'Ma'am' makes me feel old." She allowed the beginnings of a smile.

"Yes, Ma'am—Whoops. Sorry, *Dr. Mann.*"

When Marie laughed, Leon's embarrassed expression relaxed. "I'll try to do better, Ma—Dr. Mann." He shook his head. "Whew! This could be tough."

"You're fine, Leon. Ready to head upstairs, Phineas?" Marie steadied his walker for him to stand.

"Ready. ...See you...later, Leon."

"Bye, Dr. Mann and Dr. Mann."

The elevator opened on the sixth floor to reveal a man whose brawn stretched his black suit from shoulder to shoulder. He wore a crew-cut and a curly wire from behind his right ear to under the collar of his jacket. Brawny Man here was a level above hospital security.

Marie held up her hospital ID badge for the security guard's inspection. Phineas followed her lead with his. Ernest sat patiently while the man examined and patted down the service dog vest. Finally, Brawny Man gestured with his head toward the hospital floor's lounge. "They're in there." "In there" was through an open door, propped in that position by a doorstop.

Michael, the congressman's POA and "friend", was standing next to the patient, now seated in a wheelchair that was equipped with an oxygen tank. The patient wore a black silk robe, and the two men were gazing out the lounge's windows. To the side of the lounge, a young man with a bulky-lensed camera chatted with a well-dressed middle-aged woman. They wore press badges with N&O printed in large letters, Raleigh's News and Observer's label. When Phineas' walker clanked through the door, the four turned as one to study Ernest and the source of that clank.

It took Phineas a moment to recognize Quentin Tate without his eyes taped shut and a breathing tube in his mouth. The Internet images Phineas had reviewed helped. Now, Quentin was shaved, and his jet-black hair appeared freshly trimmed and combed. Makeup was subtle but unmistakable with a pale absence of it behind the ears. A narrow plastic nasal cannula dangled and whirred from the tank on Quentin's wheelchair, sending pure oxygen uselessly into the room.

He probably removed it from his nose when the press arrived.

Michael beamed. "Dr. Mann, thank you for coming." He turned Quentin's wheelchair to face Phineas. "Quentin, this is Dr. Phineas Mann, the brilliant specialist who solved your case."

Quentin glanced past Phineas, as if he expected to see someone else. Then, with his black eyebrows pinched into a 'V', he took a hard look at Phineas and Ernest. He turned toward Michael and asked, "*That's* him?"

"Yes, Sir. This is Dr. Mann. He figured out what you had."

Quentin shook his head. "This won't do."

Michael's smile dissolved. He looked puzzled. "Sir?"

"We need to cancel this meeting." Flat words, under Quentin's breath.

"But your people wanted us to do this, and both doctors came in to see you and how much you've recovered." Michael's raised pitch suggested frustration.

"We can't have pictures of me next to him and his handicap dog with captions saying I needed him to rescue me. I'll look too weak to re-elect." He glanced at the photographer and reporter then gestured with his head toward the door. "No photos. No story. You two can leave now."

Michael leaned close to Quentin and whispered, "Are you sure you want to cancel this?"

"Look at him. He's a pitiful shell of a man. We're *done* here." Quentin made no attempt to whisper.

"Congressman, ...I'm...standing...right here...in front...of you." Phineas was used to silent reactions to his appearance, but never unfiltered and out loud rudeness. Anger rose inside him like lava, ready to erupt from his stone face. "I see...a brush...with death...hasn't taught...you humility." His choppy words halted the N&O pair's exit. Phineas probed Quentin's too small dark brown eyes.

A blood vessel pulsed on Quentin's temple. "Who says I had a brush with death?" The photographer raised his camera and clicked. Quentin wiped his lower lip with the back of his hand. "I was nowhere close. —Just had a setback." More picture-taking. Quentin's eyes flashed, and he waved his hand furiously. "I said no photos! Out!"

"And Michael...here...provided us...with the...pivotal clue..."

"What pivotal clue?"

"You sanding...deer antlers...without a mask."

If Quentin, the ungrateful VIP, was going to be unfiltered, so would his consulting doctor. And the diagnosis this doctor had established, that of a manly case of blastomycosis, was already in the press, planted there by Quentin's publicist. The reporter began furiously jotting on her notepad.

Quentin slapped the arm of his wheelchair. "Who hides behind a mask? Weaklings." He pointed at Michael. "And him?" The congressman was actually smirking. "Pivotal clue? Hmph. He's just filling in. Hardly know him."

Michael looked like he'd been slapped hard. He seemed to find a reason to stare at something on the ceiling.

As if explaining the obvious, Phineas responded, "You and he...make... knives and—"

"What's that got to do with anything?"

Rude man. Interruptions and having sentences finished by impatient listeners were part of the typical Parkinson's experience, but this man's tone offended. Even Ernest's usually hopeful eyes turned glassy hard as he stared at the congressman—and for an instant, a guttural growl escaped from deep inside the belly of the previously impassive canine. Then the protective dog recalled his training and discipline. He resumed his stance as a shiny black statue and focused on Quentin's face.

"You make...knives together...for sale...from the same...address." There. *Back at you, Mr. VIP.* Phineas had seen their sales website, the one aimed at collectors, a website fully accessible in the public domain. More furious notetaking by the N&O reporter. More camera clicks. This press event had clearly been arranged by Quentin's own people. It was a sure bet that those unfortunate people would suffer under the congressman's brewing ire.

"Same address? Some of his mail came to my house by mistake. That's all. I live alone." Two denials. If Michael were denied a third time, would a cock crow?

Quentin waved Brawny Man closer. "Johnson, escort the press to the elevator." Johnson spread his arms like a male silverback gorilla and herded the reporter and photographer through the door and down the hall.

The only sound now was the hissing from Quentin's unworn oxygen tubing. Marie looked from Quentin to Phineas with an expression that suggested she was eager to escape a room filled with palpable discomfort. Michael's eyes were glistening. He glanced at Quentin, but Quentin was staring hard at Phineas.

Phineas stared right back. *Are those knives decorated with antler handles streaming from the congressman's eyes?*

Quentin muttered, "My people will be checking whether you breached my confidentiality today."

"Go ahead. ...Try to...go after what's...left of me."

Then Phineas had a thought. "Also have...them check... your knife... website and...they'll see...that it's in...the public domain." He kept a triumphant cheer private. Who better than he, someone risk-free in his last stage of life, to deliver truth? And any guilt he'd once accepted for the VIP's stormy medical course was now fully absolved.

Quentin scoffed. "That website? Like I said, he used my address. It's just for the business."

And there it is. Third denial.

Electric guitar power chords interrupted their staring contest. A heavy metal song ringtone from the past. The band Alice in Chains. Their manly Vietnam War hit *Rooster*. Quentin fumbled with the cell phone in his kimono pocket and studied its screen. "I need to get this." He furiously motioned with his free hand for everyone to leave. "Interview's over. Go. Now!"

CHAPTER 20
July 15

Saturday afternoon Mateo and Phineas faced off against each other across a *Chutes and Ladders* board game set up on the kitchen table. Phineas relished his grandson's studious expression and his total concentration on the unfamiliar contest.

Last night after the evening cooled, and the boy had gone to bed, his parents climbed the drop-down ladder to the spacious attic and discovered this time worn *Chutes and Ladders* box along with other ancient games. They'd taken more time up there than Phineas expected for simply locating stored board games among stacked bins. Had they also taken inventory of several decades' accumulation of stuff while anticipating the work to optimally sift through and distribute the family's dusty possessions? And then to drop off countless unclaimed memories at the landfill for burial?

Phineas now also warmed to the sight of Felipe busying himself with preparations for a supper feast for the entire family plus Chelsea. Their son-in-law chef gathered implements, produce, herbs and spices, and arranged them on the counter in the order Phineas guessed they'd be used. *Mise en place.* Everything in its place. This was Phineas' mantra when he'd cooked—and for his life in general—and despite his current challenges, he couldn't suppress those hard-wired impulses to stay organized.

He glanced at the frustrating tremor in his left hand, the tremor that sabotaged his own pleasures in the kitchen. At least today everyone would be gathered together for a fine meal, and there'd be lively banter—one bright spot—if only it wasn't a consequence of Iris' and his deepening miseries.

"Your turn…Mateo," Phineas murmured.

Mateo rolled the dice. "One. Two—"

Outside, two car doors banged closed.

"Someone's here!" Mateo bounded from his chair and out of the room.

"Hey! …I was…winning…this time." Phineas chuckled, relieved that their fourth straight game had been abruptly suspended. Ernest sat at attention and studied his master, his dark eyes waiting for a command.

Felipe put down mortar and pestle and wiped his hands on his bright white apron. "Let me put that game away before he comes back for more."

"A capital…idea."

"Wayla!" A toddler duet in the living room was soon followed by their invasion of the kitchen and, "Waylo!" One of them—was it Vin or Phin?—climbed up onto his lap while Felipe hurried to fold the *Chutes and Ladders'* playing board and close the box—though not fast enough.

"Play game!" pouted the twin in Phineas' lap.

Felipe hastily swiped it off the table and said, "Maybe later." He slipped the box onto a pantry shelf and closed the door.

The twin fidgeting on Phineas' lap had to be Phin, the loud twin who regularly led his more contemplative brother in and out of toddler adventures. Vin was the studious investigator contemplating his next move. Given time, Phineas could use their behaviors to tell them apart, but he had yet to spot even subtle differences in their physical characteristics, both being sturdy lads with hair the color of roasted almonds. Their parents had once tried parting that hair on opposite sides, but that had been a futile effort. Their mops never held any organization by the time they made it down I-40 to their Wayla and Waylo's house.

With the game safely stowed away, the twins descended onto Ernest, one at each end. The patient dog glanced at his master as if to say, "spare me, please," then he sat upright with narrowed eyes and a stoic air as four tiny hands vigorously patted his block head and broad chest.

"I have a better game for you two," said Felipe. "We found a crate of Duplo's in the attic."

Perfect. Plastic building blocks. Large enough to not fit up a toddler's nostrils.

Felipe addressed his son. "Mateo, will you teach your cousins how to build a castle?"

Always the clever father.

Mateo brightened at his leadership assignment. "Cool. Come on you guys. I know where it is." The three boys stormed out of the kitchen.

"How is it...two toddlers...feels like...a mob?" Was it because their grandfather was so immobile, and the twins moved at speeds he could only fantasize keeping up with? Those two were like a Hollywood action movie where the superheroes can operate at such high speeds that normal characters appear to be in agonizingly slow motion. Good thing he'd passed through parenthood well ahead of old age and infirmity.

Felipe eyed the mix in the mortar and added pinches of sea salt and a few peppercorns. "Enjoy your respite. They'll be back before you know it."

Ernest stood and whined the whine that suggested he thought this an opportune and necessary time to go outside.

"Do you...need to...get busy, Ernest?" One could always count on Ernest to preemptively announce his bathroom needs. Phineas slid his walker into position to stand himself up. The dog took cautious steps toward the kitchen door, then glanced over his shoulder at his trailing master.

"I'll let him out, Phineas. You relax," Felipe said.

Phineas released the dog from duty with, "It's okay...Ernest" then retook his seat. Felipe followed the soon-to-be 'busy' dog to the front door then doubled back to the kitchen. He sat at the table and resumed grinding herbs and spices together in the mortar. Ernest appeared outside the kitchen window and began his customary sniffing route along the edge of the lawn and into the band of woods around the lot's perimeter.

"So, Felipe...what else...did you find...in the attic?"

Forty-plus years of our lives, that's what.

Phineas had meant to go through that space and send each item to its best possible recipient, but the Parkinson's grounded him before he got to it. He'd missed a precious, healthy retirement window before disability struck. No climbing attic ladders for him now, only downward chutes. Could Dr. Grace's treatment provide a miraculous second chance to climb a ladder?

Felipe ground more slowly. "What did we find in the attic? More than expected. Martha found stuff from her childhood and started filling a box of keepsakes. And she had me make piles depending on future destinations."

Martha's discovery of the long-forgotten treasures explained the muffled squeals Phineas had detected coming from above. "I appreciate...your doing...that. And we...don't have to...tell Iris." Iris had enough sadness without adding nostalgia and more losses from their lives.

"Uh, Phineas—Iris *asked* us to start on it."

So, she was keeping it from her husband to not risk adding to *his* sadness. *Should have known.*

New action outside drew Phineas' attention to his window. Mateo must have handed off Duplo construction and his twin cousins to their parents and grandmother. The athletic six-year-old was sprinting the length of the lawn with Ernest at his heels. But then he abruptly halted at the woods' edge and bent to pick up something partially covered with leaves: a dingy, bald tennis ball that had lost its fluorescent green hue and was now weathered to a charcoal grey. Mateo held it over his head, and Ernest wagged his entire back end, then sat, his eyes locked on the ball, his powerful shoulders quivering in anticipation. Mateo heaved the ball the length of the lawn, and Ernest exploded after it, raced back, and deposited the ball at Mateo's feet.

Phineas swallowed to try to relieve a sudden thickness in his throat. That tennis ball had to be one left over from Jacob's teen years when the two of them regularly played a game they'd called Stella ball. Back then, he'd pitch tennis balls, and Jacob would bat them into the woods, one after another, to warm up for his baseball games. Stella, their Labrador retriever, a yellow, less disciplined version of Ernest, would similarly explode after each hit then drop the ball at the pitcher's feet with its fuzz soaked in slimy saliva. She'd anxiously sit and fix her stare on the ball until he pitched it again, and Jacob would launch it, a missile trailing a comet tail of dog spit. Eager Stella would fetch each ball until breathlessness and the season's heat made her settle onto her favorite cool patch of shady soil under their deck. Game over. Father and son would have worked up a lather of sweat by then.

Until five years ago, Phineas might still have been able to pitch a respectable batting practice. If he tried now, there'd be the embarrassment of a wild and feeble pitch, and he'd likely topple over and injure himself. Game truly over.

"Those two sure enjoy each other." Felipe's words dragged Phineas back to the kitchen table, where he regarded his son-in-law. The chef's contented smile brought out fine lines from the corners of his eyes.

"When...off duty, ...Ernest gets...to be...a dog." The dog looked thrilled to be allowed to play, to have a companion who was still full of life. "Felipe, let's...talk about...Ernest's future." Ernest was much more than an attic antique. "When...I'm out of...the picture." Phineas felt the throat thickness returning. He couldn't bring himself to add Iris' complicated situation to the conversation.

And for good reason. At the words "out of the picture," Felipe ceased pulverizing the herbs and spices. His smile faded and the lines next to his eyes flattened out.

"He could...retrain for...someone else, ...or you...and Mateo...could have him."

Without the slightest hesitation, Felipe responded, "If that sad time finds us, Phineas, we'd be honored to give Ernest a home." Spoken like Felipe's son wasn't the only one who adored Ernest.

But what would Ernest prefer?

He might have five or six more years of working potential, and his instincts and upbringing had programmed him for service. His current master's abilities had declined so precipitously, there'd been less and less for him to do. He'd become more a cherished family member than a working assistant. If the dog were to retrain, he'd have to return to Eyes, Ears, Nose, and Paws caregivers and the prison where he'd live in cells with inmates until he was ready for a new patient. He'd do it without a complaint, but would he be as happy? And would Eyes, Ears, Nose, and Paws even take him back for another assignment? Phineas rubbed his chin whiskers. He couldn't remember what their policy was.

Professional athletes' careers end before old age. Why couldn't Ernest's? And such a precious gift for Mateo one day, one that could help soften the loss of a grandparent. Phineas let out the long breath he hadn't realized he'd been holding. Ernest the dog, as long as *he* lived, was going to remain a cherished member of the Mann family.

"Perfect. ...Thank you, ...Felipe."

Out on the lawn, as if he'd been tuned in to his master's thoughts, Ernest dropped the tennis ball, stared into the kitchen window, and let out a happy sounding "yip." Mateo scooped up the ball, heaved it, and the dog bolted away in focused and euphoric pursuit.

Back in the house, Jacob sauntered into the kitchen. Phineas pivoted in his chair to greet his son with his best smile.

Jacob glanced at the countertop. "Whatcha' fixin', Felipe?"

"A little of this and that. Right now, I'm making a rub." He pressed his index finger vertically over his lips then whispered, "I haven't told your mother that I'm going to cook beef tenderloins."

Wise chef. Better to ask for forgiveness than permission. Phineas grinned at Felipe's words.

Iris had avoided beef since the climate crisis declared itself, and she learned how cows belch and fart massive amounts of methane. But then Phineas' grin dissolved. Was this rare treat from a short list of decadent last meals one more sign that Felipe realized that time was getting short for his foodie father-in-law?

Time. Always time. A patient from long ago had once said that time was like sheets of toilet paper coming off a roll faster at the end. How close was he now to the cardboard?

The sound of another car door closing. *Probably Chelsea this time.* Mateo and Ernest raced toward the driveway and disappeared from the kitchen window's view. In no time, the four women, their cabal reunited for yet another crisis, were speaking in animated tones in the living room as they hurried to the kitchen.

All present and accounted for now.

Chelsea led the procession and appeared almost frantic. "Finman, my Swedish disk with my MRI reached North Carolina just fine—only to disappear without a trace! Damned FedEx!" Then she glanced back sheepishly over her shoulder, probably hoping her cursing hadn't reached the children in the living room.

"You've...tracked it...here?"

Ernest crept under his master's chair, out of the crowd and its excitement, and away from a troubling Chelsea.

"The link said it was in the Raleigh distribution center four days ago and scheduled to be delivered the next day. Then they said it was rescheduled—and rescheduled—and rescheduled each day." Her usual steady television announcer's voice became a sing-song wail. "I think they lost the damned thing." This time a stage whisper. "My last hope to avoid surgery without worrying I have a cancer growing in me."

"When...is your... surgery...scheduled?" How much time did they have to wait (and wait) for FedEx to deliver her precious package?

"This coming Friday. I'm supposed to go in Tuesday for my preoperative evaluation and bloodwork. That's when I have to let them know I'm going ahead with it." Chelsea wrung her hands and stared at them. "My surgeon goes to Europe for a month next week. That esteemed professor is giving lectures at a conference in Italy and then staying there on his summer vacation."

The silence that punctuated Chelsea's frustrated pronouncement made the antique kitchen clock's loud ticking once again impossible to ignore. The clock's pulse had begun before Phineas' birth, and it seemed a certainty that its regular heartbeat would outlast his.

Martha broke the tension, responding in her unique calm, take-charge tone. "We'll just have to go and find your package." Organizing chaos was in her skill set. And the arrival of a North Carolina congresswoman in the Raleigh FedEx facility, especially a politician running for re-election in November, would pry its managers out of every one of their offices. "Shall we meet there at 8:00 AM?"

"I'm in," Felipe declared.

Iris spoke next, this time in a firm voice with her head held higher. "Same here." The gathering of her women's team for a vital quest seemed to lift her from the depths of her own troubles.

Marie put her arm around Jacob's waist and leaned into him. "Wish we didn't have to go to work and could join you."

Phineas added, "And I'll...hang out...there with...Ernest and Mateo... so you all...can spread out." Their quest had to be a long shot, but such an adventure could be just what the whole family needed to lift it from its doldrums. And under Martha's skillful leadership, they couldn't possibly be stymied by bureaucracy *this* time. Could they?

The fragrance of what Felipe described as "seared and oven-roasted herb and spice-rubbed beef" overwhelmed that of the roasted potatoes, butternut squash, and fresh black-eyed peas blanched then sauteed with garlic, onions, and a pinch of red pepper flakes. And when the chef's sourdough baguettes came out of the oven, the irresistible aroma of Felipe's fresh-baked bread brought the olfactory symphony to a crescendo. Phineas' stomach growled at a volume close to his verbal limits. If tonight's repast was meant to be one in a series of last suppers, it would be hard to top.

Marie and Jacob fed and bathed the twins with practiced efficiency, and now, in a quiet back bedroom, the parents took turns reading bedtime stories to their cleansed offspring. Phineas shuffled close enough to the closed door that he could hear their reading voices gradually soften. He hoped the infants would sleep, not just through dinner, but all the way home to their own beds.

Mateo, freed from his leadership role, circled from the dining room to the kitchen to the dining room, sniffing and repeatedly announcing "I'm hungry...I'm really hungry," until his mother helped him set the long table already covered with an amber cloth that, she explained, had come all the way from northern Italy. When her son expressed appropriate admiration, Martha promised him a seat at the table's head. He'd earned it.

Marie and Jacob, with triumphant smiles, tiptoed back to join the rest. Jacob held up crossed fingers and whispered, "They're down for now. Let's eat."

Phineas had Iris settle him at the table's foot with Ernest tucked under his master's chair. Grandfather then waved at grandson, grandly situated at the table's far end. Mateo waved back, clearly amused at his high station in the arrangement. Between them, the brimming serving platters gleamed under the Tiffany-patterned stained glass light fixture that hung from the ceiling.

Standing beside his host with a towel draped over his forearm, Felipe delivered the cork from a bottle of Bordeaux. He swirled an ounce in a stemmed wine glass and held it up for Phineas' inspection.

"Nice...legs."

He held the glass to Phineas' nose.

Perfect bouquet. Notes of berries and toast?

He held the glass to Phineas' lips.

Phineas savored a sip and nodded his approval. *Delicious and velvety. Maybe blackberries?* He chuckled. He was better at honey-tasting.

Seated at her husband's side, Iris accepted the glass and transferred its contents to a new Sippy cup, delivered only yesterday by the Amazon

Prime truck. This cup lacked dinosaurs and was comparatively elegant with clear sides and top that allowed Phineas to admire the vintage's lithe purple legs.

With great ceremony, Felipe broke a baguette in its middle, ripped off a center portion, and placed it on Phineas' plate. He then sent each half down the sides of the silent table before he went to take his seat next to Mateo and across from Martha. The bottle of Bordeaux circled among the wordless adults.

"Feels like...I should...say something...memorable," Phineas murmured. If this was going to be one of the final suppers for his clan, he should honor the moment. Reciting a grace blessing seemed cliché—and beyond his vocal capacity. A simple toast felt right. "Thank you, Felipe...and everyone." He raised his cup with its rhythmically sloshing waves of wine. "To a...week...of hope."

Iris dabbed at the corner of her eye with her napkin. "Let me add that I don't know what we'd have done without all of you coming together on such short notice to help us." She returned the napkin to her lap. "We are *so* grateful."

Chelsea cleared her throat for attention and elevated her wine glass. "And I want to say thank you to everyone for helping *me*." She held her glass even higher. "Now let's all enjoy this meal before Martha feels the need to give one of *her* speeches and all this good food gets cold." She winked at Martha and took a healthy swallow. Chuckles enlivened what had become a somber mood.

The platters were passed from hand to hand. Martha finished filling Mateo's plate then said, "I'd like to confirm our schedule for this week. It seems pretty full." Organizing people. Martha never could help herself. "Monday, it's FedEx."

"And I'm supposed to go for my preoperative visit Tuesday," Chelsea added. "—unless, of course, we find the disk with my old images Monday—and that blasted spot is old." Phineas took note that she'd made a conscious effort to avoid another "damned" in Mateo's presence.

"Tuesday, I go to the hematologist for my follow-up visit," Iris said. "—and some answers hopefully." She grimaced with her statement. Phineas knew that she had to be thinking how difficult her next steps could be. Then her expression shifted as she composed herself, probably for Mateo's sake. "Sorry one of us can't go with you, Chelsea."

"Hey, I'm a big girl. You take care of yourself."

Phineas swallowed another sip of wine. "Not sure...when I...go back." The next step in his trial would depend on his stem cells growing well in culture and producing dopamine. When enough of those therapeutic cells could be accumulated, his brain surgery would be scheduled—and that might be soon from what he'd read in Dr. Grace's grant proposal. But he'd undergo that surgery only if Iris' condition allowed him to proceed without her needing his guidance and support—and without his being swamped in guilt for putting his own needs first.

⌒

Only flakes of crust remained in the transparent pie dish that had, an hour earlier, held a raspberry tart dotted with crème fraiche. The adults sipped decaf cappuccino, while Mateo lingered over his last bite of a second helping. Phineas gripped his new Sippy cup, now mostly emptied of the rich brown liquid that had replaced red wine. His grandson's eyelids were looking heavier than they had during prior evenings. This late supper, after the added task of entertaining toddler cousins, seemed to have tired the boy more than any of the previous activities provided by his stodgy adult relatives.

Martha must have noticed too. No details got by her. "Mateo," she said, "go ahead and finish your dessert. Then you can brush your teeth, and we can pick up where we left off on your book."

With renewed energy, the boy cleared his plate and bounced off his seat.

Phineas was glad that Iris and he had kept the children's shelves intact in the family library. *Chronicles of Narnia* would be the yellowed, dog-eared copy Martha had rediscovered (and blown the dust off) for her son.

"G'night Mateo." Iris reached out her arms to gather him in for a hug. He submitted to the hug then knelt beside Ernest and, with exaggerated attention, set to patting his furry friend as if no one had said anything about his bedtime and *Chronicles*.

"Martha, I'll handle this," Felipe murmured. "You sit and talk." Father directed son away from the dining room.

Now, the only sounds were those of China coffee cups clicking on saucers. The six remaining adults each seemed to be waiting for someone else to speak.

Finally, Iris took in a deep breath and broke the silence. "You know, we've had some pretty scary times over the years." Phineas met her eye. "But I've never been as frightened as I am waiting for Tuesday."

And this husband knows enough to be frightened for her. If only he could reassure her of an easy resolution.

Chelsea offered her a hopeful half smile. "Oh, Honey, they're bound to have a treatment for your problem."

Iris appeared to force a smile in return. "They always have a treatment. I'm just not sure I'll want to take it."

Martha looked like someone had shaken her awake from a daydream. "Mom, you *have* to try to get better."

"Martha Dear, it'll depend on what we learn," Iris responded in a warm but firm voice. "I don't *have* to do anything. If there's a good chance for a cure, I'll be on board. But if all they can do is prolong me feeling lousy, I'll look for an easier path." She threw her shoulders back and sat up. "You know, sometimes a treatment is worse than the disease."

"Mom!" Martha's eyes were shining. Was it sadness, fear? Or anticipated grief?

"I don't think I'll accept a transplant if they tell me that's my only slim chance," Iris told her, "and I'm not sure about some chemotherapies." She folded her hands and stared down at them. "My next steps will depend on what I hear. Palliative care and hospice are on the table."

Phineas wished he knew something encouraging to add. This ex-social worker wife of his was well aware of all of her options. Maybe too aware.

She raised her gaze to meet his. Her dazzling blue eyes still conveyed the steady love she'd offered him over their fifty plus years together. "And if I go that route, Phineas, you still need to go on with your trial. You need to see it through. For our family. For me."

He had to look away from those eyes. Through all their years of marriage, he'd never defied her, knowing as he had that she was almost always right. But now?

Had he been focused too much on *his* needs when he'd pursued the study for himself? True, he'd initiated that quest before he'd realized Iris was gravely ill, but then he'd stayed in the study. Was staying being selfish? It sure felt like it was now.

Phineas met her penetrating gaze. If his beloved wife chose a hospice exit for herself, he would follow her lead. Eliminate his burden on family. Avoid a skilled nursing home and finish his days next to his kitchen window with Ernest at his side. Then join his forever love, Iris, in some mystical afterlife...

CHAPTER 21

July 17

When Felipe turned off Raleigh's Atlantic Drive at 7:58 AM, Phineas spotted Chelsea's red Chevy Bolt, already waiting in the FedEx distribution center's otherwise empty visitors' parking area. As soon as Felipe pulled his Nissan LEAF into the space next to her car, she shot from the driver's seat wearing jeans, a bright red WRAL News t-shirt, and matching lipstick. Phineas surmised that she'd decided FedEx needed to feel the risk of critical publicity from the local news station if they wouldn't solve her problem.

Martha exited the LEAF wearing a pin-striped business suit with her congressional ID badge clipped to its breast pocket. Felipe and Iris followed her up the ramp to the entrance. And finally, Mateo, pleased to be given a responsibility, escorted his shuffling grandfather at his right side. All business Ernest, clothed in his red vest, had already tumbled from the back of Felipe's compact SUV and heeled on his master's left.

They entered the cavernous facility in a somber line and approached the service counter. On two sides of the building, piles of cardboard boxes rested in front of the rolled-open truck bay doors lining the metal walls. Hoots and laughs echoed from workers lugging white, purple, and orange packages. They reminded Phineas of honey bees laden with brightly colored pollen clumps scurrying across frames of honeycomb. He felt a pang of nostalgia for his decades of beekeeping, now long past.

Behind a long counter, a stout, ruddy complected, grey-haired man smiled and abandoned a stack of boxes to greet them. "Can I help you folks?" He wore a purple collared shirt emblazoned with the FedEx logo.

"Yes, Sir. I'm Chelsea Bullock, and I've been getting delivery notices every day since last week—and then nothing." Chelsea held her phone so the screen faced him. "I'm worried you've lost my package."

"Let me check." The man located a handheld scanning device and tapped her lengthy tracking number into it one...digit...at a...time. "Says it's going out today. They're loading the trucks now. Should be delivered to your address later."

"It's said that for four straight days. I need it now. Can't you just give it to me here?" Chelsea pleaded in a syrupy sweet tone. She batted her eyelids and smiled her best cherry-red smile.

"That'd be complicated, Ma'am. It's already been scanned. It'd be better for you to just wait and let us take care of it for you." His tone seemed to also say, "Don't worry your pretty little head."

"We'll deliver it to your address today," he promised.

"That's just not going to work for me." *Her* tone shifted from sweet to a "don't mess with me" tone. "As I said, I need it now—could be a matter of life and death. My life and *my* death." She tugged at the bottom of her WRAL t-shirt and leaned onto his counter, into his space. A silent but toothless threat of bad publicity. At her age, would he believe that she was still on-air?

Martha displayed her ID badge between Ruddy-faced Man and Chelsea. "Sir, we'd like to help you find Chelsea's package if that's what it takes. She's not kidding about it being a matter of life or death." She'd likely sensed that he'd continue to stonewall Chelsea without further inducement.

He'd indicated he wanted to avoid "complicated." Martha, who'd once been a shy young girl, was poised to make him fear his job was about to get complicated. Martha lifted her badge to his eye level.

"Be right back." Ruddy-faced Man retreated toward a wall of glass-fronted offices along the back, suggesting that Martha's badge presented an issue above his pay grade. He returned with a taller, younger man carrying a steaming cup of coffee. This FedEx employee wore an identical shirt except for the title 'Regional Manager' listed under 'FedEx'.

"Good morning, Folks. How can we help you?" He knew why they were there.

"We'd like to help you find her package. We need it today, and you've been promising it daily for four days now." Martha declared in a confident voice. "We're concerned it's been misplaced in your facility."

At the word "misplaced," the regional manager winced like someone had insulted his brand-new bride. "Ma'am, all our packages are scanned and located." Ruddy-faced Man handed him the scanner. "It says here, yours will be delivered to your home today."

"I've read those words before—four times." Chelsea sounded disgusted. "The package has medical information that is vital to me, and we need it *now*."

"I'm going to ask you to let us look for it before your trucks leave." Martha lay her badge on the counter. "I think we can resolve this without my having to ask for other help." She'd played a nebulous government involvement card, a card no player wanted to draw.

The regional manager handed the scanner back to Ruddy-faced Man. "Charlie, let's show these folks which truck should have her package for *today's* delivery." He clearly believed in his system more than this horde of invading interlopers did.

Charlie led them through stacks of boxes past six truck bays all the way to the corner one, the one next to the row of windowed managers' offices. A young Black man in a black shirt with purple piping stood in the back of a truck half filled with packages. An equal-sized pile inside the building awaited his attention. He hurried out of the truck. "This is Joseph," Charlie announced. "He's your route driver today."

"Can I help you?" Joseph asked. His puzzled expression suggested that eager mobs descending into his workplace were not an everyday occurrence, especially ones with a child and a dog leading a handicapped old man.

"We need to find a package addressed to me, Chelsea Bullock." Chelsea jabbed her thumb at her chest.

"I don't remember seeing your name, Ma'am, but you're welcome to look." He swept his arm toward his truck and the unloaded pile. "Just please don't rearrange them. That'd complicate things for me and make me late delivering everything."

Felipe began perusing the addresses on the stack of packages still in the building. "We should start here, since he doesn't remember seeing your name when he loaded his truck." Martha, Chelsea, and Iris attacked each of the pile's other sides.

Phineas settled onto his walker seat with Ernest sitting at attention next to him. He motioned Mateo closer and held his tremoring index fingers about eight inches apart. "Mateo, we're...searching for...a flat package... about this...wide and...maybe about...this long." He spread his hands to eleven inches. Mateo scampered from corner to corner to find packages that fit those dimensions and then showed the addresses to the adults. After their disappointing head shaking, he returned each to its original location. Joseph retreated into his truck and inspected the other parcels starting with the piles in the front. They all worked silently, top to bottom, until it seemed they'd looked at most of today's deliveries. Frustrated looks replaced their earlier hopeful expressions.

"I should've known they've lost it," Chelsea muttered.

While Phineas sat and watched the tedious inspection chore, he began to feel useless and cranky. His legs stiffened enough to become uncomfortably tight in the back, in his hamstrings. Hoping to avoid a painful cramp, he straightened his legs and pressed his heels against the concrete floor in an effort to stretch those muscles. Still uncomfortable, he pushed himself onto his feet, and shuffled, with Ernest heeling at his side, along the back wall of office windows. Deskbound managers in the first two offices glanced up at the pair as they passed by. The third office was empty, its door wide open. Phineas peered inside. A padded FedEx envelope of the proper dimensions leaned against a briefcase on the floor next to the desk. Extra stickers, some colorful beyond what all the other packages carried, adorned its exposed side.

Phineas crooked his index finger at Mateo, who hurried toward him. "Mateo, ...let's have...a look at...that one." He pointed at the stickered envelope.

Mateo's wide-open eyes suggested he wasn't sure about his grandfather's bold request for such an invasion, but of course he'd never seen his family storm and search a FedEx distribution center before either.

"We'll... put it...right back, if...it's not...what we're...looking for."

Mateo spirited the envelope out of the office and into Phineas' hands so quickly and quietly, it seemed he'd transformed into a ghost child. Ernest sniffed his approval of the slim package, then Phineas held its bright stickers up to the light. The return address was in a foreign language and ended with 'Sverige', a country he didn't recognize. One of the stickers further down read 'Sweden' though, and Chelsea Bullock was the addressee.

"Good job...Mateo. ...We'll keep...this one." He hoped his instructions today wouldn't someday influence his grandson into an unsavory career. They'd talk about it later. "Now...carry it...to Chelsea." He shuffled back toward his bold and dedicated partners while the boy sprinted ahead.

Mateo handed the envelope to Chelsea, pride all over his face. She stared at it for an instant then ruffled his thick hair, hugged him until his eyes bulged, and exclaimed, "Tell me anything you've been wanting, Mateo, and I'll order it for you." She waved it at Joseph. "Got it, Joseph. Thanks for your help."

Joseph bolted from the back of the truck with his portable package scanner held high. "Let me scan it as delivered, Ma'am." The device beeped. Done.

Felipe must have been observing Phineas and Mateo's activities. He joined Phineas back near the wall of offices and whispered, "I saw you two go down there." He gestured toward the open office. "And I saw my son snatch her package from inside."

"Sorry. I...had a...hunch...and couldn't...do it myself." Guilt mixed with triumph. They'd have to sort it out later. "Someone must...have seen... Sweden...on a sticker...and hoped for...an exotic video." He'd guessed that since the return address was in Swedish, the FedEx employee couldn't have known the package was from a hospital. And they might have had second thoughts before opening it. Perhaps they feared consequences if caught—and they'd not yet had the opportunity to slip it unnoticed back into the appropriate pile—or worse, to dispose of it.

Felipe snorted. "Imagine their disappointment if they'd opened it and saw only Chelsea's MRI. Then maybe they'd deliver it—eventually. Or maybe not."

"I've got my laptop and the disk reader attachment in my car," Chelsea announced as she wasted no time heading toward the door through which they'd entered. She yelled a cheerful "thank you" at Ruddy-faced Man as she held up the envelope and rushed by. The Mann family followed at Phineas' pace. It would take time for her to boot up her computer and load the disk anyway.

When they finally reached the parking lot, Chelsea was sitting in her driver's seat with her legs stretched out sideways through the open door, her computer balanced on her lap. She rubbed her index and middle fingers up and down on the touch pad then held her device up toward Phineas. "I don't know what I'm looking at. You tell me, Finman."

"I'll need...to sit...down...to hold it." And the July morning was rapidly heating up. Drops of sweat were forming on his brow and neck, and his heartbeat pounded a steady, fast cadence in his ears. Ernest paced gingerly on the baking asphalt.

Martha opened the backseat door behind Chelsea, and Felipe helped Phineas pivot and settle. They passed him the computer and huddled around him. Under the bright morning sun, the shadows their hovering bodies created made it possible to discern shades of grey on the screen. The

MRI images weren't the same as the x-ray or CT images he was used to, but he easily identified bones, lungs, and heart. Good thing his Parkinson's medication was starting to kick in, and his hands haltingly obeyed his instructions. He purposed his shaky but steadier right middle and index fingers to scroll through multiple image slices while he focused on the region of lung behind Chelsea's heart.

Nothing. Only lung density.

The nodule hadn't been there in 2019. He needed to break the news to her that she almost certainly had a cancer. Hopefully one in its earliest stage and curable with prompt surgery.

"Chelsea...you need...to ask radiology...to load...these with your... other images."

Chelsea's eyes glistened as she stared into his, waiting for his judgment.

Best to give the news to her straight.

"Chelsea, you...should go...ahead...with the surgery...Friday. ...Sorry." Now she wouldn't back out, wouldn't allow a deadly cancer to grow, wouldn't lose an excellent chance at the cure prompt surgery offered. He handed her back her computer. "I left...the slice up...that would... show it...if it was...there before." He pointed at the empty section of lung. "It wasn't."

She studied it for a full minute without a word then said, "I know you remember the last time I set foot inside the inpatient wards of that hospital, Finman."

He did. December 2020. Chelsea had to watch her husband through a pane of glass as he died in isolation from COVID. Ron had an endo-tracheal tube down his throat that was attached to a respirator—plus an extracorporeal membrane oxygenation catheter in his neck to deliver extra oxygen into his blood. But even that technology hadn't kept him alive. The ICU team had gone through three Code Blue protocols before they'd lost him forever. And Chelsea had witnessed it all. No wonder she had every reason to avoid the inside of that hospital.

Iris rested her arm across Chelsea's shoulders. "You'll get through the surgery fine, Chelsea. Then you won't have to worry about it anymore."

Chelsea picked her head up and offered them a tight-lipped grimace. A tear slid down her cheek from the corner of her eye. She gave her head a single shake that spun her long white hair off her shoulders, as if she were clearing debris from her person. "Well, maybe some good will come of all of this trouble. Maybe I'll meet a nice man in the hospital who'll want to see more of a certain cancer-free senior lady."

CHAPTER 22

July 18

The kitchen's clock ticked its minutes away on Tuesday. From Phineas' window seat, he offered gentle updates to family members as the departure time for Iris' follow-up appointment approached. Mateo answered each update with his six-year-old's perspective and suggestions.

"Wayla says she could be with her doctor a long time. I'm packing lots of books." He looked Phineas dead in the eye. "Will you ask Papi if we can bring candy…lots of candy? We might need it." Candy. A child's remedy for uncomfortable times.

For *this* hematology appointment, Iris needed none of Phineas' prodding to get ready, and she moved through her preparations as though she also craved answers for her worsening symptoms—if only those answers wouldn't push her straight toward hospice care, a path he would likely be inclined to follow.

Ernest, clearly disappointed at the signs he'd be left behind, still sat at attention next to the front door to see them off. At Phineas' commands "that's all" and "bed", his hopeful ears flattened before he drifted back toward the master bedroom.

The midday sun's reflection flashed from Phineas' walker into his eyes as Felipe relieved him of it before folding it into the cargo space in the very back of his compact SUV. The five humans squeezed into seats, Felipe and Phineas in front, and Martha and Iris flanking Mateo in the back row. Jacob and Marie had promised to meet them in the hematology clinic. Then they'd all endure the agonizing wait for the lab to determine Iris' blood counts ahead of her dreaded follow-up visit with Dr. Moro.

Martha wheeled an even paler version of her mother back from the laboratory to the waiting area only for the next hour to linger uninterrupted except for the slow movements of other patients. A sallow-cheeked woman checked in, her scalp concealed under a flowered turban as she leaned on a cane. A slender person in sweatpants and hoodie hid behind a surgical mask and slouched into a corner chair while focusing on their cell phone. Iris glanced up at each of them then stared at the floor, her jaw muscles tightening, relaxing, tightening.

Mateo chatted with her every few minutes. "Wayla, ..." this, and "Wayla, ..." that. Maybe Mateo sensed her jitters and was trying his best to distract her. Her responses were muted, gentle, concise. When he extracted one of his books from his backpack and offered it, her smile seemed forced as she said, "When we get home, Mateo."

Phineas was relieved when Jacob and Marie arrived and provided a brief but needed distraction. Phineas couldn't hear what Marie whispered in Iris' ear when they embraced, but he hoped it gave his wife a much-needed boost. Jacob leaned over and silently hugged his mother. Words seemed to have abandoned him.

Finally, Dr. Moro's familiar nurse Gladys stepped through the door leading to the examination rooms and shook her head at the gathered Mann family. "I'm sorry, but only one of you can accompany Mrs. Mann into the examination room." Phineas pushed himself out of the chair and leaned onto his walker. He had to be that one.

Marie, still wearing her long white coat, stepped up to the reception desk. "There's a conference room in the clinic and we'd appreciate it if you'd ready it for our family."

The receptionist withered under Marie's stare and said, "I'll ask, but I can't promise anything."

Without another word, Marie disappeared through the door to the work area of the clinic, breaching their defenses in a single bold action. It was clear she had little patience for manufactured barriers during a tense day. Her family, the one she'd always wanted, was threatened.

Gladys shrugged a 'not my issue' shrug then escorted Iris through the standard check-in procedures while Phineas trailed them one careful step at a time, trying not to trip in his effort to keep up. Despite Felipe's bountiful offerings, Iris' weight was down three more pounds and height another startling half inch, but she'd stood less tall, not rising to her true height. Phineas resisted the urge to prod her higher with his words as she'd always done with him in the past. *No sense irritating her today.* She already wore a beaten aspect, from her flat facial expression down through the uncharacteristic slouch and all the way to her shuffling feet. She'd continued to share only glimpses of her internal struggles with those who wished they could help. *Stoic? Terrified? Both...And sick.*

He wanted to intervene as soon as Iris winced while Gladys overinflated the blood pressure cuff. With Iris' low platelet counts, unnecessary bruises were sure to follow. When Gladys finally opened the cuff's valve and it deflated, Phineas let out the breath he'd been holding.

He settled into the lone chair against the cramped exam room's wall, and Gladys directed Iris onto the examination table. He wished she didn't have to receive her diagnosis while isolated there on a high, barren perch. Phineas preferred her by his side, as they'd faced adult life and prior challenges together. It felt to him like she'd been told to wait alone on the edge of a rocky cliff.

"You okay...up there? ...We can share...my chair." Together their scrawny butts would barely cover its seat.

Iris opened her mouth, but before words could escape, Gladys responded, "Dr. Moro wants her up there." She was tapping the room's keyboard, documenting.

Iris murmured, "I'll be okay up here. Hopefully it won't be too long this time."

Gladys stood from the rolling stool. "I entered your status as ready. Dr. Moro will see a green dot on his schedule next to your name, and he'll see you just as soon as he can." She slipped out and pulled the door closed.

Iris said, "It must be exhausting for her, processing patient after patient with scary hematology diseases. No wonder she doesn't connect. That would be so hard."

Phineas realized that Iris' sympathetic judgment of Gladys' abrupt manner followed by the word "scary" was today's first out-loud admission of her fright. He managed to say, "She's learned... from Moro...to keep... emotional...distance." A series of soft knocks. "Speaking...of—"

The door inched open then clicked closed again as if the next person had hesitated to collect their thoughts—or was reluctant to face difficulty. Muffled words outside.

"Maybe he's avoiding us...because of what he has to report." Iris' voice lost volume with each word, and she seemed to shrink further with the delay the suspense added.

"Someone...probably...interrupted him." His making an excuse for Moro felt inadequate. And cowardly. Time to stop defending the man, even if his icy behavior was the destructive result of decades of overwork and pressure. It was time to challenge him. Phineas was surprised to see that his right hand had balled into a tight fist. He eased his fingers back open.

When Moro finally stepped inside the too-tiny room, the smell of hand sanitizer enveloped him. The bright overhead lights again exaggerated his facial scar in its serpentine route under his eye and down his cheek to the corner of his lip. He made no attempt to conceal its impact in the crease a smile would create.

"We'll talk about your bone marrow results and diagnosis after I repeat your examination." Moro's terse words suggested he might also be dreading that conversation. With barely a sideways glance at Iris, he walked past her to the room's far corner, sat on the rolling stool, and logged into the computer.

Isn't he at least going to take an interval medical history? Moro hasn't even asked whether she's deteriorated since he last saw her.

"Hello, Dr. Moro. How are *you*?" She wasn't having any of his rudeness—or was it just an acquired social ineptitude—or worse, an actual dread of delivering horrible news?

Moro finally pivoted to face her. "Fine, Mrs. Mann. Have there been any changes?"

"You might recall that it's *Dr.* Mann, *Dr.* Moro."

Good for her.

"And I'm just skinnier, weaker, and sweatier." She leaned forward in a way that made Phineas think she might be preparing to pounce on Moro. "I hope you've got a fix for me."

Moro stared at her then finally acknowledged Phineas' presence, glancing sideways at him like he hoped for an ally.

Phineas looked right back. *No ally here, Mister.*

Moro stood and spoke directly to Iris. "*Dr.* Mann, let's complete your exam, then we can review your tests. We have much to talk about."

Frightening words from a doctor, especially a cancer doctor. Phineas rubbed sweaty palms on his pants.

Moro took out his pocket flashlight, clicked it on, and shone it at her mouth. "Open." He then repeated the same lightning-fast ritual examination as in the prior visit, slowing only to have her lie flat long enough for him to listen to a few heartbeats and to estimate the size of her spleen with his cupped hand.

Iris asked, "Is it bigger, Dr. Moro?"

Phineas wanted to cheer when her voice didn't shrink this time. Moro's brusque manner had ignited her fuse.

"Maybe a centimeter." Moro stepped to the small sink in the corner. "Okay, you can sit up."

Moro kept his focus solely on his hands as he soaped, rinsed, and dried them. Then he lowered himself onto the rolling stool and clicked the computer mouse. Each of his methodical actions seemed drawn out in slow motion. Was he delaying or did it just feel that way? And washing his hands instead of using sanitizing gel? Was he more concerned about touching her? Did he want to wash his hands of her problems?

Finally, Moro said, "So, your blood counts just came back. They've declined since last week. We may need to consider transfusions of red cells and platelets soon."

"What are...the numbers?" To process Iris' situation, Phineas needed to know.

"Hemoglobin's just over 8 grams, Platelets are 35,000, and white count is down to 2800." Moro waited long enough for the numbers to sink in and worry them before he added, "We should do something right away. We need to halt the progression of the underlying condition."

At Moro's "do something," Phineas wanted to cheer. For weeks now, every time he'd looked at his fading wife, he'd wanted to "do something" to make her better—but hold on—Moro hadn't said what that "something" would be or what the "underlying condition" was.

"And just *what* is my underlying condition?" Iris was obviously ready to hear its name.

Moro cleared his throat and swallowed. "Several of us studied your bone marrow during our weekly hematology conference."

"Several of us." Not a good sign.

"And I asked Dr. Reddick to review your case."

"Who...is Dr. ...Reddick?" Someone new since Phineas retired?

"He came from Hopkins and joined the pathology faculty last year. He's our international authority on what we decided your marrow reveals."

Is Moro now pausing for dramatic effect or because he isn't himself 100% sure of the diagnosis?

"He feels that your marrow biopsy findings are consistent with a diagnosis of histiocytic medullary reticulosis—and we accept Reddick's assessment that it's HMR." Moro seemed relieved to finally spit the words out, to put the bizarre label on it, as if that would end all difficult deliberations and somehow smother the smoldering embers burning inside Iris.

Phineas' jaw muscle tightened at the words "consistent with" and "we accept." *Hedge words.*

And histiocytic medullary reticulosis brought back a terrifying memory. It had been decades since Phineas had heard that esoteric string of medical terms or its abbreviation, HMR. Back on that traumatic day, Moro's male patient, bleeding and in shock, had been emergently transferred to Phineas' ICU service. Phineas' team tried in vain for hours to resuscitate *that* hematology patient before they lost him. And Moro had been elsewhere when his patient expired. Phineas recalled the heartache of having to break the news to the man's sobbing wife and four adult offspring. When he'd reached the part where he gently suggested an autopsy, the grieving wife wanted to give permission, but the next generation united against it. She'd backed down, and the team was left to wonder if the whole story had been revealed.

So, Moro had accepted this frightening diagnosis for Iris, and apparently he'd stopped thinking about other possible causes for Iris' low blood counts. The words "accept Redick's assessment" felt like *so much* uncertainty.

Creases formed across Iris' forehead. "I've never heard of this HMR that you say I have. Please explain."

Iris' request snapped Phineas all the way back from his frightening past HMR experience to her present plight. His pulse pounded in his ears as he waited to hear what Moro would tell her. If Iris knew what her husband did, she'd surely lose all the stoicism she was mustering.

"I wouldn't expect you to have heard of it. HMR is an exceedingly rare diagnosis. Histiocytes are immune cells, and for unclear reasons, they have packed your bone marrow and interfered with normal blood cell production." Moro's words were matter-of-fact, indifferent, as though he was lecturing a medical intern and not the victim of this deadly condition.

"So...what are you going to treat me with?"

Moro shifted uneasily on the rolling stool and half-mumbled, "Since it's rare, and we don't know what leads to it, there is no standard treatment protocol."

Is he hoping to slip this important information by us without either of us reacting? Sure enough, Iris was flinching. From her prior hospital work, she had to be thinking that rare conditions, while intriguing to medical teams, were hazardous to the patients. No one knew how to treat them.

Moro appeared to be studying his shoes when he said, "Chemotherapy drugs and bone marrow transplants have been tried anecdotally without clear success. It seems that the unchecked proliferation of histiocytes replacing functional bone marrow doesn't respond to the drugs used in treating malignancies and for transplants." He glanced up at Iris. "There's a new biological agent, Histiocab, that specifically targets and effectively suppresses histiocytes." He now seemed to be reciting a prepared spiel. "It's been tried in a few cases of HMR overseas with some success."

"And you want to give it to me." Iris sounded resigned to this fate.

Phineas knew what she was saying. She yearned for *something* to be done.

"It *is* FDA approved, but as treatment for a type of histiocytic lymphoma. HMR isn't the same disease, so we'd have to provide it to you off label."

"You're sure...Iris...doesn't have...a type...of lymphoma?" Phineas couldn't believe he'd finally said that word out loud. And in front of Iris. He'd previously feared hematologic malignancy and the grueling treatment it would indicate, but lymphomas *at least* had accepted and usually effective treatment pathways. A more defined and less frightening future than HMR.

"No, not a type of lymphoma. The cell markers we tested proved her histiocytes are not monoclonal." Moro must have noticed Iris' puzzled forehead creases. "That means they didn't start with one malignant cell clone that reproduced unchecked and spread throughout your marrow—like lymphomas do."

"So, what I have isn't malignant?" She had to be searching for any positive news.

"HMR is hard to characterize. We don't honestly know what triggers it."

Phineas acknowledged that his words were likely true, but it still felt like Moro was being evasive.

"What I can say is that the proliferation of histiocytes in your bone marrow has mostly shut down your production of normal and essential blood cells." Moro sounded impatient at having to repeat this explanation. "But let's talk about treatment."

He wants to shift the discussion and hurry us toward a conclusion.

Moro pressed on. "We can have Histiocab here in a few days and give it to you intravenously in the hospital's infusion center. If you tolerate it well, you won't have to spend even one night in the hospital."

"*That* part suits me." Iris nodded her approval. "And so does not taking chemotherapy or having a bone marrow transplant."

Her affirming words brought Phineas back again. He'd been submerged under another flood of disturbing thoughts and now surfaced as if for air.

Moro's pitch came too easily. He hasn't told Iris everything.

"What…does… 'some success'…mean?" Phineas asked. Moro had casually dropped the phrase. "Some success" was not a ringing endorsement for the drug and meant it wasn't a cure.

Moro's hoping we won't press him on it.

Moro looked irritated at being called out to explain in more detail. "The declines in blood counts reversing—of course, the goal we're hoping for." His tone smacked of condescension.

Just because I look used up, doesn't mean I'm no longer capable of understanding anything complex.

"For…how long?" Should he continue to probe Moro for details? Maybe Iris would feel less threatened if she were spared such details. But he couldn't help himself. He needed to learn all he could *because* she was threatened.

"It's only been used in a limited number of patients with HMR. Remember, this is a rare condition, and the drug is new." Moro now sounded defensive. "We did discuss Histiocab at our hematology conference, and the group agreed on recommending we try it." Phineas understood that Moro was in a tough spot. He was treating a retired faculty member and former colleague's wife just diagnosed with a poorly defined condition that lacked a standard treatment protocol. That was why he'd sought group approval.

"Patients haven't been followed on it long term, usually due to interval complications," Moro disclosed as though he was obliged to.

"*What* complications?" Moro's mention of "complications" transformed Iris' recently acquired slouch, which had folded her spine into a question mark, into an exclamation point.

"You have a low white cell count, so your body's immune defenses are impaired. And histiocytes are also involved in fighting infections, but we don't know how well yours are working." Moro turned away from her gaze to the refuge of the computer screen. He clicked the mouse. "How functional those cells are in cases of HMR isn't known, and Histiocab reduces histiocyte numbers. Patients are at increased risk for infections." His eyes remained focused on the computer screen, and he appeared to be scrolling with the mouse. "I do want you to know that special stains for infectious agents in your marrow were all negative, and cultures for infections remain negative as of today's reports."

What he didn't say was that the HMR patients treated with Histiocab must have *died* from infections. Their deaths must be why there was no long-term follow-up. More importantly, cultures for some pathogens could take several weeks to grow and give needed answers.

Iris doesn't have weeks for answers.

Moro spun on the rolling stool back to face Iris. "I can order the drug for you. It'll be here in two or three days." He clearly wanted a conclusion. "That's your best option."

Phineas turned from Moro to Iris. Maybe it *was* her best option. Anyway, they didn't have time for an expert second opinion elsewhere; her illness was progressing too rapidly.

Iris sank back into her question mark and probed Phineas' eyes. The blue in her eyes flashed at him like a sunlit sea. *Does she want me to answer for her?* Now that her hematologist had provided them with a working diagnosis, there'd at least be time for Phineas to search the literature. Maybe he'd find some help with Iris' critical decision. She could change her mind if he turned up something against Histiocab.

Iris turned back from Phineas to face Moro. "It sounds like we shouldn't wait long to decide."

Phineas understood her. She really wanted *something* done—and it was clear they shouldn't wait long.

Moro pressed his lips into threads and slowly nodded.

"Then order me the drug."

"We'll call you as soon as it gets here," Moro turned back to the computer and clicked the mouse.

He'd had that order ready to send.

Moro stood and edged toward the door like he hoped to wrap up her visit and quietly escape. He grasped the doorknob.

Has he used up his daily quota of words and feelings?

"Now, I'm sure you know my daughter-in-law, Dr. Marie Porter." Iris words made Moro turn to face her. "Unless I've underestimated her, my family is waiting for you in your conference room. I want you to talk to them, Dr. Moro."

"Wish I could, but I'm backed up, and other patients are waiting." Moro closed the door behind him.

"I don't think he wishes he could. He's happy to be shed of me for now." Iris' tone suggested that she was relieved to be shed of *him*. "Let's collect everyone and head home, Phineas."

He pushed himself up and onto his walker then unlocked its brakes. The trying visit was over, and Iris had been given a diagnosis. But words like "we decided" and "consistent with" didn't inspire Phineas' confidence in that diagnosis, and the question remained, had Moro given up on considering other possible conditions?

Something was scheduled to be done. That *something* unsettled Phineas. He'd often taught trainees that they should never be in a hurry to make a mistake, never to just *do something*.

He followed his wife back toward the waiting room to face their anxious family who'd surely be bursting with unanswerable questions. He'd see what he could learn in the days before Iris was to receive the drug, except that research could take time, and time was something that lately there never seemed to be enough of.

CHAPTER 23

July 19

Dawn's fiery horizontal needles pierced the lush foliage surrounding the Manns' narrow front lawn and dotted the far kitchen wall and Iris. The mottled, flaming image of her jolted Phineas for a moment, but he forced himself to return his attention to the task he'd planned to pursue. He rotated his laptop on the table, so that the screen faced her. "Sorry... to get you...up so early. ...I wanted...to work before...everyone...got up."

"What's this?" She glanced at his computer then set the orange Sippy Cup of coffee in front of him, being careful not to step on Ernest.

"Do you...mind...signing me...into your...medical record, ...so I...can read...your reports?" The first taste of coffee scalded his tongue. He'd have to wait for a needed caffeine boost. He'd slept poorly again.

"Sure. Knock yourself out." She bent over to log in then turned the screen back to him. "Thanks for doing this for me." She kissed his forehead. "I'm going back to bed for a bit."

He held up his hand to signal she shouldn't escape yet. "You know...I *have* to...do this." He hoped today's efforts might reassure both of them. Was there more she hadn't mentioned that he could help her with? "Want to...talk about...anything...before the...others get up?"

"Phineas, you know I'm scared, and I feel lousy. Sleep and dreams are welcome escapes. Resting helps me be there more for you when I'm with you, and for our family when I'm with them. Who knows how much longer that will be?"

Her question sent a chill through him. He couldn't bear to think about what his life would be like without her. He wanted to steer her from those thoughts and back to the present. "And your...planned treatment?"

"What about it? It's the recommendation of a team of experts, and it sounds simpler than what I expected. I'm glad of that." She now appeared more animated, less sleepy. "And it *would help* if you seemed enthusiastic about it."

"I hope I...will be...after I...read about it."

"Good." She pulled a chair out from the table and sat close, facing him. "There is one detail I've been thinking about and want to mention to you while the others are sleeping."

He leaned closer.

"If things go badly, I want to talk to a priest while I still can."

Her unexpected request sent that too familiar chill back down his spine. They were both baptized Catholic and married in a Catholic church. They'd attended masses for grandsons' baptisms and Christmas and Easter high masses with family, but he couldn't remember either of their last confessions, what the church now called the Sacrament of Reconciliation. That sacrament was supposed to be completed as regular spiritual maintenance. But now, like the sorting of their cluttered attic, she seemed to be planning to check the sacrament off as another last detail, and to hedge her bet on an afterlife with a forgiven and spotless soul. She'd clearly processed Moro's words when he'd talked about "complications."

"I'll remember, ...and I'll...talk with...the priest too."

"Thank you. Now, with that off my mind, I could really use another hour or two of sleep." The sun's rays, unbroken now, warmed her pale cheeks. She squeezed his hand and left him alone.

He'd awakened her an hour or two earlier than she would have on her own, and when she'd risen, the sheet under her torso was beyond damp. Her night sweats had worsened enough that she'd begun quietly laundering the linens and remaking the bed almost daily. Add in her usual chores of caring for him—no wonder she was tired. And even Felipe's cuisine hadn't tempted her into putting lost pounds back on. Unless *something* intervened soon, her time was running out.

He reached down to rub behind Ernest's ears, eliciting an appreciative moan. "Wish me...luck, ...my friend." Back to the task at hand.

He started with Moro's clinic notes. They showed only the bare minimum: Iris' exam, a summary of lab results, the final pathology diagnosis, and the planned treatment. None of the uncertainty that permeated her case. No hints whether Moro had gone through internal reflections, whether he had any doubts. Even less of his thinking than what Moro had shared during the visit. In his notes, he'd documented only a meager sliver of Iris' background as the sum of her existence. Her social history stated that she was married and retired faculty. Not even a mention of her academic concentration, much less that she'd worked her way to the top of her field by starting in the trenches, by providing care for an indigent population on the public wards in Boston, New Orleans, and Durham, North Carolina, where she'd labored to help the homeless, the drug and alcohol users, and incarcerated men sick enough to require hospitalization. No mention of all the misery and down and out diseases to which she'd been exposed back in the '70s and '80s.

And parts of Moro's notes read to Phineas like he'd copied and pasted from their internist's documentation, more evidence that Moro had glossed past knowing her. At least his notes on Iris couldn't reach the level of fully cloned notes—notes totally copied, pasted, and repurposed from visit to visit, a shortcut technology made possible, and tempting to many clinicians. It was a shortcut that Phineas loathed. Iris' visits were for a new problem and hadn't yet *allowed* for cloned notes—otherwise, Moro might have.

Focus on what's there, not what's missing.

Iris' sets of blood counts could be viewed in the summary table but were better appreciated in graphic form. In graphic form, her counts had previously appeared as flat, normal lines until her recent life-changing visit with their primary care doctor. Each line graph now descended steeply to alarming new values—numerical lemmings plunging over a cliff's edge.

He studied each microbiology report one by one: all either negative or still pending one full week after her bone marrow cultures were planted. The abdominal CT report was as Moro had indicated, remarkable for Iris' enlarged spleen and surrounding lymph nodes. The radiologist had also dictated that the limited amount of the left lung base imaged above her spleen was unremarkable. No clues in that more than a week-old study.

He touched the side of the Sippy cup. His coffee's temperature would finally allow a careful swallow. He needed to avoid a coughing spell that would bring the household to his side. He wanted quiet, not the boisterous presence of Mateo. Quiet made him sense the thump of each of his heartbeats, and their pace accelerated as he opened the file containing Iris' bone marrow pathology report.

Its final sentence read: "The polyclonal proliferations of histiocytes replacing normal marrow elements supports a diagnosis of histiocytic medullary reticulosis."

Supports. Not a definitive word. A word inviting uncertainty. Phineas disliked uncertainty, but he knew all too well the time-worn proclamation: Medicine is an art. Diagnoses sometimes come together like impressionist dot paintings, the whole picture formed from arrangements of objective and subjective data points.

He reached down, ran his hand from Ernest's crown to his shoulders, and asked, "How can we put this together, my friend?" Ernest lifted his head and studied his master as if anticipating directions.

Phineas returned to his computer screen. The report had been dictated by Reddick, the new expert Moro seemed to hold in awe. After Reddick's digital signature, he'd copied and pasted references to add weight to his opinion, an impressive measure beyond the usual pathology reports. And Reddick was listed as a sole or coauthor on all four of these publications. The first, in the *Annals of Pathology*, was of a patient series with Reddick as the sole author. Phineas opened the link to that article. In it, Reddick reported on four cases, describing similar pancytopenia and bone marrow findings. And survival? None of the four survived six months. In none of them was an underlying trigger for the disorder identified.

The other three papers were single case reports that provided wordy descriptions of the pathology without references to possible causes. All of these patients had been diagnosed and treated in the United States, so none had received the new drug, Histiocab.

Arrggh!

Histiocab. Quick, before his family awakened, he needed to search Histiocab and what he could find on its use in HMR. Siri finally got it right the third time he stammered its novel name, and each time the wall clock ticked away precious seconds of his necessary solitude. When Siri took him to Histiocab articles, he saw at first only reviews of its use in histiocytic lymphoma. These at least documented improved survival times when it was added to standard chemotherapy, but those patients who'd received Histiocab had more complicating infections than the control group who received only the standard lymphoma treatment protocols. But lymphoma trials weren't the studies he needed to review, since Iris definitely didn't have histiocytic lymphoma. He found the trials he was looking for at the bottom of the next page of links.

Reports of Histiocab use in HMR were single case reports from Europe. As Moro had suggested, blood counts improved for weeks after patients received the drug, but each patient eventually succumbed to an infection. And some of those infections were from unusual organisms, ones only patients with compromised immune systems risked acquiring. Could those extra histiocytes invading Iris' bone marrow be proliferating in response to something undiagnosed? What if all those histiocytes were reacting to some unidentified *infectious* agent? Would that agent then spread because it was *completely* unchecked after Histiocab?

So, Moro had claimed that Reddick was recognized as an international authority on HMR. That information might have been reassuring, but to anyone who understood the profession in all its complexity, that assertion was far from reassuring. To stay an authority, Reddick needed to continue finding cases and keep publishing them—especially as a new faculty member trying to make a name for himself, advance in his field, and be awarded precious promotions and tenure. And wouldn't that provide incentive, perhaps only subconsciously, for Reddick to see HMR *too readily* in marrow specimens referred to him?

Cognitive bias. That was the term for this professional hazard. Seasoned physicians knew to guard against this type of bias that narrowed broad thinking and closed open minds. Bias that put the brakes on a journey to truth.

And, to appease the demanding bean counters, the ones who paid his salary, wasn't Reddick under pressure to read more bone marrow specimens more quickly? Of course, he'd probably put on *his* brakes and rejoiced when he'd seen Iris' marrow and felt he could diagnose another rare case of HMR. *His* disease.

Phineas had to find a way to eliminate any cognitive bias in Iris' case. He knew a seasoned pathologist, Dr. Henry Postum. Henry, a colleague and friend, was not yet fully pulled out of circulation because of his many years but was past the point in his career where he was on everyone's radar and in constant demand. This allowed him to be free of the external pressures that might influence his thinking and hurry him to make diagnoses.

Henry and he had together studied countless lung specimens under a two-headed microscope. And, while well into his seventies and nearly deaf without his hearing aids, Henry still attended pulmonary teaching conferences and remained a thoughtful and wise voice on tough cases. *He'd* help Phineas settle his angst over Iris' diagnosis. With Siri's help, Phineas composed an email and touched Send.

"I smell coffee." Martha shuffled into the kitchen hugging her laptop. She stopped short and blinked for a moment when the morning sun shone full into her sleepy eyes. "Looks like you and I are once again hoping to get some work done before Mateo keeps us busy." She set her computer on the table and glanced at his screen. "What are you working on so early *this* time?" She bent to pat Ernest.

"Your Mom. ...I'm trying...to ease my...mind." During his career, work often settled his anxiety about uncertain cases, but today's work had, so far, only amplified his worries.

"That's good. We count on you, Dad." Martha kissed his forehead then took her coffee to find a quiet corner elsewhere in the house, a corner free of all distractions.

He touched the spot she'd kissed. That forehead kiss was his second of the morning. Gratitude and affection might be expressed on the gesture's surface. But underneath, he could only wonder if Martha was humoring him, like she did when Mateo, full of pride, showed off a fresh crayon drawing? In her eyes, had her father become twice a child?

And, in view of her mother's dire situation, if Martha's hopes were pinned to *him (twice a child?)* providing a novel insight and resultant miracle, she had to be an expert at hiding her desperation.

Phineas returned to his computer. So far, reviewing Iris' records and the literature had provided less and less reassurance. He pressed on and the more he read, the more uneasy he felt about her diagnosis and planned treatment. Reddick's and others' work had been published years ago, and fewer HMR reports appeared in recent years, as though the diagnosis was being made less often. Were newer clinical tools allowing other diagnostic explanations for similar bone marrow findings? Was Reddick trying to justify the continued existence of a pathologic entity for which he'd once been recognized as an international authority?

Phineas scratched behind Ernest's ears while puzzling over how to further pursue answers. Maybe he should search for answers in letters to editors in more obscure journals? He'd need a translation app to review foreign language papers? Both options would take time.

But before Phineas could pursue those desperate strategies further, the kitchen came alive with Mateo's hungry energy. The lad had clearly dressed himself, since he sported his favorite tiger tee shirt backwards. Trivial details mattered little to the boy.

Felipe entered right behind Mateo and began taking orders. "Apple-smoked bacon, home fries, and eggs just the way you like 'em. Now, who's hungry?"

Mateo requested sunny side up with "no runny yolks." Soon a bacon grin, home fries hairdo, and two orange eyes stared back at him from his plate.

Phineas pushed his laptop aside to consume his over-easy eggs and to marvel at a six-year-old's voracious appetite. Martha, lured by the fragrance of cooked cured pork, drifted back to the kitchen from wherever she'd stationed herself to work. While Felipe fixed her a plate, she claimed a seat beside Phineas and set her laptop on the table with the screen facing him. But instead of studying the screen, his attention was drawn to her expression. Considering the straits her parents navigated, she wore a surprisingly mischievous grin. He put his fork down and waited for her to share whatever it was that amused her. He could use a chuckle and didn't have a clue what so tickled her.

"Dad, look at this piece in today's *Washington Post*." The headline read:

NC LAWMAKER ENDS PARTNERSHIP

The accompanying photo showed Marie, Ernest, and "Dr. Phineas Mann MD" standing and facing Congressman Quentin Tate in his kimono and wheelchair. A shocked-looking Michael was standing next to Tate but staring at the ceiling. The caption identified each of them and stated that Quentin Tate was recovering from a fungal disease, disseminated blastomycosis. Phineas knew well the tense moment that photo was taken, but at least the caption indicated that Tate was further recovering from his illness.

"Not a…very good…picture of me. …Ernest looks…handsome though." Phineas read the first paragraph.

The reporter explained how Quentin probably acquired the fungal infection while working on deer antlers for the knife handles he and his partner sold in their business, and that Michael, his former business partner, fashioned the metal for the designer knives' blades. The article explained that Quentin had been on life support until consulting pulmonologist Dr. Phineas Mann suggested the correct diagnosis and that the congressman was now recovering in his home and receiving the proper treatment.

The reporter had dug further and stated that Michael and Quentin had the same home address in western North Carolina until Quentin abruptly folded their knife company prior to his discharge from UNC Hospital. In a subsequent interview, Michael hinted that a memoir about his and Quentin's intimate time together might be published quite soon.

Quentin hadn't personally responded to the reporter's phone calls. Quentin's people had called Michael "a liar and a gold-digger" and declared that "people shouldn't believe anything that man says."

The North Carolina Republican party had put out the statement "We thank Quentin Tate for his service and dedication to our positions, but we'll be supporting another candidate in the coming election." The party floated two names as possible replacements for Quentin.

"Looks like Tate won't be running again," Martha said. Her grin melted. "But his district is so red, we still won't be able to flip it to blue." Spurned by his party, Quentin Tate would be only a blip in the long history of North Carolina politics as usual.

Iris sidled back into the kitchen, rubbing her eyes against the grit of sleep. She groaned, "coffee."

"Some eggs…would be…good. …Some protein," Phineas suggested.

"After coffee." She planted herself next to Mateo as if she could absorb needed nutrition through his vital aura.

Phineas' laptop pinged, indicating a new email. He turned it around to see that the sender was Annabella, his Duke study coordinator, then carefully swallowed his last bite of egg. He clicked the email open and read.

Dear Phineas,

We have great news for you! Your stem cells are growing vigorously and producing the amounts of dopamine we've hoped for.

I have scheduled your preoperative visit for this Friday at 2 PM. Surgery to implant your port will be early next week. We'll know a specific time when we see you Friday.

Cheers!

Annabella

Dopamine. The substance he craved dangled in front of him at Duke only eight miles and days away. Possible salvation. Yet, guilt and conflict followed his instant of excitement. They wanted him at Duke the day after Iris was to receive her first Histiocab treatment. His stone face must have displayed hints of emotion. Across the table, Iris' eyes narrowed, and she peered at his screen.

"What have you got, Phineas?"

He slid his computer closer to her so she could read Annabella's words. She had to turn the screen at an angle away from the sun's glare.

"It's the...day after...your treatment." He waited long enough for the news to sink in. "I can...cancel."

She leaned back into her chair and shook her head. "No. My treatment's as an outpatient. You've come too far to abandon your hope. One of us will get you there Friday."

He couldn't tell her, after this morning's literature search, how much more worried he was about *her* treatment, about life-threatening complications from it—or from her obscure disease. What Iris hadn't said was that she wanted him to go ahead with his trial in case she died soon. If his intervention went as hoped, it could make him more independent.

And if his procedure went poorly, he might shortly join her in death. He probed her eyes the way she did his when she wanted more and felt that he could confirm these messages. She wasn't saying them out loud. She'd spare Mateo having to process her death, for now.

Martha put down her fork. "We'll make sure you get there, Dad." His inquisitive and capable daughter had, days earlier, perused his folder of Parkinson's disease research studies and seen the reasons he'd selected such a desperate step. She also seemed convinced that he should proceed.

Iris reached for his computer. "I'll tell her you're looking forward to seeing her Friday." She typed his response for him and hit Send.

CHAPTER 24

July 20

Phineas waited at his kitchen window seat as Mateo supervised his father. "Not too much mayo, Papi, or it'll squirt out when I bite."

Felipe wrapped three chicken sandwiches and added them to the basket already packed with a fruit salad, potato chips, and oatmeal cookies. It was the least a chef could do for Martha's friend, Jenny, who'd offered to take Mateo for a play date and spare the lad having to witness Iris' IV stick and Histiocab infusion. And Jenny's six-year-old daughter, Emma, was a bonus. Mateo could finally hang out with a peer and have a break from the stodgy adults.

As Jenny's SUV pulled into the driveway, Mateo asked, "Please can Ernest come with us?". The boy's last-minute plaintive expression would have been hard for Phineas to resist.

But Felipe shook his head. "You know that Ernest is a service dog, Mateo. Waylo will need him this afternoon." Mateo gave Ernest a generous parting hug and was rewarded with a lick on his cheek.

"Have fun, ...Mateo." Phineas waved as Felipe escorted his son outside. One less worry. Phineas had enough of those. He patted Ernest. "Shall we gather everyone and go to the hospital, my friend?"

Marie, radiant in her bright white coat, waited curbside in front of UNC Hospital for the Mann clan's arrival Thursday afternoon. She and Leon, the now familiar security guard, appeared to be chatting amicably as Felipe's electric car crept silently toward the hospital's entrance.

Good for her. She'd obviously taken Phineas' comments to heart and made peace with Leon, an olive branch that had to have made his day.

Felipe hustled around his vehicle to retrieve Phineas' walker from the back and unfold it next to the front passenger door. He held it steady as Phineas relived the dreaded sensation of descending into that too-familiar bottomless pit until his feet found the firm asphalt surface. Ernest then tumbled out while somehow appearing composed and professional. At the command, "heel," he took up his preferred post at his master's side. His service vest had been freshly laundered.

Iris climbed out and joined the men and dog. While still slouching, she seemed resolved to accept whatever the hematologist and fate offered today. Under the penetrating midday summer sun, her weight loss made her facial bones appear prominent enough to sear a frightening image of her skull's bony planes into Phineas' brain. The longshot mission he'd arranged for today *had* to succeed. It just *had* to. His desperate hunch *had* to be right.

"So, let me get the plan straight, Phineas." Marie sidled up protectively next to Iris. "I'll begin escorting Iris to the Infusion Center for her treatment, while Martha parks the car, and you and Felipe go looking for your pathologist friend."

When Phineas had told Iris his desperate plan of attack, she'd reminded him of how he'd called himself Don Quixote on the day they'd met fifty-plus years ago. Was he tilting at windmills today? He couldn't just sit idly by as a spectator watching his wife's frightening battle for her life.

"Should we...synchronize...our watches?" His pitiful attempt to ease the mood while appearing deadly serious. He raised his shaky wrist and tried to angle his eyebrows down as much as his neurologic condition allowed,

Iris answered, "They texted that my medicine was sent for. You men go on with whatever idea you hatched, Phineas."

He shuffled to her side and leaned in for a peck on her pale cheek. "I love you, ...and I'll see...you soon." Even in the sun, her face felt hotter than expected.

Leon looked stunned as he took in Iris' sickly appearance and heard of her Infusion Center treatment. "Sorry to hear you're not feeling well, Ma'am. Please let me know if I can be of any help."

Phineas responded for her, "Thank you, ...Leon. ...We will."

Felipe, Ernest, and Phineas caught the lone aged and shaky elevator that descended all the way down to the subbasement labyrinth of pathology offices and laboratories. They walked and shuffled to the dimly lit far end of the hallway and stopped outside the last office. Its plaque read "DR. HENRY POSTUM MD." So, administration had delegated Phineas' old friend to the farthest outpost in the hospital. Was their message saying that Phineas had pinned his last hope on someone also on the far side of his best years?

Phineas rapped his knuckles on the door's glass pane and waited. And waited. The heartbeat in his ears throbbed at a pace well above that of a mechanical clock.

"Felipe...knock harder... He might have...forgotten...his hearing aids."

Felipe administered a hearty pounding with his fist to the wooden bottom half of the door. Within seconds, Henry Postum appeared from an inner room and eased the door open. The remnants of his hair consisted of a few tufts over and behind his ears which indeed lacked hearing aids. Bifocals were secured with a lanyard midway down his oversized nose. He glanced at Ernest and took in Phineas with an up-and-down appraisal then held out a liver-spotted hand.

"It's been a long time since we worked together, Phineas." The boisterous greeting of a nearly deaf man.

"You can see...why I had to...retire, Henry." Retire before he made some last, terrible mistake he'd regret for his duration on the planet's surface. Phineas wanted so much to chat and catch up with Henry, but risked rudeness to press his case forward. He spoke as loudly as he could, trying to reach Henry's handicapped ears with his handicapped voice. "You're the...only one I...thought of...who could...help. ...Can we look...at the slides...now?" He gestured with his head toward Felipe. "Where should...Felipe, wait?"

Dr. Postum studied Felipe with a curious expression. "There's an extra chair in the microscope room, if it's okay with you for him to be there."

"Felipe's family. ...Lead on."

Postum led them one door back up the hallway into a tiny room furnished only with a small table, its two chairs, and a separate chair in the far corner. He motioned for Felipe to wait there while he and Phineas took the seats across the table. A bulky two-headed binocular microscope was secured on its center. A cardboard folder, purposed to protect a dozen glass slides from breakage, lay open next to the instrument.

The command "under" directed Ernest to settle beneath Phineas' seat. His walker was at the ready beside them.

"I was saddened to hear of your wife's illness, Phineas." Postum peered at Phineas over his glasses.

"Thank you, ...Henry. And...thank you...for helping us."

"I hope I can somehow," Postum responded. "I've been going over her bone marrow reports. You do know that the pathologist who read them is considered an authority on the condition he diagnosed? He's published series of patients with histiocytic medullary reticulosis."

"That's...exactly why...I wanted you...to look at...her specimens...with me."

Postum's scalp creased in parallel furrows from its shiny apex down to his bushy eyebrows, suggesting that Phineas' comment had puzzled him. "Go on, please."

"Cognitive bias. ...If Reddick...subconsciously wants...to make a...certain diagnosis, ...he's more likely...to believe...that's what...he's seeing. ...I need you...to be...*unbiased*."

Postum's scalp creases smoothed out, and he beamed at the compliment. "Ah, the wise old clinician always keeping his mind open. Well, you and I are definitely *old*." His face turned serious. "Let's hope we're as wise as we need to be."

He opened the folder, carefully extracted the first slide, and secured it in the clamp on the microscope's platform. He peered into his side's binocular lenses and turned a grooved dial. "I'm in focus now. You should adjust your eyepieces." He waited for Phineas to adjust his side then spun separate dials to move the biopsy images side to side then forward and back, scanning the cells under low power magnification. "On this slide, you can see numerous histiocytes stained pink, many more than is normal, replacing the usual marrow precursor cells which stain blue."

The pink histiocytes vastly outnumbered the marrow's expected dark blue blood cell precursor lines. Those pink areas clumped into nests that swirled and resembled miniature threatening storms clustered across the field. Their dominance of Iris' vital marrow cells made Phineas' pulse pound faster in his ears.

"Okay. ...I see lots...of histiocytes. ...That's not...specific. ...Can we look...at the special stains...for infections?" *Something treatable, please.* Like his hunch.

"Sure. I'm sure you saw that those stains have already been looked at, but I did as you requested and had the technicians make as many micro-biologic slides as they could from what was left of her tissue specimen. What are you thinking?"

Was Postum humoring this elderly colleague? Easier than calling him an old fool.

"That history...sometimes repeats."

Postum's scalp creases returned. When he removed the slide they'd just inspected, it slipped from his fingers, landed on the table's edge, and bounced onto the floor, breaking into three sections. He shrugged. "At least we've got more of those tissue stains." Felipe carefully gathered up the pieces and lay them on the table.

Phineas watched with apprehension and concealed impatience as Postum arranged the next slide for inspection. "Here's the first AFB stain." The AFB stain was for acid-fast bacilli, the organisms of the genus mycobacterium, which among its many species include the tuberculosis bacterium.

Phineas concentrated on every bit of the visible field while they scanned back and forth as if they needed to peer into each tiny pigeonhole of a grid. He saw only the background sea of the blue-green counterstain taken up by Iris' cells. No red-staining microbes, the 'red snappers', clinicians' slang for TB germs. Postum removed the slide and arranged another. He repeated the laborious inspections. A third slide with the AFB stain. Nothing. Only the same turbulent blue green sea.

The inspections were taking too much precious time. Iris would soon be receiving the intravenous Histiocab infusion. Phineas' hopes were plunging like the last grains of sand in an hourglass.

"You know, Phineas, they look at three AFB slides before they release the report." Postum looked up from his eyepieces, apparently checking to see if Phineas had seen enough to satisfy him.

"How many...more do...you have?"

Postum sighed. "The lab techs were able to get three more from what was left. They're from the tip of the biopsy, the deepest part—and the last of it."

"All the...better. Deeper...samples."

Postum settled the fourth slide on the platform, and they repeated another thorough inspection. Then the fifth. Postum opened the clamp holding the slide.

"Stop. Henry, ...I saw...something." *Was that something a speck of red?* "In the last...field. In the...corner. Please...go back."

Postum complied without comment, at first with low magnification then under highest magnification. The blue-green sea had almost consumed a tiny red dot.

"That...could be... the tip of...a mycobacterium." The pounding in Phineas' ears rose to deafening. "Let's look...at the...last slide...same area... deeper in." His last hope.

The pathologist's hands trembled ever so slightly as he secured the last slide in place and found the corresponding corner using low power. Was that more red? Postum switched to the highest magnification and centered the suspect area.

There. Two tiny bacilli, elongated rods crisscrossing—and taking the crimson stain in a beaded pattern—typical for tuberculosis organisms. Diagnostic.

Iris has tuberculosis.

Not histiocytic medullary reticulosis, but miliary tuberculosis, so named for presenting with tiny millet seed sized clumps of the surrounding immune response to disseminated TB germs. Miliary is the form of TB that begins with a single event and scatters bacteria through the blood stream seeding organs one bacillus at a time. And TB is a *curable* disease. But a deadly disease without proper treatment.

"Jesus, Phineas." Postum sat back and stared slack-jawed across the table at Phineas. "Thank God you persisted. What on earth made you do so?"

"The doctors didn't...persist in...Eleanor Roosevelt's...case, ...and she died from...miliary TB." Phineas hastily summarized how Roosevelt was also treated for pancytopenia but with steroids that impaired her immune defenses and accelerated her death from miliary tuberculosis. Roosevelt's TB had been consuming her "bite by bite" until she'd been prescribed steroids. Then, because she'd taken them, she'd died, not by bites, but by gulps.

Because she'd been a president's wife, a disease like TB that, in the United States, mostly infected immigrants and the poor, wasn't considered in her case despite her work with impoverished groups, groups that her doctors forgot—that time forgot. Another deadly example of cognitive bias.

And Moro, a distinguished fellow faculty member, hadn't aggressively pursued TB for Iris because he hadn't taken a complete history. And Iris' history, like Roosevelt's, included work with the impoverished. Iris' histiocytes weren't merely proliferating, they were *fighting* the infection, and her low blood counts were collateral damage.

Phineas shuddered at the immediate realization that the drug Moro planned to give Iris would knock out her immune defenses to those TB germs, allow them to proliferate unchecked—and soon kill her—but a proper antibiotic treatment regimen started now could cure her tuberculosis, reverse her pancytopenia, and save her life.

"Now we need...to save Iris."

As Felipe listened to Phineas' hurried explanations, he'd sat bolt upright. "Uh, Phineas. Should we be concerned about Mateo catching TB, as much time as he spends close to his Wayla."

"Miliary TB...where Iris...has it so far...is unlikely...to be contagious." *For now.* There wasn't time to elaborate.

Phineas patted Postum's forearm. "Henry...I need you...to call...Dr. Moro...right away...to stop...the treatment...he's ordered...for Iris Mann." Phineas tried to push himself into a standing position but, in his haste, toppled onto his forearm on the microscope's table and struck his chin on the microscope eyepiece. The knifelike pain turned his legs to rubber.

Felipe shot across the room and rescued his father-in-law from a more damaging crash to the floor. Ernest pushed himself from under the chair, stood at attention, and stared at his master, waiting. Phineas wiped a thick band of bright red blood onto his shirt's cuff. Something to deal with later.

"Let's...hurry there...Felipe." He pushed himself up onto his walker and took one step toward the door. "Heel, Ernest."

"I'll page Moro now," Postum announced.

"Then...call the...infusion center...nursing station...to stop...the infusion."

"Not sure they'll accept my order, Phineas. You'd better hurry."

Phineas pushed his body at what felt like a snail's pace in his race to head off the deadly drug. Felipe slipped ahead and pressed the subbasement's elevator button over and over like he was sending a desperate line of Morse code to Iris. The numbered lights showed that the elevator was moving in the wrong direction, rising from the second floor to the third. Fourth. Finally, the seventh.

"I can carry you, Phineas." Felipe held out his arms in front, an invitation.

"The infusion center... is in a...different building. ...Too far to...carry me."

Ernest sat and let out a whine that seemed to say he understood time was their foe. His sturdy shoulders were trembling.

Felipe extracted his cell from his pants pocket and held it up. "I can call Martha."

Movement in the lights. Sixth floor. Fifth. 4. 3. 2. Lobby. Felipe pocketed his phone. The 'L' light stayed on. And on. Felipe pressed the button again. Finally, the 'SB' light. DING. The doors slid open to reveal......a mixed crowd of white coats and civilians in street clothes packed shoulder to shoulder in the steel box. No one shifted except to glance at Phineas and Ernest then to stare at the floor. They clearly expected the old man, his dog, and his walker to catch the next train.

Felipe loudly cleared his throat. "Some help, please. It's urgent." He gestured toward Phineas' bloody chin.

A tall man in the back, his head above the rest, sounded disgusted with his fellow travelers as he muttered, "Excuse me. Coming out." But before he could part the unyielding crowd, the elevator's doors slid closed.

"Sorry about this, Phineas." Felipe bent at the waist, hoisted his father-in-law, and folded him stiffly over his shoulder like a side of beef. "We'll retrieve your walker later."

With each step up the two flights of stairs, Felipe's shoulder bones painfully poked Phineas in his soft midsection. The level surface of the lobby offered modest relief. Every pair of eyes turned to stare. No one moved to assist.

"Wheelchair," Felipe said. With Phineas' elevated backside leading the way, Felipe pivoted and strode toward the entrance doors.

"Leon!" Felipe yelled. The familiar security guard was holding a sliding entry door in the open position for an elderly woman.

"Is Dr. Mann okay?" With a surprising burst of speed, Leon hustled toward a corner of the lobby where an empty wheelchair sat parked and ready. Felipe met him halfway and bent to lower his father-in-law onto the padded seat.

"It's...that way." Phineas hoisted his shaky left hand off his lap and pointed at a crowded hallway. Felipe pushed. Ernest trotted beside them, alternating looking ahead and at his master for a command.

Leon took the lead and waved his arm ahead. "'Scuse us. Emergency. Coming through." He glanced at Phineas over his shoulder, worry and puzzlement on his face. "Emergency Room?"

"Infusion...Center. Got...to stop...Iris' treatment." Phineas leaned back in the wheelchair to straighten his right thigh then inserted his hand into his front pocket to extract his cell phone. "Siri, ...Dr. Moro's...cell number." He touched the call icon and waited.

No answer. The voicemail message, "You've reached the voicemail of Dr. Moro. Leave a message and I'll call back as soon as I get a chance."

"Dr. Moro, ...it's...Phineas Mann. ...Stop my wife's...infusion. I'll... explain later."

"I saw Dr. Moro hurry out of the hospital an hour ago." Leon slowed for an instant while he spoke. "He's usually out of the hospital on Thursday afternoons. Once I heard him tell another doctor that he'd meet him at the tennis court."

Did Moro schedule Iris' treatment when he was unavailable on purpose? So he wouldn't have to answer more of her and her husband's troubling questions?

Leon resumed his frantic pace. "'Scuse us. Coming through."

Focus on the task at hand, Mann.

Who to call next? Marie? She was likely busy on work rounds having handed Iris over to Martha's care. "Siri, I need...to call Martha." Ten digits appeared. He struggled to press a shaky left index finger onto the screen while they rolled on. The trio entered a long, less crowded windowless hallway. Phineas' cell screen read, "No Service."

"Dead zone," Leon explained. "Center's at the far end, off to the right."

Dead zone. Horrible phrase. Phineas slapped his thigh in frustration.

Felipe picked up the pace. They shot out of the hallway into a glassed-in lobby with Leon scanning. "Where is Mrs. Mann?" he shouted at the desk. Double glass doors led in opposite directions down long hallways from the lobby. They didn't have time to pick the wrong ward.

The lone receptionist glanced up from her computer screen. "Who's asking, please?" She inspected the irregular trio over half-frame reading glasses and lingered suspiciously on Ernest. Ernest sat and narrowed his eyes back at her.

"I'm...her husband." Phineas summoned all the volume he could. "We need to...see her now!"

Felipe leaned onto the counter. "It's an emergency."

She looked from Phineas' chin to his bloody sleeve. "Well, the emergency room's back near where you came from." She offered a half smile and rested her hands on her lap.

"Iris Mann's the emergency," Felipe barked.

Ernest tilted his head back and sniffed, at first a calm sampling of scents in the lobby, and then vigorous, deep inhalations followed by soft whines and cautious tail-wagging. He stood and stared at Phineas.

The receptionist returned her attention back to the screen, typed something, clicked her mouse, and peered back at them. Was she about to ask for ID now? Phineas began reaching for his wallet, but she waved her finger at the set of doors to her left, their right. "She's in there. Bay seven."

Leon triggered the automatic doors to open. Felipe threaded the wheelchair through and stopped in the endless, empty hallway lined by an ocean of identical silky drapes pulled closed. Phineas' hopes sank. How long would it take to locate Bay Seven?

"Iris...Martha?" Phineas pleaded. His weak voice disappeared among the numerous conversations escaping the surrounding fabric enclosures.

Ernest's sniffing pace and volume intensified. His shiny nose pointed at the ceiling at first, then down the hall. He let out a single soft bark as if to say, "I got this. Release me." He studied Phineas for a response.

"Ernest, ...find Iris," Phineas commanded.

The service dog sprinted a beeline down the hall and stopped past halfway, wagging his entire back end in front of a set of drapes on the left. Felipe raced after him pushing Phineas' wheelchair. Ernest gripped the drape in his teeth and dragged it open.

Iris' eyes were closed, her head pressed into the pillow and her silver braid tucked out of sight. A sheet had been pulled under her chin. She held her left arm out, exposed and rigid. An IV line from a hanging bag of fluid was taped above her wrist. A nurse opened a valve in the IV line and watched clear fluid begin its descent toward Iris.

Phineas lurched from his seat and tumbled onto the bed beside Iris' covered legs. He extended his right arm, then stretched it farther, to its limit, grabbed the IV line and pinched it closed.

Iris startled; her wide-open brilliant blue eyes fixed on his face. "Phineas! You're bleeding! What happened? Are you okay?" Forever sublimely squeamish, she covered her mouth with her free hand.

"Never better...my love," he answered.

CHAPTER 25

Three Months Later

Phineas' euphoria evaporated into mist like summer rain on hot asphalt. A red-orange screen unfurled and replaced the total darkness as a searing pain declared itself from a point on his scalp behind his right ear. He opened his eyes. *Damn, it's bright!* His eyelids slammed shut, a reflex, defending.

"Well, look who's back." Each time he'd reimagine this scene, Iris' voice would come from his left.

He'd always reach for the pain and feel gauze.

"Don't fool with your bandage, Phineas."

Iris hates bandages. Hates what's underneath them worse.

The glorious anesthetic propofol would clear from his brain, and the smidgen of fentanyl the anesthesiologist had added never fully killed the sensation where they'd cut him to remove the port and catheter to his brain.

Nothing foreign in him now. Only his own useless reprogrammed stem cells—his futile hope for a future. They'd failed him in reality, but not in his dazzling daydreams.

From her chair, Iris would reach over to squeeze his hand. Weeks ago, after her treatment for TB had begun, her bone marrow awakened, and a healthy pink tint replaced the pallor in her cheeks. Those pretty cheeks were filling out, gaining flesh back, gaining Iris back. He'd had the woman he loved a while longer. If only his Parkinson's disease trial had succeeded and also given him new life.

Next, the stocky recovery room nurse would hurry to the right side of his stretcher. Her nametag read Miriam. "Well, hey there Sleeping Beauty."

They call everyone waking up after anesthesia Sleeping Beauty.

"You did well. Ready to get up?" Her breath would smell of coffee, and he'd long for a fresh cup. Always did when he was waking up.

He imagined his lips forming a full and easy smile, not a forced and pitiful excuse for one. Until he'd lost his face's ability to show emotions, he hadn't treasured that sensation like he should have, and now it was forever gone, at least in what was left of this life.

"I can't wait, Miriam. Thank you." He'd fantasize his words flowing out, not requiring effort. They'd contain strength, and the sound of his restored voice would recruit a happy tear. He'd effortlessly wipe his cheek with the back of his steady right hand.

"Let me get some help." She'd beckon to the tall, slender orderly leaning against the nurses' station, busy checking his cell phone. She'd say, "Timothy, need you here."

Then Phineas would hold his left hand, the erratic problem child, in front of his face to inspect his index finger and thumb for a return of the pill-rolling tremor, a motion like testing an unpicked blueberry for ripeness, the first sign he'd had of Parkinson's disease. In his fantasies, his hand would be as steady as it was years ago.

Miriam would slide his gown's front down and peel ECG leads off his chest, plucking a hair or two in the process. *Ouch!* She'd ease his light blue UNC sweatshirt down over his raised arms while protecting his scalp's bandage.

"Dr. Mann, you'll have to keep the paper booties over your shoes until you're out front." She'd motion for him to pivot his legs and dangle them over the side of his perch. Slender Timothy would apply a surprising iron hand under one upper arm while Miriam would hold the other gently, poised to firm her grip.

He'd hoped the frightening feeling of stepping into a black hole would recede with the first of his stem cells, but the sensation of what terra firma felt like in his time before Parkinson's disease remained only a distant memory outside of his daydreams.

"How about a walker—until the anesthesia's out of your system?" Miriam would suggest.

"I'm hoping I won't need one for a good while. Since I've got you two, let's try out these refurbished legs once again." He'd imagine standing and allowing his full weight to rock heel to toe and back.

Secure.

"I'm ready." He'd take healthy strides toward the entrance with renewed confidence. Miriam and Timothy would release their grips and let Iris come to his side.

The recovery room's automatic door would always slide open and reveal his superhero team, Dr. Grace and Anabella. They'd study him, mentally sketch his face, measure his balance, then focus on his steady hands. Each time, their broad smiles would replace their concentration when they met his and Iris' gazes.

"Your family is waiting," Dr. Grace would announce, and she and Anabella would flank Iris and him. "We'll walk with you." His cherished neurology team would escort them down the hallway, nodding and marveling at each of his steps—steps so light and sure; it was as if he'd sprouted wings from his ankles. Then, when they'd step through the next automatic door, Chelsea and the entire Mann family, including Ernest, would look up as one.

Dr. Grace, with pride all over her face, would sweep her arm in front of Phineas and declare, "We give you back your Phineas Mann."

He'd bow deeply and motion for Annabella and Dr. Grace to do the same. Each time, applause and cheers would fill the small waiting room.

His people faded into a damp, gray fog. His imagination was faltering; his brain's morphine levels had to be climbing.

If only the novel Parkinson's disease study had concluded as triumphantly for him as he'd hoped it might. Instead of enjoying such a celebration at his last follow-up appointment with Dr. Grace, she'd reported that they'd instilled the highest and final dose of his programmed stem cells, and she was unable to objectively measure an improvement in his motor function, his tremor, or see any hint of a rewarding smile. Then the catheter had come out, the last sign of abject failure, of admitting that his stubborn Parkinson's disease had beaten them. He'd witnessed tearful defeat in Dr. Grace's downcast eyes instead of pride in a resounding success, a success he'd later imagine over and over to create fleeting cheerful moments.

During those precious moments, Iris and the hospice nurse timed the oral morphine drops so perfectly that his myriad discomforts, especially the brutal cough, were subdued, but he wasn't so sedated that he slept. He could then fantasize victorious scenes at the end of the Parkinson's disease trial. And the touch of a tincture of medical marijuana that the hospice nurse had also suggested gifted him with vivid sensations. At times he could even relive how it might feel to cast his walker aside and stride confidently from the recovery room into a waiting room packed with celebrating family and friends. At least the Parkinson's disease hadn't stolen his imagination.

But the greatest thrill in Phineas' life came from watching life re-enter Iris, pound by pound and gram of hemoglobin by gram of hemoglobin. Her energy and stamina rose daily as the tubercle germs died and the immune cells in her bone marrow calmed.

During her recovery, he'd explained to her how decades ago during her time in the hospital trenches with indigent and coughing patients, a single tubercle bacillus had floated through the air, and she'd innocently inhaled it. Her body's robust defenses had surrounded it and walled it off in a nearby thoracic lymph node. Over the decades that followed, the bacillus had ever so slowly divided again and again to form a microscopic colony, and as she'd aged, and her immune system gradually weakened, that collection of organisms smoldered until it finally ruptured through that lymph node and spilled into a nearby pulmonary vein. Her circulation had then, in a single event, distributed those bacilli throughout her body where they'd stealthily multiplied until they manifest initially in her bone marrow. Untreated, the tuberculosis infection *would* have soon manifested in her lungs and other vital organs. But lifesaving treatment had been initiated in time and she'd responded as he'd hoped. Now, whenever she appeared at his side, her presence gave him such tremendous joy.

Phineas was also granted the rare honor of being eulogized in a crowded forum *while he was still alive.* With Iris' permission, Phineas' friend Henry Postum had organized a medical grand rounds to discuss her near fatal case. Her course, laboratory studies, and the initial bone marrow pathology were presented as a puzzle for the audience to solve. Then, on the auditorium's big screen, Postum revealed the key slide with the crisscrossing tuberculosis germs. The beaded red X marked the spot.

An infectious disease specialist discussed tuberculosis in detail, including famous people who'd succumbed to it. Iris sat next to Phineas' wheelchair throughout, and she'd allowed an emotional interview about her first-hand experiences. Postum then spoke of Phineas' involvement in Iris' salvation and other challenging cases over his long career. A standing ovation followed with Phineas the only one remaining seated. At that moment, he realized that he *had* contributed, if not to the basic knowledge of medicine, but to the education of medical learners of all ages. And he'd cared for *so many* patients over his lifetime, even curing some of their afflictions.

He'd scanned the audience for Reddick and Moro, but it appeared they'd found reasons to be elsewhere that day.

Only weeks after this tribute, Phineas learned that Dr. Grace's team had identified the reason his and the other study subjects' stem cells had shut down their dopamine production soon after they were instilled in participants' brains. Dr. Grace and Annabella paid Phineas a visit at his home. They explained in molecular terms how they planned to alter the DNA sequence to be inserted in future subjects' stem cells. They said they were now confident the next study would be successful at correcting the symptoms of Parkinson's disease, and they hoped to launch this new trial within a year or two. Phineas' and the other subjects' invaluable participation in the Phase One trial had been crucial for the research team to gain both procedural experience and necessary knowledge at the molecular level. Believing that future patients would benefit provided Phineas solace.

But by then, Phineas' swallowing, despite applying the measures taught by speech therapy, posed such a challenge and risk that his diet had to be shifted to one of thickened liquids and pureed 'solids'. Felipe, God bless him, had prepared his tastiest offerings, loaded them in a blender, then frozen away cubes of French cuisine to be warmed for future meals. But trouble with *all* liquids, including his own saliva, soon followed, soiled his lungs, and caused an incessant and painful cough.

How ironic for me, a pulmonologist, to be taken down by a cough! His trusty ribs now ached most of his waking hours like they'd been beaten with a hammer. If he'd been stronger and able to take a full breath, his brutal cough would have broken at least one of his ribs.

Constant thirst told him that he was dehydrated. When questioned again about a gastrostomy tube to bypass his taste buds and feed him directly into his stomach, he'd again declined. He'd at least kept wits enough to recognize that his care had become more than Iris could hope to handle. With his encouragement, she'd hired nursing assistants who took care of most of the degrading and embarrassing necessities, but Iris still pitched in to help and witnessed how far her husband's body had fallen. She left his side only for her own obligatory appointments. He had become her prison.

In recent days, his signal to her that he wished for relief for his parched mouth was to run the tip of his shaky tongue over his lips. She'd then press an ice-cold, soaked swab against his dry oral tissues and provide a few moments of relief. Some days, she indulged him with a hoppy ale on the swab. Other times, she'd dip it in a memorable Bordeaux wine.

A body can only last so long without enough liquids to replace those that evaporate from skin and breath, and those that carry toxins out through the kidneys. He'd be leaving soon. His family hovered.

He felt Ernest's cold, wet nose nuzzle his hand. His furry friend whimpered and rested his heavy head on the sheets wrinkled by his master's intervals of uncomfortable fidgeting.

Iris signaled the nurse. One last generous dose of morphine would hold Phineas in its comforting embrace.

His life had been full and now was complete—better than complete. Could there be more after?

Iris was kissing his forehead, his cheek, her lips so cool and silky. He could only whisper, "It's okay, ...Iris. ...I have...your love, ...and you... have...mine."

It was time.

Acknowledgements

My editor and coach, Dawn Elaine Von Wald of Rewired Creatives, Inc., once again helped with book revisions and my education as an author.

Christy Day and Maggie McLaughlin of Constellation Book Services designed the cover and interior, produced the e-book, and supported *The Desperate Trials of Phineas Mann*'s publication.

Martha Bullen, of Bullen Publishing Services, once again guided me through the complex publishing and book marketing process.

Jeremy Avenarius of Real Avenue Design designed and has supported my website.

My Osher Lifelong Learning Institute novelist group has supported me and provided helpful suggestions. They are one of the reasons I keep writing. Thank you, Carol Hoppe, Bonnie Olsen, Phil Goldberg, and Sara Strassle.

I am grateful to Sneha Mantri, M.D. (Parkinson's disease specialist), Craig Rackley, M.D., (pulmonologist), and Bob Christopher (engineer and service dog expert) who read early drafts and brought up ways to improve my book.

I greatly appreciate the busy authors and doctors who wrote endorsements prior to my novel's publication. Their kind comments are in the Praise section at the front of the book.

My sister, Vicki Powers, once again pored over a final draft looking for typos. My mother, Irene Powers, who just turned 99, disliked my original title and started me thinking about better options.

My wife, Karen Lauterbach, remains my main sounding board and early reviewer. I am grateful for her steady encouragement and love.

About the Author

MARK ANTHONY POWERS grew up in the small town of West Lebanon, NH. At Cornell University, he branched out into Creative Writing and Russian while majoring in engineering. After receiving his M.D. from Dartmouth, he went south to the University of North Carolina for an internship and residency in Internal Medicine, followed by a fellowship in Pulmonary Diseases and Critical Care Medicine.

After almost forty years in clinical practice and teaching, he retired from Duke University as an Associate Professor Emeritus of Medicine and began his exploration of other parts of his brain. Writing classes, writers' groups, and growing fruit and vegetables were some of the enjoyment that followed. A deep dive into beekeeping led to his presidency of the county beekeeping association and certification as a Master Beekeeper.

Two cups of coffee and two hours of writing most mornings produced the medical thrillers in his Phineas Mann series: *A Swarm in May, Breath and Mercy, Nature's Bite,* and *The Desperate Trials of Phineas Mann.* To learn more or connect with Mark, please visit hawksbillpress.com.